A HEART FOR ANY FATE

A HEART FOR ANY FATE

Suzanne Lyon

CHIVERS

British Library Cataloguing in Publication Data available

This Large Print edition published by AudioGO Ltd, Bath,
2012.
Published by arrangement with Golden West Literary
Agency

U.K.   Hardcover   ISBN   978 1 4458 2868 8
U.K.   Softcover   ISBN   978 1 4458 2869 5

Printed and bound in Great Britain by
MPG Books Group Limited

Let us then be up and doing,
With a heart for any fate;
Still achieving, still pursuing,
Learn to labor and to wait.
Henry Wadsworth Longfellow

■ ■ ■ ■

PART I
VIRGINIA,
1790–1798

■ ■ ■ ■

CHAPTER ONE

Hannah slept late on her wedding day. When she finally woke, it was to the music of meadowlarks. Drifting, she let their sweet notes, like the sound of church bells, lull her into semi-consciousness. The smell of wood fires burning and meat roasting finally brought her fully awake. Rolling over, she peered out the tiny attic window. The sun was fully up! A quick glance told her that her sister Phoebe, who shared the rope-strung bed with her, was long gone. As were Martha and Mary, who shared the other bed.

The late sleeper's sense of having missed something important momentarily overtook her. But then, sinking back into the sheets, she pulled the quilt to her chin and burrowed with a wicked sense of slothfulness. Anticipation needled her stomach, spreading its slow warmth from head to toe. Tonight she would share this very bed with

9

Temple! What would it be like, lying with a man, feeling his skin next to hers? She knew enough about mating to know the basics of the sex act, but what would it feel like? Would it be slow and tender, like a lazy summer sunset? Or crashing and tumultuous, like a heat-induced thunderstorm?

Heart pounding, she flung aside the covers and quickly dressed. Taking fresh linens from the animal-hide trunk, she carefully prepared her marriage bed. At the last moment, she slipped her wedding present to Temple under the straw tick pillow — a tiny wreath woven from a lock of her own hair and tied with a bit of blue ribbon.

Downstairs, the Allison women bustled about preparing the day's feast.

"Hannah! I thought perhaps you would sleep the day away and miss your own wedding!" Nancy Allison, Hannah's mother, smiled up from the dough she kneaded.

"And well I might have! Why didn't you wake me? There's so much to do."

"In faith, that's the truth. But you will have the rest of your life for rising early and doing chores. A girl should let others do the work on her wedding day."

"Oh, Ma, you know that's not my way. Now, put me to work." Hannah rolled her long, dark hair into a knot, secured it with a strip of rawhide, and tucked it up under her mob cap.

Mrs. Allison pointed a mealy finger outside. "Very well. Your job is to greet all of the guests as they arrive. My heavens, I believe your father has invited every family in the valley. And I just got news that some cousins of the Coles who are visiting all the way from Philadelphia will be here. Can you imagine?"

"Philadelphia! What are city folk doing all the way out here in the Blue Ridge?" wondered eighteen-year-old Rhoda. Although two years younger than Hannah, Rhoda was already married and the mother of a baby girl.

"They say many people leave the city in warmer weather to escape the pestilence." Nancy separated the dough into biscuits and turned them into the bake kettle.

"Well, I shall certainly look forward to meeting them," said Rhoda. "I am sure they will be wearing the latest fashions. I have heard that skirts are much fuller these days."

"Much good it will do you," muttered Phoebe. At sixteen, Phoebe was a frail and petulant girl, given to dark moods and cutting remarks. "Where would you ever wear a fancy dress around here?"

"Ah, Phoebe, always looking for the dark

cloud on a sunny day." Rhoda gave her sister a good-natured nudge on the shoulder.

"Where's that no-account Lucy? I sent her for some eggs an hour ago." Nancy shook her head in disapproval. Lucy, their thirteen-year-old slave girl, was notoriously unreliable. It seemed no amount of whipping would bring her into line.

"I'll get them, Ma," offered Hannah, grabbing a basket as she headed out the door. Once outside, she was almost sorry she had not accepted her mother's offer to while away the day. For what a day it was! Bright sunshine bathed the fields blooming with spring's rebirth. White and pink crab apple blossoms dotted the woods like a delicate first frost.

The Allison property sloped down to the banks of the New River where she spotted her brother reclining with a fishing pole. Near the river rose a mighty white oak tree under whose embracing leaves she and William Temple Cole would soon take their vows. Their vows! What a wondrous thing it was to pledge yourself to another person for the rest of your life. And how lucky she was to have found such a fine man. At twenty, Hannah was well aware that some considered her an old maid. Other young men

12

from the valley had sought her hand, and her father had urged her to consider them favorably. But they had all lacked some indefinable quality — that spark that would set her heart on fire. Hannah knew she had set a high standard, perhaps impossibly high. She could only thank God that her father held the enlightened view that a girl ought to have a say in whom she married. Although both her parents had warned her that the valley would likely run out of eligible bachelors before she found the man of her dreams.

But then Temple Cole entered her life. She first saw Temple at a barn raising. He was tall and carried himself with a bit of a swagger. His buckskin shirt had clung to a pair of broad shoulders and his thick arms had swung an axe faster than any man there. His auburn hair, tied back in a queue, had glinted gold in the sun. They had said only a few words to each other that day, but the intelligence in his sunny blue eyes had spoken directly to her soul.

Within days, Temple showed up on her doorstep, courtship on his mind. He succeeded in charming her parents, particularly her father who was pleased that the young man was a property owner, having recently purchased 100 acres on Peak Creek.

"Quite enterprising for a man of only twenty-two," Holbert Allison had declared.

Temple had proposed marriage on a cold November afternoon beneath the bare branches of the stately white oak tree. When he had kissed her, a white-hot flame inside her had leapt to life.

Snapping out of her reverie, Hannah picked through the chicken house searching for eggs. Her basket full, she ducked out the door, nearly colliding with Lucy.

"Land sakes, gal," she warned. "You nearly made me drop these eggs."

Lucy stepped out of the way and stared at her bare feet.

"Where have you been, you little varmint?" Hannah inquired. "Ma said she sent you out here quite some time ago."

"Marse tol' me to shovel out de ho'se stalls," mumbled the slave girl.

"That is a lie. Pa left early this morning to fetch the preacher. If I were not in a particularly good mood this morning, I would turn you over for a whipping when he gets back."

Lucy said nothing, her gaze fixed on her mud-caked toes. A tall, strong girl, Lucy was a recent addition to the Allison ledger books. She had come to them in trade for a pair of fine horses, a transaction Holbert Allison was beginning to regret given Lucy's indolent ways.

Relenting, Hannah handed over the basket of eggs. "Here. Take these to the kitchen. And next time do as you're told."

"Yes'm." Lucy trudged off toward the house.

Hannah watched her go, shaking her head in frustration. Was there anything worse than a slave who was too smart for her own good? Hannah could tell by the way Lucy watched them all, like a wise old owl, that the girl possessed a sharp mind. No doubt she was of the view that she deserved better in life. And maybe she did. But the world was what it was. It was not Hannah's place to try to change a system that was as old as time itself.

A cheery "Halloo!" brought her back to the present. Temple Cole, astride his big black mare led a group of horses and wagons into the yard. Hannah picked up her skirts and ran to greet him. Sliding to the ground, he encircled her waist with his huge, farmer's hands and swung her in a circle.

"My sweet! Did you order this fine day just for us? Certainly you've got me securely under your spell, but, in faith, I did not know you had such sway with Mother Nature!" Laughing, he set her down.

Hannah welcomed his father and mother, brother and sisters. "But where is Stephen?" she asked, referring to Temple's missing brother. "I had so hoped to meet him today."

Temple suppressed a frown. "He will be here. He has been on a hunt for the last two weeks, but he promised to be here for our wedding." Reaching up, he assisted to the ground a diminutive lady who appeared to be close to Hannah's age. "Dearest, may I present my cousin, Dolley Todd, and her sister, Anna Payne?" Temple indicated a pretty young girl of about ten peering over the wagon rim. Beside her, a portly black woman mopped her brow.

"Are you the folks from Philadelphia?" Hannah took in Dolley's plain linsey-woolsey dress and modest cap. Rhoda would be disappointed if this was what the fashionable set was wearing in the city these days.

"Indeed. Though as Temple has perhaps told thee, we are originally from Hanover County, Virginia. Please accept my congratulations on thy marriage to Temple. Imminent marriage, that is."

Now that Dolley Todd had spoken Hannah realized the reason for the plain attire — she was a Quaker. The "thees" and "thous" gave her away. She also noticed a telltale swelling under the lady's empire style gown.

"Thank you. Are you traveling without your husband, Missus Todd?"

"Dolley, please. Yes, John had business to attend to in the city. But he urged me to visit my family in Virginia as I am accustomed to do every year. Anna, come meet Temple's lovely bride!"

Hopping down from the wagon, the little girl performed a small curtsey. "Pleased to meet thee, Miss Allison."

"Likewise. I am sure you must both be tired. Let me show you inside where you can rest up."

"Yes, a drink of water would be most refreshing. Temple, would thee see that Mother Amy is given some assistance stepping down from the wagon? She's not as limber as she used to be." Dolley reached up to pat the old black woman's hand.

Hannah led the Philadelphia ladies to the kitchen where Nancy made sure they were comfortable and Rhoda peppered them with questions about city life. Returning to Temple's side, she joined him in greeting all the arriving newcomers. Many brought pies and cakes, jugs of cider and, Hannah suspected, a few stronger concoctions.

At last it was time for her to dress for the wedding. With a final squeeze of Temple's hand, Hannah climbed the stairs to her attic room. Fast asleep on Martha and Mary's bed lay Dolley Todd. Hannah tried to move about the room quietly, but in a moment the lady stirred.

"Oh, dear," she said, rubbing her eyes. "I did not intend to fall asleep. I only meant to put my feet up for a little while. I seem to become fatigued so easily these days."

"That's natural, I am sure," said Hannah. "When will you have your baby?"

"Thou noticed? Well, I suppose it is hard for a woman of small stature to conceal her condition for long. Our blessed event should occur in the autumn." Dolley swung her legs over the side of the bed and straightened her clothing.

"Have you been married long?" Hannah unlaced the bodice of the everyday dress she wore and hung it on a peg.

"Hardly. John and I said our vows in January." She patted her round belly. "I am sure thou art thinking we did not waste any time in making a baby. Well, after all, it only takes once. Who knows, perhaps thee and Temple later tonight. . . ." She wiggled her brows suggestively.

Hannah turned away, blushing like a rose

18

in bloom.

"Oh, dear, I have embarrassed thee, haven't I? I fear I have a penchant for doing that. People expect a Quaker lady to dress plainly, but not to speak plainly. I do apologize."

"That's not necessary." Hannah slipped a clean chemise over her shoulders and sat on the bed opposite her guest. "It's just that I have wondered what it will be like to . . . to be with a man."

"I am sure it will be quite glorious with a fine specimen such as thy Temple. I would counsel thee, however, not to expect too much at first."

"That could be rather difficult for me," Hannah admitted. "Patience is not one of my virtues."

"So Temple has said."

Hannah looked at her in amazement. "Temple has spoken about me to you?"

"My heavens, yes! Talked my ear off on the way here. Rarely have I heard a man wax so poetic over his betrothed. Let's see if I remember it all . . . thy raven hair and alabaster skin, thy hazel eyes and cherry lips, thy sharp mind and dulcet tongue. The man is quite smitten with thee."

Hannah brought her hands to her burning cheeks. "No more than any man is over his intended, I'm sure."

"*Hmm,* I see innocence is another of thy admirable traits. My dear, consider thyself lucky. Temple and thou are starting out life together just as thou should . . . deeply in love with each other."

Hannah smiled. "Yes, you are right. It is a wonderful feeling, is it not, to have found your one and only love?"

The young mother-to-be averted her eyes. "Indeed. Now, is that pretty dress hanging over there to be thy wedding frock? May I help thee with it?"

Hannah stepped into her petticoat and turned to let Dolley lace up the back of her new blue cambric gown. Her mother had purchased the fine linen fabric at market and had labored for months to have it ready for her daughter's wedding day. As Dolley threaded and tugged the laces, Hannah pondered why her newfound acquaintance had so abruptly changed the topic of conversation. It hinted at a lack of fervor in Dolley's own marriage. Although it might be considered rude, Hannah was tempted to draw out the young Mrs. Todd. After all, by the lady's own admission she admired plain speaking.

"Dolley," Hannah ventured, "is your own marriage all you had hoped for?"

20

Dolley gave the laces a last tug and tied them together. She crossed her arms across her chest, considering the question. "That depends, I suppose. When I was a young girl living at Scotchtown, I dreamed of marrying a fine Virginia gentleman, a man of property and importance. A gallant blade who possessed lofty ideas and would cut a fine figure on his mount. Had we stayed in Virginia, perhaps I would have found such a man. But my father chose to free our slaves, even Mother Amy though she chooses to stay in our employ, bless her heart. We moved to Philadelphia where Quakers are not considered such an oddity. Father began a dry cleaning business which was never much of a success. Our fortunes very much in reversal, it became clear that my duty was to seek an advantageous match. John Todd fit the bill quite nicely. He is of good family, a respected lawyer who will provide well for me and our children, and he is a kind and decent man. So when thou asks if my marriage is all that I had hoped for, I can only say that it does not quite fulfill the romantic notions of a silly young girl, but it completely satisfies the desires of a grown woman."

Hannah did not know what to say. Her heart went out to Dolley Todd, who was clearly determined to make the best of her marriage of convenience. Hannah was quite certain she would never have been able to be so self-sacrificing.

"Now, let's see." Dolley led her back to the bed and sat her down. "I have noticed quite a lovely new hair style among Philadelphia's fashionable ladies. Perhaps I can replicate it for thee."

Dividing Hannah's waist-length hair into several sections, she began a complicated braiding procedure.

"Dolley," Hannah mused, her head bobbing with the occasional tugs on her tresses, "I am so glad you are here today. I shall never forget meeting you."

"Nonsense, dear. Thou shall remember many things about thy wedding day, but meeting Dolley Todd likely will not be one of them."

"But it will! I feel as though I have known you forever. I can talk to you more freely than I can talk to my own sisters."

"There." Dolley fastened the last pin in place and stood back to admire her handiwork. "Lovely, if I do say so myself. Does thou have a mirror so thou canst see? No? Well, take my word for it, thou are the prettiest bride the valley has ever seen."

Hannah rose and gave the tiny lady a

spontaneous hug. At the bottom of the stairs Nancy Allison called up. "Hannah, your father and the preacher have arrived. Are you ready?"

"Yes, Ma, we'll be there directly."

"Before thou goest, I have a gift for thee." Dolley opened her satchel and pulled out a beautiful leather-bound book with gilt-edged pages. "Does thou read and write?"

"Yes," Hannah said proudly. "My father engaged a tutor for the boys, but I kept sneaking into the lessons. Finally he gave up and let me stay." She opened the book and flipped through it. The pages were empty. She looked at Dolley, puzzled.

"It is a journal for thee to write in. I have found that it sometimes helps to record my thoughts. A woman's life is mostly toil, sunup to sundown. But if thou canst find time occasionally to reflect in these pages, it will give thee strength."

Hannah clasped the journal to her breast. "What a treasure! Thank you, Cousin. I shall write in it faithfully."

"That would be lovely. But should thou findest that the days and months go by without thy opening its pages, do not despair. Think of this journal as an old friend who, though sometimes forgotten or neglected, will always be there, ready to share thy secrets. "Now" — Dolley reached for Hannah's hand — "there is a young man down below who is waiting for his bride. Shall we?"

CHAPTER TWO

Dolley Todd had never spoken truer words when she described a woman's life as filled with toil. In 1790, in the frontier of southwest Virginia, everyone's life was toilsome, male or female. It was no wonder, then, that folks welcomed the opportunity to gather for celebrations. On a beautiful spring day people traveled for miles not just to witness the exchange of vows between Hannah Allison and William Temple Cole, but to leave behind for a day or two the burdensome drudgery of daily life.

Hannah and Temple were united by the circuit-riding preacher under the white oak tree, and the party began. Nancy Allison outdid herself, serving a feast of roasted beef, pork, and fowl, boiled potatoes and cabbage, hominy, and cornbread. While the older folks retired to the shade of a beckoning tree, small children raced around playing games of Weevilly Wheat or Sister

Phoeby. The younger men set to work laying down a temporary split-log floor in the barn for that night's dancing.

Hannah felt as high and light as the clouds, but her bliss was tempered with impatience. Heaven knew she reveled in the frivolity, yet she yearned to have Temple all to herself. Her husband seemed to feel the same urgency, for he rarely left her side all through the afternoon. His hand strayed again and again to her waist, his touch more insistent, more possessive now that she was his own.

As dusk settled over the valley and the surface of the river rippled with fish rising to the surface, the fiddlers tuned their instruments. The bride and groom led off the first dance, a Virginia reel. Soon the others joined in for three- and four-handed reels, jigs, and square sets. The dancing was continuous, with parties cutting out when they became tired, their places filled by rested members of the company. Only the weariness of the fiddlers ever brought the music to a halt.

After a good hour on the dance floor, Hannah and Temple finally cut out, retreating to the sidelines, breathless and sweating.

"I believe I have worn a hole in my shoe!" Laughing, Hannah bent over to examine her tattered slipper.

Temple knelt beside her and playfully tugged at the shoe. "Shall I remove it, milady?"

"Thank you, no." Hannah yanked her foot away. "I do not care to get my feet full of splinters."

"That's all right. You will not be on your feet much longer. Not if I can spirit you away." Temple glanced around to see if people were looking and, satisfied that several were, kissed her on the lips. Shouts of approval went up from the crowd.

"Temple!" Hannah protested, although the kiss pleased her. "It is too early to leave. You must be patient."

"A dubious virtue on a man's wedding night." He spoke softly into her ear, grinning as her cheeks colored. "Well, if I can't convince you to come away with me, reckon I will go in search of something to quaff my thirst." Kissing her hand, he wandered out into the night. Hannah had no doubt he would not have to look far to find friends passing around a jug of whiskey, but it did not worry her. Temple was a man of temperate habits.

"Mercy! Has the bridegroom abandoned the bride?" Dolley Todd walked over trailed by Phoebe who, like Hannah, seemed drawn

27

to the Quaker lady.

"Only temporarily, I hope. Are you enjoying yourself?"

Dolley's religion forbade her from taking part in dancing or other frolics. Hannah could not imagine why God would disapprove of such pleasures. But Dolley appeared perfectly content to stand on the sidelines. Perhaps, in her condition, she would have abstained from dancing in any event.

"Yes, indeed. Phoebe and I have had a lovely talk."

Hannah's eyebrows rose. How on earth had her new cousin been able to coax interesting conversation out of her churlish sister? Phoebe glared as though she could read Hannah's uncharitable thoughts.

"I am glad you have been keeping Missus Todd company, but perhaps you had better take a turn out there." Hannah nodded to the dancers. "Plenty of nice young men, and sixteen is not too young to find yourself one of them."

Phoebe narrowed her eyes in a familiar look of distrust. "You waited long enough to find one. Why should I be in any hurry?"

"I would not have waited if I had found Temple earlier. Who knows, perhaps the man you will fall in love with is here tonight, in this very place. Yet if you spend all your time hugging the wall, you will never find him."

"I will never find him anyway!" cried Phoebe. Nearly in tears, she turned and ran.

Hannah instantly regretted goading her sister. On this, of all days, she should have made an extra effort to be kind. She apologized to Dolley for her thoughtless comments.

"Do not worry. She will come 'round. It is just that thou art leaving tomorrow to begin a brand new life and she will miss thee."

Hannah laughed. "Miss me! Phoebe will miss me like a bad itch. Reckon she's been counting the days until she can have the bed all to herself."

"Odd. That is not the impression she gave me at all." Leaving Hannah to ponder that, Dolley moved on.

The musicians struck up another tune and Hannah was drawn back onto the floor. Smiling and clapping, she twirled from one partner to another, so familiar with the traditional old folk dances that her feet moved automatically to the beats and rhythms.

In the middle of the Pea Straw her partner, a particularly vigorous lad, sent her tumbling into the crowd. Off balance and on the verge of losing her feet, a pair of strong arms reached out to set her right. She turned to thank her rescuer, and felt a sudden shock. The man who held her bore a striking resemblance to her husband. Yet on closer inspection he seemed nothing like him. His eyes were the same shade of blue, like the sweet william that grew near the river, but where Temple's were merry and open, these were veiled. His features were poured from the same mold as Temple's, but were sharper — the brow more prominent, the cheeks more angular, the jaw more pronounced. His chin sported a scraggly beard that was a shade or two darker than his long, light brown hair.

The man dropped his buckskin-clad arms and nodded politely, his eyes never leaving hers.

"You . . . you must be a Cole," Hannah stammered. "You look so like my husband."

The crowd jostled her closer to him and she smelled wood smoke and dried sweat. He backed into a darker corner of the barn, and, without thinking, she followed.

"And you must be my brother's wife," he said.

Suddenly Hannah knew. This was Stephen, Temple's younger brother.

"Yes, I am Hannah, your new sister-in-law. My, it is remarkable how you and Temple resemble each other."

Stephen smiled, or perhaps it was a grimace. "In some ways, I reckon."

"Temple will be so pleased that you are here. He very much wanted all of his family to be with him on his wedding day. Now everything is perfect."

Stephen looked doubtful. "Temple don't need me to make things right. All he wanted was to marry you. Now I see you, there ain't no mystery why."

Hannah colored at the homespun compliment. He continued to stare at her with a look in his eyes that seemed vulnerable and, at the same time, dangerous. It reminded her of the time she had been in the woods and came upon a panther. The animal had crouched, uncertain whether to pounce or run, until her brother's shouting had driven it off. Here in this room full of festive folks dressed in their finest, Stephen Cole seemed out of place, yet completely self-contained. She realized he would not care a hoot what people thought of his smelly buckskins and unkempt beard.

"Have you eaten yet?" Hannah asked, uncomfortable under the perusal of those eyes.

"No, ma'am."

"There should be plenty of fixings left. Let me show you." She turned to lead him outside and saw Temple coming toward them, his arm around Phoebe's shoulders.

"Stephen, I am glad to see you. I had about given up hope that you would grace us with your presence." The brothers shared a stiff embrace. "Look who I found, pouting, all by herself. I told her it was high time she danced with the bridegroom." Temple introduced Phoebe whose red-rimmed eyes grew huge at the sight of the rough-looking young man.

"Don't be afraid, little sister. He does not always look so frightful." Temple leaned over and took a good whiff. "Or smell so frightful. No time to clean up from your hunt, eh, Brother?"

Stephen shrugged, unfazed by Temple's friendly joshing.

"He has not yet had a chance to eat," said Hannah. "I thought I would fill a plate for him."

"Ah, Stephen, see what a fine woman I have taken to wife. Always eager to serve others, even on her own wedding day." Temple bussed her cheek, then grabbed Phoebe's hand. "Come, little sister, let's show these folks a thing or two!"

Phoebe stumbled after him, glancing over her shoulder to keep Stephen in her sights.

Outside, in the glow of the fire, Hannah handed her brother-in-law a pewter plate and watched him stack it high with food. He ate with his fingers, occasionally using his hunting knife to spear bites of meat. When he was finished, he wiped his knife and hands on his buckskins. "Thank you, ma'am. I ain't had vittles that tasty in some time."

"Stephen, we are related now. I do think you should call me Hannah."

"Thank you, ma'am. It is a beautiful name." For the first time, he smiled, the corners of his mouth and eyes lifting ever so slightly.

Hannah felt the same as when she peeked under the towel to check her bread dough rising — anticipation and satisfaction all at once. She tilted her head, finding herself unexpectedly taken with his understated charm. "Shall we return to the dancing? I hear a reel beckoning."

"You go ahead. I ain't much for dancing."

"Surely you don't mean that. Everyone likes to dance."

"I never learned it," he admitted.

"Well, I never. . . ." Hannah was dumbfounded. Didn't everyone know how to

33

dance, just like they knew how to hoe a field or sew on a button? Why, Temple was a wonderful dancer, and here his own brother professed never even to have learned.

"Teach me," he said.

She frowned, not sure she had heard right.

"That is, I'd be honored if you would."

"Well, I . . . I don't know. I have never tried to explain to anybody how to dance."

He stood awkwardly, his hands turned up at his sides in invitation. He looked like a shy little boy begging a sweet.

"All right then." Hesitantly she held out her own hands. He grasped them in a strong grip. His fingers were long and lean — a hunter's hands, not a farmer's hands. She cleared her throat. "The couples stand opposite each other, men on one side, women on the other, in two lines. The pair nearest the caller is the lead couple, and, when the set is finished, they go to the end of the line and the next pair takes over. Do you follow?"

He nodded.

"Very well. First, you hop on your right foot and swing your left forward and to the side, like so. . . ." She moved slowly through some steps while he did his best to follow. "Then you turn, like so . . . no, don't let go hands, that's right, and then make an arch

34

with your arms for the head couple to go under, and then it starts over again." Laughing and slightly out of breath from dragging him after her, Hannah brushed a stray strand of hair from her cheek. "Do you think you have got it?"

"One more time." He held out his hands.

They went through the steps again, and then once more. He learned quickly, gaining confidence with each repetition.

"Bravo! Let's show the others how well you are doing."

"No, Hannah, I. . . ."

"Come on, now." She pulled him along to the barn. "I must show off my prized student!"

They joined a reel in progress, and, although Stephen was still a bit fumble-footed, he was game, falling back into step whenever he missed a beat. Hannah informed everyone that he was just learning, and soon all the young ladies, particularly the unmarried ones, were vying to be his teacher. Like baby chicks sparring for the worm, they fought over him for each dance and would not hear of him giving up until he had attempted them all. Even Phoebe joined in the fun.

Back on the sidelines, Hannah once again found herself standing next to Dolley Todd.

"Cousin Stephen is certainly the center of attention," Dolley noted. "Poor thing, he is most likely a bit flummoxed by the young ladies' interest. But it is good for him. He needs a little social leavening."

"How well do you know him?" asked Hannah, watching as Stephen and Phoebe ducked under a tunnel of arms. She was not sure when she had ever seen her sister look so happy.

"I couldn't have been more than twelve or so when I saw him last. And he was still just a boy, although even then he had quite an independent streak. It was not uncommon for him to go off on his own for days at a time. He always came back with meat, or a brace of birds. He was far and away the best hunter in the family, even at such a tender age." Dolley chuckled and leaned in to share a confidence. "I think I may have been a bit infatuated with him."

"Do tell," Hannah said. "He seems a rough sort for a person of your tastes."

"Yes, well, that was all part of the attraction. I probably had some girlish fantasy of trying to tame the wild beast in him. Thankfully it was a fleeting notion."

"Don't you think it would be worth the effort?" Hannah winced as Stephen came down hard on Phoebe's toes, although

Phoebe laughed it off.

"Indeed I do, but it will take a woman with more fortitude than I possess to succeed. Such a woman is to be both envied and pitied."

Hannah gave her a questioning look.

"It is hard to explain. Just look at him. Stephen Cole is all man, a man's man, more at home around a campfire than in a drawing room. Yet he has that spark about him, so appealing to women. Whoever he marries will lead a life full of passion and excitement, but I venture to say a lonely life as well." Dolley laughed self-consciously. "Oh, dear, how I do run on at de mouf, as Mother Amy would say."

Hannah started to assure Dolley that her confidences would go no further, when a cacophony of noise interrupted the musicians. Half a dozen or so young women paraded into the barn, whooping and shouting as they pounded together pewter plates and tin cups. Having been part of a shivaree before, Hannah knew what was expected. Laughing, she pretended to hide and look dismayed when they found her out. The girls shepherded the new bride out of the barn and into the house, depositing her in her marriage bed. Within minutes, Temple had joined her there, courtesy of a similar gang of rowdy young men.

At last they were alone, and reasonably certain of at least a few hours of privacy. The revelry would continue throughout the night, and as the Black Betty continued to flow it was likely the groom's friends would pay them another visit, but for now they were blessedly alone.

Hannah lay back on the bed, her nerve endings flickering like tiny fireflies. Temple propped himself on an elbow and bent to kiss her.

"My wife," he whispered, stroking her cheek.

"My dearest husband."

His hand strayed under the pillow and brushed the wreath of hair Hannah had placed there. "What's this?"

"My gift to you," she said. "So you will always carry a part of me with you,"

He pressed the wreath to his lips. "Sweeter than honey. But I fear I have no gift for you."

"Oh, Temple, you have given me everything . . . your name and your heart. That is all I desire."

He kissed her tenderly. She rose to douse the candle but he pulled her back. "Not yet," he said. "I don't want darkness yet."

Slowly she reached her hands up and unpinned the braids that Dolley had wound around her head, unplaiting the strands until her hair fell free.

"You are so beautiful." Temple brushed aside her hair and kissed the back of her neck.

Her back arched and she trembled all over. "Temple, I don't know what to do. You must show me."

"We shall learn together," he murmured, his fingers fumbling with the laces of her bodice.

"You mean . . . ?" Could it be that he was as inexperienced as she?

"*Shhh,*" he whispered, burying his lips in her hair.

Down below, the merriment continued, only now the couples brushed a little closer, laughed a little louder, teased a little longer. When not engaged in the dance, young men offered their laps as seats and the girls boldly accepted. The night flowed on with a sensuousness like the river itself.

Phoebe Allison searched the crowd, looking for Stephen. In the confusion of the shivaree she had lost sight of him. She wandered outside and circled the bonfire, but he was nowhere within its arc of light. Glancing toward the house, she saw a dim glow in an upper room, the room she shared with Hannah. Suddenly it went out. Averting her gaze, she finally caught sight of Stephen. He stood on the path holding the reins of his horse, his eyes locked on the same window. Before she could call to him, he mounted up and melted into the night.

CHAPTER THREE

Hannah fell in love with the home Temple had built for her. Modest it was, as he had warned during their courtship, but she would have been happy in a crude lean-to as long as it sheltered just the two of them.

They set to work planting a small patch with crops to be used for their own subsistence. Then they tackled the larger task of clearing additional acres for the planting of wheat, flax, and hemp. Most of this harvest Temple planned to take to market, hoping to trade for useful items.

Felling trees and digging stumps from the ground was the most laborious work Hannah had ever undertaken, yet she toiled right alongside her husband. In later years she would see this as the happiest time of her life. Rising before dawn, she would stir the flames in the hearth and begin preparing breakfast while Temple tended the stock. Then, if they were working in a distant field, they would ride the black mare to the site and work, side-by-side, until the sun was high in the sky. Midday, they returned to the cabin for a quick meal and attended to other chores — Hannah might do some washing while Temple made lead bullets or repaired tools. Then it was back out to the fields for a few more hours. Finally, in the worst heat of the late afternoon, when the insects buzzed around them like tissue-paper combs, they would climb back on the mare and amble home. Sometimes Hannah was so tired she would rest her head on Temple's broad back and fall asleep, rousing only when he would gently lift her down from the horse.

Too tired to eat right away, they would sit on the bank of the creek and bathe their hot, dust-covered feet. On the very hottest days, they stripped all the way down and immersed themselves completely. Rejuvenated, Hannah would fix a meal, usually nothing more than a roasted rabbit or opossum, some corn pone, and whatever fresh vegetables were available, and then they would fall into bed in each other's arms.

They were completely content in their own company. Hannah gloried in their peaceful privacy. Both of them had grown up in large families and had never known what it felt like to be surrounded by silence and space. Although their cabin measured only twelve feet square, it seemed as large as a palace. Soon, they were confident, they would fill their home with children, which was as it should be. But for now they embraced their lovely isolation.

Like the languid river, summer meandered by, and soon fall brought frosty mornings and flights of geese overhead. For the first time in her life, Hannah looked forward to the cold days of winter, knowing she and Temple would stay warm and cozy in their snug cabin of love.

On a day in early October, Temple harnessed the mare to a wagon and made preparations to haul a load of grain to the gristmill. He asked Hannah to come with him, but she had a long list of things to do and could not see whiling away the day to no purpose.

"But you will serve a most important purpose," Temple insisted, sliding his arms around her waist and pulling her close. "Keeping me in good humor."

"That is exactly what I fear," Hannah said, wiggling free. "If I keep you too happy, we would never reach our destination."

"Now there is a thought." He reached for her again and began playing with the laces on her bodice. "After all, what's the hurry? The mill can wait another day."

Laughing, she batted his hands away. "Go, you rascal. Go and hurry back home to me."

Sighing dramatically, he gathered his things and climbed aboard the wagon. "Do you realize, my love, that this is the first day of our marriage that we shall spend apart?"

She reached up to squeeze his hand. "I shall count every second until you return." Hannah watched him roll out of sight, a knot forming in her throat. Was there ever a woman with a kinder, more handsome husband? What would she ever do without him? Pushing away this unpleasant thought, Hannah turned to her main task for the day — making soap. She had previously prepared the lye, and today she would mix it with lard, then pour the concoction into trays to harden. The trick was mixing the ingredients together at a consistent temperature — not too hot, not too cold — so that it would thicken properly.

Temple had helped her position the heavy kettle over the fire pit in the yard. She got the flames going, poured in lard, added lye and some water, and began stirring. Every now and then, if the mixture seemed to be getting too hot, she threw some dirt on the fire to tamp it down.

44

Concentrating on her work, she failed to notice movement in the bushes at the edge of the clearing. Suddenly the back of her neck tingled. She held perfectly still. The only sound was the wind rustling the tops of the trees. Slowly she turned around. Not ten feet away stood an Indian brave, staring at her with eyes as black as char. He was young and tall for an Indian. He wore only buckskin breeches and knee-high moccasins. At his waist was a knife, a tomahawk, and a long, stringy thing that she realized with horror was a scalp. His head was shaved but for a roach that traveled down the middle and ended in a long, unkempt queue down his back. His cheeks were marked with gunpowder tattoos.

Hannah gripped her arms, felt her muscles burn and twitch as fear flowed through her body. She had seen Indians before, at the trading places. They had mostly looked old and pathetic, not threatening in any way. Not like this brave in the prime of his manhood who could not be here for any explainable reason other than to steal something, or do her harm.

Images flashed before her eyes, stories she had heard of captured female settlers and the things that had been done to them. But those kinds of depredations had not oc-

45

curred around here for years, to her knowledge. The Indian troubles were in Kentucky and Ohio country now. Yet this was surely trouble standing before her.

She glanced around, peering into the bushes and trees that lined the clearing. Was he alone? If he was, maybe she could run for it. But how could she possibly outrun him? And besides, she did not want to die with a tomahawk in her back. If death was to be her fate, let her meet it head-on, defending herself and her home. If she could only make it back to the cabin, she could grab the loaded musket Temple left hanging over the fireplace, and send this heathen to hell where he belonged.

She started to take a step backward, when the Indian said something, gesturing at the kettle. He repeated whatever he had said and then mimed reaching into the kettle and bringing something to his lips. Hannah realized he was asking for something to eat. Could it be that he was simply hungry and had sought out their cabin in search of food? Yet his sleek, well-muscled belly did not look as though it had been empty for too long. Perhaps this request was a ruse of some sort. Nevertheless, if she could get to the cabin for food, she would be that much closer to the gun.

"No food there," Hannah said, her voice trembling. She pointed to the kettle and shook her head. "That is not for eating." She turned and pointed to the cabin. "In there. I can get you some food in there." She repeated his gesture of bringing food to his lips.

The Indian grunted assent and motioned for her to lead the way. He followed closely behind, dashing her hope that he would let her enter the cabin alone. At the door, he pushed her aside. Tomahawk in hand, he kicked the door open and peered cautiously inside, checking for other occupants.

Now he knows, thought Hannah. *I am completely alone.*

They entered the small room. Hannah went about preparing whatever food she could put her hands on, some pemmican and hominy with gravy still lukewarm in a pot by the hearth. She tried not to glance at the musket over the fireplace for fear the heathen would guess her plan. The Indian stood in the center of the room watching her every move. Now that they were in close quarters she could smell him — a dank smell, like blood and earth.

Ladling the food into a wooden bowl, she offered it to him with hands she willed to be steady. He took it and ate, watching her over the rim. Hannah found herself wondering what he could be thinking. What did a creature like that think about? What was behind those angry eyes? What had she ever done to deserve his wrath?

He finished and offered the empty bowl back to her.

She pointed to the table. "Set it there."

For a split second he took his eyes off of her to set down the bowl. Hannah whirled and reached for the musket. But he was right behind her, his hands covering hers. Yanking the gun from her, he shoved her against the table, shouting something incomprehensible.

Hannah reached behind her, desperately seeking a weapon of some kind. He came toward her, still shouting, his fist pounding his chest. He was so close now she could smell the food on his breath. Suddenly her hand found a wooden cabbage stomper. Grunting with the effort, she swung the heavy club at the heathen's head. He ducked and the blow glanced off his shoulder. Enraged, he wrested the club from her and threw it across the room. Pinning her against the table, his loins crushing her pelvis, the Indian unsheathed his knife and held it to her hairline, exerting just enough pressure for the tip to pierce her skin. A drop of blood trickled down her temple and into the hair above her ear.

She stared into his eyes, only inches from hers. So this is how it would end. Scalped while she yet breathed. By God, she would not give this heathen the satisfaction of hearing her scream. She clenched her jaw and glared at him with hatred.

He increased the pressure on her abdomen, eyes narrowed as though waiting to see what she would do. Her mouth too dry to spit, Hannah settled for struggling beneath him, although it was no use. Suddenly a smile spread over the Indian's dusky face. He said something in a low voice, and then pushed himself off her.

Stunned, Hannah raised herself from the table. Blood trickled down her forehead, but she resisted wiping at it, her eyes on the knife in his hand. Neither of them moved. Then, in one quick motion, the Indian grabbed Temple's musket and rushed out of the cabin. She heard the chickens squawking, and then silence.

Staggering to the door, she bolted it and slid down its length to sit like a rag doll on the dirt floor. With every shuddering breath, she prayed for Temple to come home soon.

Hours later, Hannah heard noises in the

yard. Petrified that the Indian had returned, she raised her head and listened closely to creaking wagon wheels and jingling harness. Then there was the muffled sound of voices speaking in alarm. Someone pounded on the door.

"Hannah, are you in there? Hannah!"

"Temple!" She scrambled to her feet. Flinging open the door, she collapsed into the arms of her husband, sobbing with abandon now that she was safely in his embrace.

He held her tightly, shushing her with soft words of comfort. Taking a deep breath, she raised her head from his chest and noticed for the first time that they were not alone. Stephen stood behind his brother, outlined in the doorway.

"What happened?" Temple demanded. "You let the fire go out and the soap hardened in the kettle. Something must have frightened you."

Hannah wiped her face and eyes with her apron. "An Indian," she gasped. "I was busy tending the fire, and suddenly he was just there. He wanted food, so I fed him. But he looked so angry I was certain that food was not all he had come for. So I went for your gun and he . . . he pushed me down and held his knife to my head." She raised a

50

shaky hand and felt the dried blood on her forehead. "I thought he was going to kill me, but then he just let me go. He took your gun, Temple. I'm sorry."

"Forget the damn' gun!" he said, drawing her back into his arms. "When I think what could have happened. . . ." He hugged her hard, swaying back and forth with an emotion that surprised even Hannah.

After a while he turned to look for Stephen, but his brother had disappeared. Setting Hannah on the edge of the bed, he wet a piece of cloth and began to clean the cut on her head. He asked if she were hurt anywhere else.

"No, I don't think so. A bruise here or there, perhaps." She grabbed her husband's hand. "Why did he come here, Temple? I have never seen a lone Indian brave around these parts. I thought they had gone over into Kentucky and Ohio."

"They have, mostly." Stephen stepped into the cabin and closed the door. "Every now and then you'll see a hunting party back this way, even though the game's pretty sparse around here. This one may have been scouting ahead of the others, or maybe lagging behind. I checked around . . . couldn't see any sign of a large group."

"This is my fault," Temple said. "I should

51

never have left you alone."

"Don't say that. You could not have fore-seen anything like this. As it happens, there's no harm done. Except for the loss of your gun."

"And a few chickens, by the looks of it," said Stephen. "There's feathers all over the yard."

Hannah shuddered, remembering the feel of the dark heathen pressing against her body. "I suppose I should simply be grate-ful, but I can't help wondering why he left so suddenly. He seemed so angry, and then he just smiled and ran out the door."

Stephen walked over to the bed and crouched before her. "I reckon it's because he respected you. You didn't give up . . . you fought back, like running the gauntlet and coming through it with your head held high, so he decided to let you live. There's many a brave man couldn't have done what you did."

Hannah looked into her brother-in-law's eyes and saw a huge measure of admiration shining there. Her own started to well with fresh tears.

Stephen stood and checked his musket's load. "The bastard's most likely gone, but I'll stand watch tonight, just in case."

As he shut the door, Hannah breathed a

sigh of relief. No harm would come to her tonight with Stephen standing watch and Temple by her side.

Dear Cousin Dolley,

A year and a half has passed since Temple and I were joined together. A year and a half since I met you and you gave me this journal. Yet, I am shamed to say, not until this moment have I set pen to paper. The days pass so quickly, each filled with endless tasks, that by the time I think to pull out your gift and note down the day's events I am most likely already abed and halfway to slumber. Yet, if I were to be completely truthful, as I know you would want me to be, I would admit that fatigue and lack of time are not the only reasons for neglecting my journal. Rather, it is a sense that I have nothing of import to inscribe. Shall I waste precious ink and paper to record that the sow gave birth today, or that Temple traded the hemp crop for plow irons and harrows? These insignificant details do not seem worthy of commemoration, although they comprise the warp and woof of my life.

But then I remembered that on my wedding day you instructed me to use this journal to record my thoughts, and

I realized that even as my hands are busy with whatever task they have taken up, my mind is often engaged in entirely different pursuits. Indeed, my dear cousin, such was our ease of communication the first and only time we met that I frequently find myself composing letters to you in my head, and sometimes, pray forgive this liberty, even imagining your responses! It occurred to me that those are precisely the sort of reflections that ought to be set down in this volume. Thus, I have determined to address myself to you in these pages.

The first, and most important, thing I wish to tell you is that I received word of the birth of your son, John Payne Todd. How happy you and your husband must be! It is my fervent hope that you and baby Payne, as I understand you call him, will soon pay your Virginia relatives a call, though I would not blame Mr. Todd one bit for wanting to keep you at his side in Philadelphia. My Temple rarely lets me out of his sight, for reasons I shall explain in due course. I have concluded that it is in the nature of men to protect those closest to them. This I welcome, for who can deny that the world is a perilous place? Of course, I must remind Temple every now and then that his wife is not as helpless as he might think!

I suppose Temple is especially solicitous of late due to my delicate condition. Yes, dear Cousin, we are expecting a child this summer! My heart is so full of this news that I feel like telling every peddler or stray wanderer passing by, though, of course, I cannot. We have not even had a chance to tell our families, so for now it is our secret.

Having a baby shall be the completion of Temple's and my love for each other. Yet, in a way, I shall miss this time when it has been just the two of us. Will we ever love again as freely and fearlessly as we do now? Will we still have those moments when we sit together before the fire, holding hands, not saying anything because words are not necessary? I fear that a baby will change all that, and yet it seems that our love will mean so much more because of the life it will have created. I pray that it will be so.

Lest you think Temple and I have become hermits, let me assure you that is not so. We have had a few visitors here on Peak Creek including Temple's brother Stephen, who passed through on his way to the Kentucky country. He was to join a hunting party whose number included Daniel Morgan Boone, son of the famous long hunter himself. He was gone nearly a year and graced us with a visit this past September on his way home. The hunt was not terribly successful as Indians stole a large part of their hides and pelts, but Stephen nonetheless is quite taken with the land to the west. Indeed, to hear him describe it, it sounds like heaven — all rolling hills and lush valleys with game so plentiful all one need do is step outside, point, and shoot.

Temple listened to all this with what seemed to me no more than polite interest, so imagine my surprise when he told Stephen he would accompany him to meet the great Daniel Boone. Colonel Boone was passing through the valley on his way to Richmond where he serves as a county representative to the Assembly. He had agreed to meet with men from the New River area at the home of John Draper. Stephen, who has been an ardent admirer of Daniel Boone ever since the publication of Mr. Filson's book, convinced Temple that this was an opportunity not to be missed. So we all piled into the wagon and took ourselves to Draper's Meadow to hear the great Colonel Boone.

I must admit to a certain disappointment at first meeting this legendary tamer of the frontier. He is, for one thing, much older than I had realized — in his late fifties, I later learned. He is also slighter of build than I had expected, and so soft spoken as to make one lean forward to hear all his words. For all that, he appears quite vigorous, to which his charming wife, Rebecca, can no doubt attest. She has, you see, borne him numerous children including little Nathan, their ten-year-old son, who accompanied them to Richmond. (Perhaps the number of Boone progeny is more of a testament to Rebecca's vigor than the master's. Certainly she must be an extraordinarily strong woman to have endured such a nomadic life. By her husband's own admission he has moved his family no fewer than ten times, often for no better reason than an aversion to seeing his neighbor's smoke!)

The men, perhaps twenty in all, began to gather in the Drapers' parlor, at which point Colonel Boone declared the room too stuffy for his liking. So they repaired to the shade of a hickory tree where Boone sat upon a stump with the men arrayed on the ground before him like a teacher and his pupils. I joined the women in the kitchen, but found several excuses for tending to the party outside, and so overheard snatches of the colonel's comments. Temple later filled in for me what I had missed.

Colonel Boone began by stating his support for the admission of Kentucky as a sovereign state. Someone asked if conferring statehood would encourage more settlement. He replied that so many people were already streaming into the Bluegrass that statehood would likely not affect things much.

"They're comin'," he said, his voice scratchy like the sound of scraping hides. "No matter what we do, or don't do, people are headin' west."

"Is it already too crowded, then?" asked another.

He rubbed his chin before answering. "I would not say that, no."

"But, sir," the questioner continued, "you have abandoned Kentucky yourself, have you not?"

"It's true," Boone admitted. "You see, I am a hunter and a trader. For me, the woods and rivers are my livelihood. Kentucky is fast becoming a place for planters, and, I dast say, lawyers."

At that, a rumble went up from the crowd.

"Lads, lads, settle down." He waited for calm to return. "Here's the thing. Everything you've heard about the Bluegrass country is true. The land there is fertile beyond anything you can imagine. Why, you can clear sixty bushels of corn per acre! If I were a farmer, I'd be buying up every parcel I could get my hands on. But getting your hands on it ain't as easy as it sounds."

More rumbling, then he went on. "You have to buy warrants, or certificates, you see, and these allow you to make claim on a piece of property. Then you must defend your claim, and, often as not, someone else comes along claiming that property is rightly his, not yours. That's where the lawyers come in. But it's worth a shot, boys, it surely is. For there ain't no healthier land on God's green earth than the Bluegrass country."

Temple was looking at the old man like a starving man looks at a juicy roast. I don't mind saying my insides started to churn. Then someone asked about the

Indian troubles.

"It is a matter of concern, there can be no doubt," Boone said. "You all know what happened to Harmar's troops last year . . . over a hundred regulars killed. And that's nothin' compared to the numbers of settlers that have been slaughtered or captured. My own sons. . . ." Here he paused to collect himself. Everyone knows, of course, that the Boones have lost two sons to murderous Indian attacks. Oh, how my heart bleeds for the mother of those boys.

"The Indian problem ain't to be taken lightly," he continued. "But there will soon be more of us than there are of them. They'll see that we will not be turned back. Many of you know I spent years as a captive of the Shawnees. I feel I know them well, and I am sorry for what must become of them. But there ain't no other way. They must either learn to live with the white man, or move on."

We were a quiet group on the way home to Peak Creek. I could tell that Colonel Boone had stoked the fire in Stephen by the look in his eye. He tried to sound out Temple on the matter, to no avail. Temple seemed to be mulling it

61

all over in his own inscrutable way.

That night, alone in our cabin while Stephen bunked outside, I asked Temple what he made of Colonel Boone's comments. He sighed and admitted that it had crossed his mind to seek out the fertile pastures of Kentucky.

"But why?" I asked, raising myself up so I could see his expression. "Why should we leave our home and our families, especially now when we've put so much work into this place and are just starting to see results?"

He was quiet for a moment, his arms crooked behind his head as he stared into the fire. It was one of the few times when I had no idea what he was thinking, and it scared me. Finally he spoke.

"You are right," he said. "It would be foolish to risk our lives when there is no guarantee we would even be able to claim any land in Kentucky. Besides, I reckon we'll do well enough here."

His tone did not match his words and I began to feel a bit guilty, as though it was I who was holding him back. I told him that I would follow him without question wherever he decided to go, be it Kentucky or the South Seas.

"Aye, I know you would," he said,

tucking my head under his arm and holding me tightly. "But I would not ask that of you."

Which brings me, dear Cousin, to the explanation I promised regarding Temple's protectiveness of me. I was attacked by an Indian who snuck up on our cabin while Temple was away. Thankfully he did me no real harm, but it was a frightening experience, the memory of which can even now, over a year later, cause me to tremble. I know that such an occurrence is unlikely to happen again, as this area is generally considered safe from Indian attacks. Still, I am glad that Temple stays nearby or, if he must leave, takes me with him. And I am glad that he has come to his senses and dismissed the allure of Kentucky, for, despite my brave words, I do not know if I could follow my husband into a country still overridden with savages.

The situation in the Northwest Territory continues to deteriorate, as I am sure you are aware. Just last month our army and militia suffered a horrible defeat at the hands of that monster Blue Jacket. Can you imagine a white man, even one who had been adopted by the Shawnees as he was, leading the charge against his own people? Even women and children within the army camp were mercilessly slaughtered. It is too awful for words! Now they say this victory has emboldened the savages to undertake even more attacks on the Kentucky settlements.

Well, call me a coward, but I want no part of that. I do not want to be like poor Rebecca Boone and see a child of mine fall victim to such unspeakable atrocities. Especially now that we are expecting a baby, I am sure that Temple is of the same mind and is convinced of the wisdom of his decision to stay on Peak Creek.

As for Stephen, I am rather surprised that he has not joined the tidal wave heading west, given his enthusiasm for the Bluegrass. But he stays on in the valley, except for frequent trips into the woods to hunt. Sister Phoebe moons over him, yet he remains oblivious to her affections. Perhaps that is just as well since, as you once said, he will be a tough one to tame. My heart tells me Phoebe is not the one to do it.

I am, as always, your affectionate and
loving cousin,
Hannah

CHAPTER FOUR

Temple secured the last of his provisions behind his saddle and turned to his wife. Gathering her hands in his, he held them to his chest. "You know I would not leave you had I any choice in the matter. And if it were not so close to your time, I would take you with me."

"Oh, Temple, you needn't worry about me. I am feeling fine, and Stephen is here to help take care of things." Hannah could not bear to admit that Stephen was there to take care of her, as though she were a cow that needed constant tending. Yet there could be no doubt that Temple had arranged for his brother to stay with her in order to protect her in his absence.

"Damn this court session!" Temple's grip on her hands tightened. "I ought to tell them I won't serve on their blasted jury. My wife is about to give birth, for God's sake!"

"Not for at least a month," Hannah reminded him. "It is better that you satisfy this obligation now, rather than after the baby is born. That is when I shall really need you with me."

"Meaning you don't need me now?" Temple cocked an amused eyebrow in Stephen's direction. "Do you hear that, Brother? I believe my wife is trying to get rid of me."

"No such thing," Hannah said. "You know you will not be out of my thoughts for one moment." She threw her arms around his neck and hugged him tightly, her swollen belly pressed to his. Suddenly the baby gave a lusty kick.

Temple leaped back in surprise. "Good Lord, woman, what was that?"

Hannah laughed. "Your son, silly. I guess he is trying to send you on your way as well." She reached for Temple's hand and placed it on her stomach so he could feel the baby rolling and tumbling inside her.

Cradling her belly with both hands, Temple bent his head and gave her a soulful kiss. "I love you," he whispered.

Embarrassed, Stephen averted his eyes from the tender moment. Hannah blushed at the display of such intimacy in front of her husband's brother. Temple was so accustomed to it being just the two of them that he must have forgotten the rules of proper behavior. She gave him a chaste peck on the cheek.

Temple reached out to clap Stephen on the back. "Watch over her, now. She tends to get prickly with too much attention, but don't let her run you off. Stay close."

Stephen nodded his assent.

"I shall expect to see you and Phoebe in three days," Hannah said.

With a sharp salute Temple mounted the mare and trotted out of sight.

"What's that about Phoebe?" Stephen asked.

"Oh, on his way home Temple is going to stop at my parents' home for my sister Phoebe. You remember her, don't you? The two of you met at our wedding. Anyway, she is going to come stay with us for a spell to help when the baby comes."

Stephen had a blank look on his face. Hannah wondered if he truly had no memory of meeting her sister. If that were so, poor Phoebe would be crushed.

The baby kicked again. Hannah's hand automatically touched her stomach and she gave a little gasp. Blushing at having once again acknowledged her condition in front of a man not her husband, she picked up her skirts and scurried toward the house.

67

"Hannah." Stephen's bemused voice stopped her. "It's all right. I've seen women with child before. Reckon it's nothing to be ashamed of."

She dropped her eyes. "But . . . before . . . with Temple . . . it seemed to embarrass you."

"Temple ain't here now. Besides, to me you look beautiful."

Hannah's heart thumped inside her chest. "You should not say such things."

"No, reckon I shouldn't. But dancing ain't the only thing I never learned. I'm afraid I never learned how not to speak plain what I mean."

Later that evening, after supper had been eaten and cleared away, Hannah stepped outside looking for some cool air. She was tired, but the cabin's sweltering heat would preclude sleep for another hour or two. Fireflies blinked their fairy lights in the dusk. Across the yard she spotted Stephen, his back against a tree, rubbing the barrel of his musket with a piece of cloth. She wanted to go sit with him, but suddenly felt shy. *What is wrong with you,* she thought. *You have been around this man many times before and never felt uncomfortable. Of course, Temple was always there. Temple was the buffer. Now, it is just you and he.*

68

Steeling herself, she ambled over to the tree. He rose and offered to help her sit.

"I don't know," she laughed, indicating her swollen belly. "I might not be able to get up again."

"Stay here," he commanded. He dashed into the cabin and returned with a three-legged stool that he set at her side. "Madam," he said, with a courtly bow.

"Thank you, kind sir." Hannah perched on the stool and Stephen resumed his seat against the tree.

They sat silently, watching the stars make their appearance one by one. By and by, a three-quarter moon sneaked over the tops of the trees. Hannah realized with relief that her shyness had disappeared. She felt no awkwardness in their companionable silence.

Stephen resumed cleaning his gun, rubbing it down with a sure and gentle touch. She watched his long, well-shaped fingers fit themselves around the curves of the weapon, like a virtuoso handling his instrument. His ruffled sleeves were folded to the elbow, and he had removed his neck cloth so that his shirt fell open to the middle of his chest. Hannah knew he had done this to seek relief from the warmth of the evening — a perfectly natural thing to do. But also rather bold to expose so much of one's skin to a woman. Of course, they were kin so it did not matter.

As the darkness deepened, tree frogs set to chirping, underscoring the night with their rhythmic beat. Stephen finished with his gun and set it aside.

"Thank you for coming to stay with me," Hannah said. "I am sure it is nothing but a nuisance to have to look after your brother's wife. But it does ease Temple's mind that you are here, and for that I am grateful."

"I am glad to do it," he said simply.

"When Temple returns, shall you stay with us for a while? We would be pleased to have you for as long as you like."

"I promised to help Pa for the rest of the summer. Then . . . I don't know. Reckon I'll go west for winter hunting." He leaned his head back against the tree trunk. Hannah could almost see a vision of the beautiful bluegrass of Kentucky marching through his brain. "Stephen, it is obvious you are quite taken with the Kentucky country. Why don't you go there for good?"

"Reckon I will, someday," he said. After a moment he added: "When the time is right."

"Yes, I am sure your father still needs your help. It is good of you to stay on at home. When you have married and started a fam-

70

ily that is when you will no doubt seek your own place over the mountains."

Stephen made a skeptical sound.

"Perhaps it seems to you unlikely that you will find a wife," Hannah prattled on, "but I am certain of it. I have not forgotten how all the young ladies clamored to dance with you at my wedding. You know, there are plenty of girls in the valley who have their eye on the dashing Stephen Cole. My sister is one of them."

Hannah immediately wished she could take back that last part. Phoebe would be mortified if Stephen knew of her attraction to him. On the other hand, what harm could it do? Perhaps knowing how Phoebe felt would help him to overcome his shyness.

"Forgive me for dwelling on such delicate matters, but I suppose I am rather like you . . . I have never learned how not to speak plainly. I feel you should know of Phoebe's interest so that, if you are at all inclined in that direction, you can be confident of success."

Stephen was quiet for so long that Hannah became certain she had overstepped her boundaries. Finally he said, with more than a touch of irony in his voice: "I'll cogitate on that."

Hannah cringed inside. "I am sorry if I

71

have made you uncomfortable. It was not my intention."

"Think nothing of it." Stephen stood abruptly. "I'll say good night now."

Sighing, Hannah retreated into the still stifling cabin. After a few moments she peeked outside. Stephen had thrown some blankets a few feet from the door. He lowered himself to the ground, checked his musket's load, and lay back with his hands behind his head. Despite his apparent displeasure with her, he was taking his bodyguard duties seriously. Nothing and no one would get past him tonight.

Hannah rose on the third day fully expecting to see Temple and Phoebe by suppertime. She made extra portions of rabbit stew and heated water for a bath. By sunset they had not arrived. Setting the stew by the hearth to stay warm, she wandered outside. Stephen sat on a bench, whittling on a piece of wood. "What are you making?" she asked.

"Pipe stem."

She watched the pile of shavings at his feet grow for a minute. "I thought Temple would be back by now," she said.

He turned the stem over, admiring his work. "Maybe by tonight."

"But it is almost full dark. I don't think

he would travel at night. Not with Phoebe."

"Reckon he was delayed," Stephen said, showing not the least bit of concern.

"Perhaps," she sighed.

The following day she was certain Temple and Phoebe would arrive, but the hours passed with no sign of them. She tossed in bed all night long, fretting in sheets damp with sweat.

When she rose on the morning of the fifth day Temple had been gone, Hannah was convinced something had gone awry. She found Stephen in the barn, shoeing one of the horses. "I think you should go look for them," she announced.

Stephen glanced up from the hoof held between his knees. "It ain't nothing, I'm bound. The court session lasted longer than expected, most likely."

"But what if it is not nothing? What if they met with an accident, or, God forbid, some savages overtook them? You must go look for them."

"I can't do that, Hannah. I can't leave you here alone."

"I am in no danger here. But they might be in grave danger. Please, Stephen."

Stephen stepped around the horse, wiping his hands on his waistcoat. "I promised

Temple I'd stay close to you. Would you have me break my word?"

"What does your word matter with my husband's and sister's well-being at stake?"

"No, Hannah." Stephen shook his head. "What you are asking me to do makes no sense. Temple's plenty capable of taking care of himself and Phoebe. I ain't leaving a defenseless woman all alone to go looking for an able-bodied man. Don't you remember what happened the last time you were left alone?"

"Then take me with you," Hannah pleaded.

"In your condition? Think what you are saying."

"I know exactly what I am saying." She stepped around him and reached for her saddle. "Either you shall find them, or I shall find them, or we shall find them together. But I will not sit by idly while my husband may be in peril."

Stephen took hold of her, his strong hands gripping her forearms. "You have lost all reason, woman! You can't ride. You would be risking the baby."

"We must find them," she insisted, her panic growing. "If I can't ride, then I shall walk."

"All right, then. All right. Lord, what a

hard-headed woman you are." He gave her an exasperated look. "I'll go look for them. But promise me you'll stay inside the cabin while I'm gone, with the door bolted and a loaded rifle close at hand."

"I promise," Hannah said, her heart swelling with relief.

Still, he held her in a painful grip, his hands squeezing her arms.

"Let me go, Stephen," she said, confused. "You are hurting me."

He dropped his hands and looked away, his face flushed. "I'll follow the road toward town," he said, "but, if I don't find them, I'll turn around and come back before nightfall. I won't be leaving you here alone all night."

Agreeing to these conditions, Hannah hastily prepared some provisions for him. As soon as he left, she bolted herself inside the cabin, despite the heat, and tried to keep busy. No more than an hour had passed when she heard noises in the yard. Peering through a hole where some of the chinking had fallen out, she saw Temple at the reins of her father's wagon, hitched to the black mare. Beside him, on the wagon seat, sat Phoebe. With a squeal of delight, she unbolted the door and waddled out to greet them.

"Temple, oh, Temple, where have you been? I've been in such a state. You should have been home three days ago."

Temple hopped down and gathered her into a hug. "I am sorry, my dear. The court session lasted an extra day, and then, when I went to fetch Phoebe, your father didn't have a spare horse for her to ride, so he lent me this wagon. But the damn' wheel broke, halfway here, and I had to ride back to town to get the smithy to fix it. I knew you would be worried, but I had no way to send word."

"It doesn't matter now. Just so long as you are safe." She nestled in his familiar embrace.

Climbing down from the wagon, Phoebe stood to one side, looking tired and disheveled. Extracting herself from Temple's arms, Hannah gave her sister a quick hug. "You are looking a little peaked. This trip has been hard on you, hasn't it? Come along, let's get you something to eat."

She took Phoebe to the cabin while Temple led the horse and wagon toward the barn.

In a few moments he joined them, frowning. "Where is Stephen?" he asked.

"Oh, I completely forgot," Hannah said. "He went looking for you hardly more than an hour ago. How could he have missed you, I wonder?"

Temple's frown deepened. "He left you here alone, against my instructions?"

"Well, I was quite insistent that he do so. I was fearful something had happened to you. Please don't be angry with him." Hannah dished up a plate and set it before him. Temple ignored it and stormed out of the cabin.

"You never told me he has such a temper," Phoebe needled.

Hannah pursed her lips. "He is actually quite even tempered. I am sure he will be fine."

But Temple spent the rest of the day pacing in the yard, one eye on the path as he waited for Stephen to appear. It was evening before his wait was over. As Stephen rode into the clearing, Temple strode forward to meet him.

"Explain yourself, you half-faced varmint! What do you mean by leaving Hannah all alone?"

Stephen dismounted and held the reins of his sweating horse. "Well, Brother, glad to see you're plenty chirk. Too bad I missed you on the road. I thought I saw some fresh tracks leading into the underbrush, so I followed them for a ways. That's when you must have passed me."

"Answer me! How could you abandon her?"

"Temple, please." Hannah came up behind him and placed a hand on his arm. "I told you that I insisted he go. It was all my idea."

"And a damn' bad idea it was!" Temple shook her off, pushing closer to Stephen. "So now you allow yourself to be ordered around by a woman, is that it? I counted on you having better sense."

Stephen's eyes darkened even as his voice remained steady. "I did what I thought was right."

"You did a damn' fool thing. I trusted you with the care of the person most precious to me in the world, and you let me down. I will not forget that . . . *Brother.*" With a disgusted shake of his head, Temple stalked away.

Stephen's fists clenched as he started to follow.

"Let him go," Hannah pleaded.

He paused and without a word retreated to the barn.

Phoebe sidled up to Hannah's side. "Did you see that? They almost came to blows. I don't think much of your husband's even temper. Seems to me Stephen's the cool-headed one."

78

"Oh, hush, Phoebe." Hannah hurried after Temple to see if she could calm him, although she considered that her first duty should be to apologize to Stephen. She wondered why he had not placed more of the blame on her, as would surely have been justified. Perhaps he had been trying to protect her from her husband's wrath, and so let that wrath be spent on himself. A new appreciation for Stephen Cole bloomed in Hannah's mind.

CHAPTER FIVE

Before the day was out Hannah succeeded in convincing Temple to apologize to his brother. The apology was accepted, grudgingly. Hannah then prevailed on Stephen to stay until the end of the week, on the pretext that his help was needed in the fields. In truth, Phoebe had been so down-hearted when she learned of Stephen's plan to leave immediately that Hannah had agreed to do what she could to keep him around for a while.

Phoebe's presence, although meant to be gainful to her burdened sister, soon proved to be exactly the opposite. Rarely did she undertake any chore without complaint of some sort. She refused to do any heavy work, pleading frailty, yet she did not seem to find it untoward that Hannah, due to give birth at any moment, was thus left to do much of the lifting and toting. Phoebe was a small girl, Hannah kept reminding herself, with a history of illness. Yet there did not seem to be anything specifically wrong with her besides a constant, dry cough that seemed to arise more from habit than necessity.

Remarkably Phoebe's anathema to work disappeared whenever Stephen was around. Suddenly the soul of sweetness, she would bustle about importantly, trying to capture center stage. And she never failed to volunteer for, or invent, any duty that would place her in close proximity to the younger Cole. Many was the time that Hannah sought out Phoebe, needing her assistance, only to discover that she had left to tag along with the men.

None of Phoebe's preening seemed to have any effect on the object of her desire. Stephen steered clear of her, as best he could. And when forced to deal with her, there was none of the spark about him that cousin Dolley had noted. It puzzled Hannah, because her sister was really quite lovely — small and dark, with the sort of pixie features that so many men found appealing. Nothing at all like Hannah who, although considered handsome and well proportioned, was altogether a more robust woman. Part of her wished Stephen would show some interest because, after all,

Phoebe was her sister and she wanted her to be happy. Part of her was relieved at his indifference because she somehow doubted that Stephen Cole could ever make Phoebe Allison a happy woman. Or *vice versa*.

She longed to talk the situation over with Temple who, having expended his anger at his brother, was now feeling magnanimous toward him. But with Phoebe's arrival the opportunity for private talks had vanished. Temple had constructed a loft — no more than a few slabs of wood elevated over their own bed and reached by climbing a ladder — where Phoebe slept. Every word they uttered, even in a whisper, could be heard throughout the tiny cabin. It was odd, Hannah thought, how during the first twenty years of her life, when she had almost never been alone, she had never craved privacy, but now, after two years of idyllic seclusion with her husband, she mourned its loss. If it was true that one does not miss what one never had, it was also true that one doubly misses what one had and can never have again. For even though Phoebe's visit was only temporary, soon they would have a baby sharing their lives and, Hannah prayed, many more after that. She would simply have to treasure those two unforgettable years with Temple, taking them out every now and again, like keepsakes from a box, before lovingly placing them back in the recesses of her mind.

On the day before Stephen was to depart, Hannah stood in the yard dressing out a wild turkey. The men were in the fields and Phoebe, as usual, had invented some excuse to visit them there. She smiled, remembering Phoebe's reaction when Stephen had arrived home yesterday with the turkey slung over his back. The girl had made quite a fuss, declaring it to be the largest turkey she had ever laid eyes upon and praising his hunting skills to the skies. Stephen had eyed her suspiciously before plopping the bird on the table and asking Hannah if she needed any help dressing it. Surprised at the offer, since food preparation was normally a woman's chore, she told him not to bother, that Phoebe would be glad to help. He gave her a look, unnoticed by her sister, that said — "You and I both know better." — before taking his leave.

That look probably explained why Phoebe seemed to hold no charm for him. Despite her best efforts, he had seen through the façade she had constructed of a hard-working, attentive helpmate. Stephen Cole had no use for a lazy, argumentative woman.

It was a pity, because Hannah was certain

that deep down Phoebe possessed reserves of strength that had never been tapped. As the third daughter behind Hannah and Rhoda, both strong-willed and energetic workers, Phoebe had been allowed to indulge her alleged frailty. Although there was plenty of work to go around, Nancy Allison had fallen into the habit of assigning the least onerous tasks to her "fragile" daughter. This, of course, had only served to feed Phoebe's own notions of herself. Yet, if truly tested, Hannah was hopeful that her sister would not fail. Unfortunately it appeared that Phoebe would never get the opportunity to prove her worth to Stephen Cole.

Hannah finished plucking the bird and was preparing to gut it when a strange sensation rolled through her mid-section. Ever since the midday meal she had felt a bit uncomfortable — indigestion, she assumed — but this was different, a painful and very strong tightening of her abdominal muscles. Suddenly a wet warmth engulfed her legs and feet. Lifting her skirts, she looked down to see that she was standing in a puddle.

"Heavens!" she exclaimed, then laughed at her surprise. "I was not expecting you, little one, for another few weeks, but perhaps no one told you that."

84

Waddling into the cabin, she cleaned herself up, and then turned to preparing for the birth, laying an oilcloth sheet over the bed and setting out the few implements that might be needed.

Temple had fashioned an iron triangle that she could clang to summon them in from the fields, but she saw no reason to yet. Having attended several of her mother's birthings, she knew it could be some time before anything much happened. In the meantime, she might as well finish dressing the turkey; her family still had to eat, after all.

Two hours passed before the men and Phoebe returned. They found Hannah pacing the cabin, stopping every so often to breathe her way through the pain.

"Ah, there you are," she said, reading all of their expressions at once — Temple's shock, Phoebe's fear, and Stephen's concern. "Phoebe, be a dear and boil some water. I've laid out everything, so there's not much to do but wait. It should not be too long . . . the pains are coming regular as rain now." She bent over with a fresh spasm as everyone scurried into action. Phoebe raced to fill the water kettle, Stephen, feeling useless and out of place, retreated to the yard to finish the day's chores, and Temple rushed to place a supportive arm around his wife.

"Good God, why didn't you call us in earlier? How long has this been going on?"

"Not that long," Hannah replied, coming out of her pain. "I would have called you if I had thought it was necessary. Everything seems to be fine."

"Come, lie down." Temple steered her toward the bed.

"I reckon I shall keep walking for as long as I can. They say that hurries things along."

After another half hour of pacing, Hannah could no longer stand through the pain. Temple helped her to the bed and kissed her sweating brow. Then she sent him away.

She looked over at Phoebe standing hunched into herself like a cornered animal. Hannah tried to remember if the girl had been on hand for any of their mother's birthings, deciding that she might have been old enough to help out with their youngest brother's arrival. Still, that was not the same as being the sole midwife. No wonder she looked nervous and scared. But anybody who grew up on a farm was familiar with birth, and death for that matter, so even sheltered Phoebe would have some knowledge of the process.

Another pain, the strongest one yet, racked her body. She tried to breathe through it, but it lasted so long that she lost her concentration. A tearing sound escaped from her throat. Phoebe stood paralyzed, wringing her hands. Hannah motioned her over and pulled her down on the bed next to her.

"You will have to help me, Phoebe," she said, panting as the spasm passed. "I know Temple can hear if I scream or cry out, and he will be beside himself. So whenever the pain comes, I want you to hold my hands, look right at me, and help me to breathe. Breathe with me all the way through the pain. Can you do that?"

Phoebe looked away, chewing at her lip.

"What is it? What's the matter?"

"I'm scared," Phoebe whispered, tears welling in her eyes. "I don't know what to do."

"Well, my dear, I shall be doing the bulk of it, after all. And I am sure you know more than you think you do. It is not too different from pulling a calf or a foal, when you get right down to it."

"Yes, it is." Phoebe's face had gone white as a snowdrift. "What if something goes wrong?"

Hannah's reply was cut off by searing pain. She grabbed the younger girl's hands and forced her to meet her gaze. Phoebe hesitated, then, following her sister's lead, began breathing loudly and rhythmically. Maintaining the rhythm, Hannah got through the contraction without crying out.

"There, you see? You did just fine," said Hannah when it was over, thinking how peculiar it was that she should be offering comfort and encouragement to Phoebe rather than the other way around. "It should not be long now," she promised.

But things seemed to stall. The pains kept coming strong as ever, but not with any greater frequency. Hannah worked through them, gritting her teeth and breathing in time with her sister, but she could feel herself tiring. Temple stuck his head in the door at one point; she shooed him away, not wanting him to see her in this condition. It was not vanity that concerned her, but a desire to spare him undue worry.

Finally, after what seemed an eternity, the tempo and severity of the pains increased. Hannah could no longer bear them in silence. Pulling her knees up, she pushed, her muscles bearing down with a will of their own. Phoebe, wide-eyed and colorless, trembled by the side of the bed.

Hannah thrust out an arm and pushed her toward the foot of the bed. "He's coming! Help me! Help me!"

Stumbling, Phoebe took a position between Hannah's sweat-streaked thighs. She inhaled sharply and clapped a hand over her mouth.

"My God, Hannah, the head isn't coming out first! It's . . . it's backwards!"

Hannah's moan rose to the rafters of the hot, fetid-smelling cabin.

"What do I do? What do I do?" Phoebe backed away, her hands shaking as though palsied.

"Try to turn him," Hannah managed to grunt just before the uncontrollable urge to push came upon her again. She rose on her elbows and bore down with all her might. A sound that began as a wail and ended as a scream, like some crazed loon, escaped her lips.

Phoebe turned and ran.

Within seconds, Temple was at her side. He dropped to his knees, stroking her brow, his eyes wide with fear.

"Help me," Hannah cried, her heart pounding so hard in her ears that her voice sounded distant. "He's coming out the wrong way."

Temple moved between her legs. As she once more tried to expel the baby, the color drained from his face. When the spasm passed, he sat next to her and took her hand.

"The baby is in a breech position," he confirmed, his voice cracking. "Next time you have to push, hold back while I try to turn him around. If that doesn't work, I will try to hold on to him and help pull him out, but it will not be easy."

Hannah nodded, although she barely heard his words. His form wavered before her, framed by darkness and pulsing stars. She tensed again, and he returned to the foot of the bed.

"Don't push, not yet, not yet!" Palpating her belly, he attempted to turn the baby, but he did not really know what he was doing, and he hated the thought of hurting Hannah even worse. With a groan of frustration, he gave up. "All right, my love, now push. Harder now, harder!"

With a cry, she fell back on the bed, defeated. She was tired, so tired, and it hurt so much.

Temple bathed her forehead and spoke in a low voice. "Hannah, you must push harder. If you can push him out a little more I might be able to get a grip on him. If my hands were smaller, I could try to reach up inside and pull . . . I've done it with calves before, but I am afraid I would hurt you too much."

Hannah whimpered with the onset of

90

another contraction. Once again, she raised herself up and pushed, but she could feel her strength leaving her.

Temple looked up, his face ashen. Laying his head on her chest, he listened to her wildly beating heart. "Try, my love, try," he pleaded. "Don't give up!"

Hannah reached for his hand, her eyes black as a bottomless well. "Get Stephen," she rasped.

"Stephen? I don't understand."

"His hands. . . ." She tried to explain, but words were too hard. "Get him."

The next thing she knew, Stephen stood at her side. She saw herself through his eyes — body slick with sweat, hair tamped to her cheek, eyes bloodshot — and did not care. "Help me," she mouthed.

He stepped between her legs and knelt, his voice speaking soothing words she could not understand. She felt the pain come and rose to meet it, like an army streaming across the battlefield to join the enemy. Her loins were on fire as though someone had ripped her with hot tongs. The cry on her lips died as she fainted dead away.

Hannah floated in cool water, rising and falling in gentle swells. The sound of her breathing echoed in her ears like the tide crashing

91

on the shore. Sunlight warmed her face and turned the water's surface into a carpet of stars.

She went under and felt herself sinking, pulled by some irresistible force. Deeper and deeper she went, the sun receding as the depths of the water closed about her. Soon the darkness was complete, save for one shaft of light that penetrated the murky waters. Her body undulated with the ebb and flow of unseen undercurrents.

Suddenly a shadow obscured the shaft of light. Hannah reached out, desperate to bring it back. She could feel that it was still there, even though all around her was blackest black. She strained upward, breaking the surface of the water in a spray of rainbow-colored drops.

There, sitting on the bank of the river, was Temple, smiling and laughing as though she had just performed a marvelous trick. She stood and came toward him, her naked body streaming with diamond-like droplets of water. Still smiling, he rose and started walking, gesturing for her to follow.

She could see where he was headed — the towering white oak where they had first kissed and where they had become man and wife. Underneath its sheltering boughs, he paused. She came up behind him and encircled his waist, pressing her body against his strong back. He turned in her embrace and, to her amazement, she found that it was Stephen who she held so close.

His strong, supple hands moved up her back, over her shoulders, down her arms, caressing her like he caressed his weapon, taking pure pleasure in the feel of a thing he knew intimately. . . .

Hannah opened her eyes and saw Temple looking down at her. The worry lines on his face eased a bit as he watched her come back to herself. He leaned over and kissed her gently on the forehead, then moved aside to place a softly wrapped bundle in the crook of her arm.

"Meet James, our son," he said.

Hannah's Journal
October, 1794, Peak Creek

Dear Cousin Dolley,

Must I begin every entry in this journal with an apology for neglecting it? Many times have I meant to add to it, only to be brought up short by the inadequacy of words. What to say to a young wife and mother who, in the space of a few hours, loses both husband and baby? Yet Mother Cole has just paid a visit and tells us there is, finally, happy news from your quarter, so that it seems possible, at last, to speak of the unspeakable.

Even now, dear Cousin, my heart breaks for you. How cruel, how cruel is fate! So often have I thought how wonderful it is that you and I seemed to be following almost identical paths — each marrying fine men and each becoming mothers to two fine boys. And then to learn that the cursed fever heartlessly took your husband and youngest boy, William Temple. It is too awful!

My own Temple and I were so honored when you christened your son with that name. It has a long history in your family, of course, but you will forgive me for believing that you had my own dear

94

husband a little bit in mind when you chose it. And now his namesake is gone, God rest his innocent soul.

I have tried to put myself in your shoes to imagine what I would do were I to lose Temple and my baby, Holbert, who is the same age now as was little William Temple. I cannot. My mind simply cannot imagine a life without them.

And yet, what choice have we but to carry on? You have married, Mother Cole tells us, a gentleman who boarded near your house in Philadelphia, by the name of James Madison, a Congressman from Virginia! Dearest Dolley, I know nothing of this gentleman, other than that he is lucky indeed to have won your hand. But I pray that he is something like the man of your girlhood dreams. Do you remember? You dreamed of marrying a man of property and importance, a man who possessed lofty ideas and cut a fine figure. Surely a Congressman must be all of those things, though perhaps what was foremost in your mind was finding someone to be a good father for little Payne. I pray that your Mr. Madison is up to the task.

Mother Cole conveys to us another loss you have suffered, that of your lifelong servant, Mother Amy. Perhaps you mourn her passing as much as that of your husband and son. If that seems a vile notion to you, then I am sorry. For some, I am sure, the feeling one has for a servant, no matter how devoted and loyal, cannot compare to the love of family. Yet I sensed a special bond between you and Mother Amy, and for good reason. More, perhaps, than the woman who birthed you, she was the woman who raised you, cared for you, tucked you in at night, and woke you in the morning. She was the one who shared your triumphs and wiped the tears from your cheeks when you despaired. She was with you every day of your life. You must miss her terribly.

It is a puzzling thing, this link we Virginians have with our Negroes. I have come to ponder it by and by because our own household now includes a Negro, Lucy, who was recently given to us by my father. He did not care for her attitude and was on the verge of selling her when my mother suggested he send her to us. She is only seventeen, but is, I must admit, a Godsend. A big, strong wench, she carries her own weight with Temple in the fields, though, commonly,

I use her to help me with the boys and with all of my work around the house.

Her attitude is a mite troublesome, though it is nothing I can call her down on. As a child she was often a lazy thing, running off to hide whenever someone had a job for her. Father took the whip to her more times than I can count. She is settled down now, mostly doing her work without complaint. But I don't care for the way she looks at me sometimes, like she would not flinch if I dropped dead before her eyes! Why should that be? She is treated well here — far better than most Negroes, if you ask me. She has a warm, dry place to sleep, she eats the same food we eat, and I have never asked her to do any piece of work that I have not done myself. But is she grateful? No indeed. She acts like she is simply enduring life until something better comes along, though what that might be for a Negro wench I would not know. I can tell you this, though. If I ever took a notion to give Lucy her freedom, like your father did for Mother Amy, she'd be gone quicker than a cat can pounce. But never mind my domestic troubles.

Dear Cousin, how lovely it would be

to see you again. Mother Cole says that when you are not in Philadelphia, you and Mr. Madison will be busy managing his ancestral home in Orange County. It sounds quite grand! Temple and I could never hope to own such a large estate, but we are quite pleased with what we have accomplished here on Peak Creek. In four year's time, we have managed to clear enough land to plant three different crops — corn, wheat, and hemp. In addition to the slave cabin, we have added a corncrib and a summer kitchen, and Temple is making plans to build another room onto the house since he is sure we shall continue to increase our family. I told him it was too soon, that we should wait to see what the Lord has in mind for us. Holbert came easily enough, but James was a hard birth. In the end, it was Stephen, of all people, who helped me deliver James. An odd rôle, I am well aware, for a woman's brother-in-law to play, but things were becoming quite desperate and I knew I needed Stephen's capable hands to ease my precious baby into this world. Not to take anything away from my own dear Temple, naturally, but his brother did perform admirably.

Anyway, if two babies are all God intends for me to have, then so be it. I just don't know if I am a woman, like my mother, with the strength to bear many children.

It pleasures me to see Temple putting down roots here on Peak Creek. He seems to have given up the notion of moving to Kentucky. Not so Stephen. When last he called upon us, he was full of the news of something he called the Battle of Fallen Timbers. General Wayne, he says, crushed the redskins for good, making all of Kentucky and the Northwest Territory safe for settlement. Temple said he hoped that was true, but that it would be wise to wait and see. Bless him, I sometimes think that if it were not for me, he would pick up stakes and leave tomorrow for the western country. But he knows that I don't want to leave, that I am wary of taking my boys to such a dangerous place. So he says nothing about going, and seems content to work his land on Peak Creek.

Stephen, on the other hand, is the picture of discontent. He is gone most of the year to hunt, but still calls his father's house home. At twenty-four, he is certainly of an age to strike out on his own, yet something holds him back. Temple thinks he is waiting to find a wife. To my mind, that is about as likely as the pig having puppies. Stephen Cole is not the marrying kind, to Phoebe's everlasting dismay. Besides, he needn't be married to stake a claim in Kentucky. Plenty of single men have done so. Well, whatever holds him here, I am not sorry for it. Though we only see him once or twice a year, we know that sooner or later he will show up at our door, bearded and as gruff as a bear, bringing us game to eat and pelts to keep us warm. If he left for good, I would miss him.

I am, as always, your loving cousin,
Hannah Cole

CHAPTER SIX

Temple removed his hat and ran a hand through his sweat-streaked hair. Retying the club at his neck, he washed up and sat, shoulders slumping, at the hearthside table. Carrying the food for the noon meal in from the summer kitchen, Hannah directed six-year-old James and four-year-old Holbert to take their places on either side of their father. She served up the stew to the three males and stepped back, waiting for them to take their fill before eating herself. Folding her hands over her belly, just beginning to swell with her third pregnancy, she watched with pride as the boys kept their hands in their laps. She had trained them to wait until their father said grace and began eating before they ate themselves. Wearily Temple picked up his spoon and dished into the stew.

James cast a questioning glance at his mother, wondering if he was allowed to eat

101

without a prayer being said. Hannah smiled at him. "Your pa is plumb tuckered out today, Son. The Lord understands. You and Holbert dig in, now."

Temple proceeded as if he had not heard her, his elbows propped on the table, his head bent to the bowl as he shoveled in the stew. Hannah regarded him closely. He had spent the morning harvesting the wheat crop, tiring work to be sure, but not the type of thing that would bring him this low.

"You feel all right, do you?" she asked, setting cups of milk before the boys.

He nodded, but let loose with a sigh as he reached for another slice of bread.

"I'll help you this afternoon, Pa," said James, his childish eyes bright.

"You are pert near big enough to be a help to me," said Temple, summoning a smile for his son. "Next year you can work in the fields. Right now you are a bigger help to your ma around here."

James's face fell but he answered with a — "Yes, sir." — as he had been taught.

"Well, something is troubling you," said Hannah. "You look lower than a bottom feeder."

Temple scraped the bottom of his bowl and pushed it away. Hannah started to refill it, but he waved her off. "Sit down and eat," he said.

She pulled up a stool and served herself even though she had suddenly lost her appetite.

"Reckon the reason I am looking low is due to discouragement," Temple said. "The wheat crop is the worst since we've been here. Be lucky to get thirty bushels an acre. And the corn and hemp are not much better. Don't know as I am going to clear enough hemp to even make it worth my while sending it East."

"Maybe we planted too late this spring because of all that rain," said Hannah, shaving off some sugar for her johnnycake.

Temple shook his head. "No, we got the seed in at just the right time. Weather conditions were near perfect all season. It just seems like the land is played out. Like it is too tired to grow anything any more."

Little Holbert, finished eating, began playing with his spoon, bringing his fist down on its bowl and giggling as it flipped into the air.

Hannah grabbed it away. "You boys take the rest of this stew out to Lucy in the kitchen. Then go check the chicken coop for eggs. James, keep an eye on your brother."

"Yes'm," they muttered.

Hannah waited until they were out the door before speaking. "What are you trying to say, Temple?"

He looked her in the eye. "I am trying to say maybe it is time we moved on."

There it was, out in the open. Hannah could not honestly say she was surprised. She had been expecting something like this for the last two or three years as each succeeding crop yielded less than the year before. She knew it had been burdening her husband and had meant to bring it up with him but had put it off, afraid to hear the words he had just uttered.

"Where were you thinking?" she asked, hoping against hope he had his eye on some place still in the valley.

"Kentucky."

Hannah realized from the instant he named it that his mind was made up. He must have been planning this for quite some time. Looking back, she remembered certain things he had said, hints dropped, openings given inviting her to discuss it with him. But she had ignored them, hoping the problem would just go away.

"It will be a hard thing to do," she said, tears pricking the backs of her eyes, "leaving our families, everything we are used to.

And what about the new baby? Will he be born in a strange place, away from everyone we know?"

Temple reached across the table and took her hand. "He will be with us wherever he is born. That is enough."

But was it? Was it enough? What if her child grew up never knowing his grandparents, his aunts and uncles, his cousins? What if something happened to her out there in the wilderness? Would Temple try to raise motherless children? Would he bring them back to Virginia to their family? Would he — perish the thought! — remarry so that her children would be raised by some strange woman?

Hannah realized her imagination was running away with her. She squeezed her eyes shut, telling herself that Temple was only trying to do what was best for them. A single tear trickled down her cheek.

Temple rose and came to stand behind her, his strong hands kneading her shoulders. "Dearest, I know it will be hard for you. If you would like to wait until the baby is born, we shall. But it would be better to do this quickly so that we can get settled in time for next year's planting. There is a group leaving next month that we could join. That would get us there in plenty of time to raise a cabin and clear some land before the spring."

"Next month! Temple, why haven't you said anything until now?"

"I thought it would be best to have a plan in place so you would not worry about the details." He pulled up a stool and leaned forward excitedly. "As I said, we can go with a group that is leaving in September. We'll cross the Gap and stay at Boonesborough just long enough to pick up supplies. Then we'll head on to Fleming County."

"How do you know all this?" Hannah asked, amazed.

"Your cousin, John Allison, has some army warrants for land in Fleming County. He has been to look at it and he says it is beautiful, right on the Licking River. There are lots of meadows, he says, perfect for farming. He is willing to transfer the warrants to me. So, you see, we already have a place waiting for us."

"What about this place? Can you sell it?"

"I am sure of it. Don't you see, my dear, how right this is? Our sons will inherit the most fertile land in the country, not a used-up plot good for nothing but growing cattle feed."

"What about . . . the danger?"

Temple looked puzzled. "Danger? From

106

Indians, do you mean? That's all over with. Ever since Fallen Timbers most of Kentucky has been as safe as . . . as the streets of Richmond. Kentucky is downright civilized now."

"That is not what I hear," Hannah countered. "What about that Indian chief, Tecumseh? I heard he refused to sign the peace treaty and that he is trying to bring all the tribes together to fight the settlements. Is that true?"

Temple gave her a surprised look. "Why, Hannah, I had no idea you followed events in the news so closely."

"Don't you make fun of me, Temple Cole. I have eyes and ears. Do you think I don't listen when you and the men folk all get together and talk? Do you think I can't read the concern in everyone's eyes when the subject turns to Indian matters? Things are not as settled as you make them out to be." Hannah picked up her uneaten bowl of stew and emptied it into the slop bucket. She felt awful challenging Temple like this. Never before had she questioned one of his decisions. But this was such a big step — leaving all she held near and dear to move to a far and dangerous place.

Calmly Temple rose and pulled her to him, stroking her back as though comfort-

107

ing a child. "My dear, do you think for one minute that I would let any harm come to you or the boys? I don't blame you for being scared. I have not forgotten what that damned redskin did to you." He ran his thumb over the tiny scar at her hairline that was the only visible reminder of that awful day. "But I have been assured that the area along the Licking has been free of Indian attacks for years. And even if there were trouble, there are plenty of forts where we could find protection. It is worth taking a little risk . . . for us and for the boys."

Hannah dropped her head to his chest. She could not refuse, of course. Temple was her husband and she must go wherever he led. Straightening her shoulders, she gave him a shaky smile. "Then I think you are right that we should make haste. This babe has a hankering to be born in Kentucky."

Having bowed to her husband's will, Hannah threw herself into preparations for their leave-taking. The group they were to join in their trek across the mountains was gathering at Fort Chiswell at the end of September. That gave her a little over a month to pack and say her good byes.

The first person both she and Temple thought to tell their big news was Stephen, who they hoped would consider coming with them. But he had been gone from the valley for almost a year on some sort of expedition, and nobody knew when he would be back. The best they could do would be to leave word of their destination and trust that he could find them if he cared to.

Both sets of families accepted the news with apparent equanimity. Temple's father agreed that the once fertile land of the New River Valley seemed to be played out and declared he would head west himself were he a younger man. He offered to oversee the sale of Temple's property on Peak Creek and send the proceeds on with Stephen or some other trusted messenger. Hannah's parents were down-hearted at the prospect of losing their favorite daughter to the "wilds" of Kentucky, but understood that her duty was to follow her husband.

Phoebe, now twenty-four and still a spinster, had finally accepted that she would never marry Stephen Cole, and so had reluctantly agreed to wed an older widower with several small children. It seemed to Hannah like a life filled with drudgery and despair, but the widower was a man of some minor wealth and was thus considered to be a good catch. Their wedding date was moved up so that Hannah and Temple could take part, but then postponed when the groom was called East on some pressing business. Phoebe seemed not to care — if she could not have Stephen, it mattered not to her whether she married today or a year from today. The only reason she had agreed to marry at all was to escape her parents' house where, in her mind, she was still treated like a child. At least as a married woman she would be the mistress of her own home.

The person who was the most despondent about the upcoming move was Lucy. She had formed an attachment to Rufus, a slave on a neighboring farm. Although not officially married, they considered themselves to be husband and wife and were devastated at the prospect of being separated. Sympathetic to their plight, Hannah asked Temple if it would be possible for them to buy Rufus from his owner, a Mr. Campbell. Temple told her it was beyond their means, but that he would offer to sell Lucy to Campbell if Hannah thought she could do without her.

"There will be much to do . . . building a home and starting in a new place, all with a new baby to boot . . . but I suppose I can do without her," said Hannah. "She would not be much good anyway, constantly in the doldrums over losing Rufus. Go ahead and offer her to Mister Campbell."

But it turned out Campbell had no interest in her purchase. Indeed, he was making plans to sell Rufus down south. Evidently Rufus was a bit of a troublemaker, and Campbell intended to get rid of him before he poisoned the rest of his slaves.

When Temple brought this news back to Hannah, she was saddened, but not particularly surprised. "It stands to reason that Lucy would choose a rabble-rouser for her man," she told him. "Seems like she would come to a bad end with that Rufus. She is better off staying with us."

They agreed that they would say nothing to Lucy about Campbell's plans for Rufus. If Lucy knew he was to be sold down south, she might try to run away to follow him. Nothing good could come of that.

Preparations continued without a word said concerning Lucy's fate. Then, a week before they were to leave, she found out that Rufus had been sold south. Beside herself, she stole away in the middle of the night. Temple found her only a few miles from home. He brought her back, tossed her into her tiny shack, and went looking for his whip. He had never taken the whip to a

111

slave before, but runaways had to be taught a lesson.

Hannah crept into Lucy's cabin and found her crumpled on the floor, legs and arms trembling as she silently wept. "Lucy" — Hannah crouched by her side — "you must gather yourself. This will not do."

Lucy rolled away and continued to weep.

"Where do you think you were going?" Hannah persisted. "To find Rufus? Do you realize how hopeless that is? He is gone, Lucy. You will never find him."

"Didja know?" Lucy mumbled.

"Know? Know what? That Rufus was to be sold?" Hannah considered whether a lie would serve better than the truth, and decided it did not matter. "Mister Campbell said he was thinking of it, yes. That is why he was not interested in buying you. You see, we did try, Lucy. We did try to do something so you and Rufus could be together. It simply was not meant to be."

Lucy raised up, hatred blazing from her streaming eyes. "You could 'a' give me mah freedom. Iffen I had mah freedom I'd 'a' found him."

Stunned, Hannah reeled back. "Your freedom! What good would that do?"

"I'd work till I'd earned enuf to buy him back!"

For a split second, Hannah was full of admiration for this slave girl who was so brave and hopeful in the face of such insurmountable odds. If only life could reward such bravery, instead of crushing it. But the reality was that Lucy's brashness was simply näiveté. One day, she would thank Hannah for having protected her from her own excesses.

Hannah came to her feet and looked down at her rebellious property. "You will get over this, Lucy," she said, not unkindly. "You will come to Kentucky and help me look after James and Holbert and the new baby. You will help master in the fields and me in the kitchen just as you have always done. Why, we could not possibly do without you."

On her way out the door she met Temple brandishing his whip. "Go easy on her," she told him. "She said she is sorry for what she did."

The day of their leave-taking came all too soon, and yet, when Hannah rose that morning, she found herself eager to be under way. Her cozy cabin, the cabin Temple had built just for her, whose doorstep he had carried her over as his new bride, no longer seemed like home. All its contents, from the four poster bed to her spinning wheel to the kitchen tools, had been loaded into the wagon or packed on the back of a horse. At least she had been spared, now that the road to Kentucky had been widened and improved to accommodate wagons, from picking and choosing which of their belongings to take with them. The only thing she was leaving behind was a large piece of her heart.

As she closed the door behind her for the last time, she allowed herself one small moment of regret. Never again would she set foot in the house where her children had been born. Never again would she bathe her hot feet in the cool waters of Peak Creek. Never again would she lay eyes on these golden hills. But there would be a new home, and new country that she would learn to love. As long as she had Temple and the boys, she could live anywhere.

She tied her bonnet firmly on her head and climbed onto the wagon seat. James and Holbert had made little nests in the back out of quilts and robes. Lucy stood by the wheel, her eyes downcast, her expression blank. Since her attempted escape she had not uttered more than a few words, and the familiar flash in her eyes had disappeared. Hannah found herself almost wishing the old, spirited Lucy would return, as trying as

114

that person had sometimes been. But what was done was done. Lucy would get over her grief in time.

Temple stowed the last of their supplies into the wagon, and then took his place next to Hannah. He lifted her hand from where it rested in her lap and threaded his fingers through hers. "This place was good to us," he said, giving it a last look. "There is a part of me will miss it."

"Me, too," Hannah said. They looked at each other and smiled.

Temple picked up the reins and, with nary a backward glance, they were off.

PART II
KENTUCKY,
1798–1807

CHAPTER SEVEN

It had all happened so quickly. In the space of a few short years, travel along the road to the west had gone from a perilous undertaking of several weeks to a relatively comfortable journey of several days. Gone were the constant threats of Indian attacks, the nights of camping in fair weather and foul, the taxing crossings of raging rivers. The Wilderness Road to Kentucky had become a regular thoroughfare. There were inns where one could rest every night if one chose, and even a tollgate established at Cumberland Ford to pay for continued improvements.

When Hannah saw the size of the group gathered at Fort Chiswell, perhaps 300 in all, she was stunned. "My Lord, Temple, is all of Virginia moving to Kentucky?"

Temple parked the wagon in a clearing already chock full of conveyances of every description. He let the reins fall lax in his hands as he joined her in gaping at the hustle and bustle that surrounded them. The fort was home to a militia company, but most of the activity centered on the trading post and tavern that accommodated the travelers.

James and Holbert peered over the wooden slats, their eyes wide. "Ma, can we go?" asked James who had spied some children playing a game of leapfrog.

"I suppose so, but stay in sight."

"Most of these folks hail from Pennsylvania," Temple explained as he helped Hannah alight from the wagon. "They are members of a congregation that decided to pick up stakes. When I heard about them, I thought this would be just the group for us to join. Plenty of protection traveling in such large numbers. Not only that, but the man who signed on to lead us is Colonel Knox. Have you heard of him?"

Hannah shook her head as she directed Lucy to begin erecting the lean-to that would serve as their shelter for the night.

"No one knows the trail west better than Knox," continued Temple, busy unhitching the horses. "He has led countless groups into Kentucky, and he was one of the commissioners that laid out and built the new road a few years ago. We could not be in better hands."

Hannah smiled to herself, noting how even now Temple was trying to convince her of the wisdom of his decision. Although she had not expressed a single doubt since that first day, he knew she was still worried. Considering all the stories she had heard about Indians murdering, mutilating, and kidnapping white settlers she could not quite believe Temple when he said there was no danger on the road ahead. If only Stephen were with them, she would feel so much safer. The unbidden thought brought her up short. She glanced toward Temple, afraid her disloyalty showed on her face. Luckily he was still busy with the horses. Making haste, she shouldered the bucket yoke and went off to find water.

The banks of the stream were crowded with women filling their pails. She greeted a few of them, but was too disturbed by her thoughts of Stephen to carry on conversation. Why would she doubt that her own husband could protect her? Why did the notion of Stephen at her side seem so appealing? As she knelt at the water's edge, a memory, hazy and half formed, came to her — a vision of the river at home, and of Stephen turning toward her with a smile on his chiseled face, running his hands over her body.

She gave an involuntary jerk, spilling water out of her buckets. The woman next to her gave her a curious look. Refilling the containers, she started back to the wagon, walking slowly and steadily so as not to splash any water. The memory nagged at the edges of her consciousness, a troubling and unexplained intruder.

Get a hold of yourself, Hannah Cole, she chastised silently. *Your thoughts are turning to Stephen only because of his experience in these wilds we are heading into. He knows its dangers far better than Temple. But that does not mean Temple isn't fully capable of protecting his family.*

Back at their campsite, she found her husband engaged in conversation with a burly, older gentleman wearing breeches and a knee-length waistcoat.

"Hannah," Temple called, "come meet our expedition's leader, Colonel Knox!"

Hannah set down the buckets and went to stand next to Temple. "My husband tells me we are lucky to be led by such an experienced guide," she said. "We thank you for allowing us to join your group."

Colonel James Knox, although well versed in the ways of the wilderness, had never forgotten his Virginia-bred manners. He removed his hat and bowed to the lady.

"Madam Cole, the honor is all mine. Our party is delighted to have the company of such a fine family. You may rest assured that I will deliver you safely to your destination."

"You ease my mind considerably, sir. Though I trust my husband in all things, I do confess to some concern about this journey."

"Quite understandable. May I say you bring to mind another young mother who made this trip some fifteen years ago in a company under my direction? Back then, traveling the road was a bit hazardous. I would never have been able to make the assurances I have just made to you. This young woman attempted to cross the river with her two children. Unfortunately the river had become swollen with recent rains and her horse foundered. The brave woman grasped the horse's mane in one hand, her baby in the other, and shouted to her little boy to hold on tight. Somehow, she guided them all safely to shore. The very next day we came upon the remains of eight men who had passed us up. Poor souls, they had been massacred by the redskins. I shall spare your sensitive ears the details, but it was not a pretty sight. If that were not enough misfortune, we also endured an outbreak of the measles. Altogether, an unfortunate journey."

Hannah cast a wary glance toward Temple. If Knox had meant to reassure her with this story, he had utterly failed.

"Naturally," he went on, "you need have no fear of any of these things occurring on this trip. The Indians are contained, the river crossings are largely done on ferries, and disease is, of course, unlikely."

"Of course," Hannah said. She noted he had called the Indians contained, not defeated, and wondered if there was a difference. Before she could say anything, he had pulled out a small ledger book and asked Temple to itemize their belongings.

"Let's see," Knox said when Temple had finished, "the toll at Cumberland Ford will be nine pence for you, sir, nine pence for each horse and mule, and six shillings for the wagon. Women and small children are free." He snapped shut the book and once again bowed. "A pleasure to have you with us, Mister and Missus Cole. Good day."

They watched Knox march away.

"A good man," Temple commented.

"A confident one, at any rate."

Ten days later, after a trouble-free journey as promised, they reached Hazel Patch in Kentucky, a fork in the road. Most travelers veered to the west, headed toward Crab Orchard and Harrodsburg. Colonel Knox went with this group. The Coles and a few others continued north to Fort Boonesborough.

Hugging the banks of the Kentucky River, the fort seemed more compact than Hannah had expected. Still, she was pleased to see it. Although the trip had posed little in the way of hardships, it would be nice to rest in the same place for a few days.

They halted outside the huge, timbered gate, hanging open on its sturdy hinges. People streamed in and out at will: men with their shot pouches and powder horns slung around their necks, women going to and from the river, some with babies riding their hips. Temple unhitched the horses and turned them and the rest of the stock out to pasture. Posted sentries guarded the fields. Hannah and Lucy gathered the few things they would need for their temporary stay. Then Hannah took the boys' hands and followed Temple into the fort. Lucy stayed with the wagon as Hannah was not sure what accommodations there were for slaves.

Enclosed within the walls of the fort lay an entire village. Cabins lined the ten-foot walls, and two-story blockhouses anchored the corners. A blacksmith's furnace belched smoke. In the middle of the yard goats and sheep nipped at the sparse grass within a tiny pen. Over all lay a haze of smoke and the stink of too many people and animals living close together.

Hannah crinkled her nose as she navigated herself and the boys through the muck. Perhaps she would become accustomed to the smell and dirt after a while. Or perhaps she would suggest to Temple that they shorten their stay here. A long rest suddenly seemed like an unnecessary luxury.

They were directed to the cabin that housed Colonel Benjamin Cooper's family. Colonel Cooper was away from the fort, but his portly wife, Anne, graciously offered to let them stay with her and her five sons until they were ready to move on. Lucy was to be housed in a cabin with the other slaves.

Cooper, a commander of the local militia, had made a name for himself fighting the Indians. Temple was honored to be his guest, while Hannah was simply grateful to Anne for letting them become additions to her already crowded household. To show her gratitude, she insisted on doing her share of the chores and made sure Lucy pulled her weight as well, although the slave girl dragged herself through her chores, silent and mopey.

"That's a right dozy-looking gal you got there," said Anne one afternoon as they sat at the table with their sewing. She concentrated on stitching up a corn-shuck mattress.

Hannah looked up from her own needlework. "Lucy? She is always like that. Well, perhaps worse now than usual. She is pining after a no-account field hand that got sold away. Some days I'm bound I should have left her in Virginia. But she is a help to me even if she does pull a long face. I will certainly need her when the baby comes."

Anne eyed her guest's expanding belly. "Which will be about mid-winter, I'm guessing?"

"Thereabouts," said Hannah.

The cabin door swung open and James dashed in followed by Anne's son. They grabbed a pewter cup off the table and ran back out.

Anne chuckled, speculating aloud that the cup was to be used in some game of their devising, but Hannah was barely listening. Foul air fanned by the swinging door engulfed the cabin and it was all she could do to keep from gagging. Hannah had lived all her life on a farm and was used to barnyard smells, but this was worse than anything she had encountered. How could Anne not seem to notice the awful stench?

"Do you ever think about leaving the fort?" she asked, trying to broach the subject politely.

"Oh, we've moved out a few times, had our own places here and there. But those redskins wouldn't leave us be. Every time there was an attack close by, we'd have to fort up. Then, too, Ben was always marching off to fight somewheres, so me and the young 'uns would have to stay here till he got back. Reckon you could say after all this time I call Boonesborough home."

"But aren't the Indians gone now? Isn't the danger past?"

"Don't know as they are gone for good. We've pushed 'em back over the river into Ohio, but who's to say that's where they'll stay?" Anne bit off her thread and stood to shake out the mattress.

Hannah's heart thumped in her chest. "Are you saying that the Kentucky settlements aren't truly safe?"

"Safe as they can be." Anne placed a plump hand on Hannah's shoulder. "Now don't you fret. There's plenty of militia keeping an eye out for trouble, and you've got a good, strong man to protect you. You'll do fine."

■ ■ ■ ■

It took Temple only a few days to obtain all the supplies he thought they would need. He traded in the wagon, as it could not have navigated the narrow trail to Fleming County. They repacked most of their belongings onto the horses and mules. What did not fit, they sold or traded to residents of the fort.

On a fine fall day, the hills gleaming red and gold, they left Boonesborough. Hannah was more relieved than she could say to be shut of the noise and smell of the fort, although she had grown fond of Anne Cooper and knew James and Holbert would miss their new playmates.

Over hills thick with trees, through streams too numerous to count, they made their way, Hannah and the boys riding, Temple and Lucy on foot. Occasionally they came upon a settler who would offer them food and shelter and assure them that they were headed in the right direction. Hannah began to relax. The country was beautiful, the people friendly, and not once did they see any sign of Indians.

At last, they reached their destination. It was just as John Allison had described — a lovely piece of land right on the river with gentle hills that swelled like waves stirred up by the slightest of breezes. They camped by the river that night and the next day Hannah and Temple went out to scout a site for their cabin.

They settled on a plot that was open enough to have space for a house, a barn, and a garden patch, but that had enough trees to provide good shade in summer. It was far enough back from the river to be safe from flooding, and was fed by a clear spring. Temple stepped off the probable dimensions of the house and placed a stone in each corner. Then he drew Hannah inside the imaginary walls and wrapped her in his strong arms.

"Are you happy, my dear?"

"It is more than I could have hoped for," Hannah admitted. "Now get busy and build me a house."

Get busy he did, for although it was an exceptionally warm autumn, the snow would soon fly and he had no intention of housing his expectant wife in a tent all winter long. The first thing he did was to build a travois-type contraption for hauling rocks. When they had gathered enough, he laid out the foundation, taking care to make it as level as possible.

Hannah thought this to be hard work, but it was nothing compared to the next step — cutting down and hewing out the trees for the log walls. Ordinarily Hannah would have willingly assisted in this task, but Temple refused to hear of it.

"You might lose the baby . . . it is not worth the risk. Lucy can spell me when I get tired. What I really need is another man. Two men could chop down all the trees we need in no time."

No sooner had he uttered these words than a "Halloo!" sounded. They turned and gaped. Out of the trees rode Stephen, and behind him, a triumphant smile on her pinched face, came Phoebe.

"Don't look so surprised," said Stephen. "You didn't think I would let you move to Kentucky without me, did you?"

"But . . . Phoebe?" said Hannah.

Stephen gave her a level stare. "We are married."

Chapter Eight

Hannah tucked the blankets snugly around her sleeping sons. Peering out of the lean-to, she could just make out Temple and Stephen standing in the dusk by the horses, smoking their pipes. Pulling her shawl tighter about her shoulders, she marveled at how similar the brothers seemed at this distance. A small surge of happiness welled up in her at the prospect of having Stephen with them again. And yet, this time it was so different. This time he had brought a wife with him. And not just any wife, but her own sister — poor, frail, cantankerous Phoebe. Hannah feared things would never be the same between any of them again.

Phoebe ducked into the lean-to, removed her bonnet, and began to comb out her hair. She had walked around all day with an annoying smirk on her face. Not sure whether Stephen was privy to information about her sister's engagement to the wealthy widower,

Hannah had forbore asking questions, but, now that she had Phoebe alone, she got right to the point. "What happened to Mister Major?"

Phoebe dismissed her ex-fiancé with a shrug.

"Come now, you were engaged to marry the man. You had given him your promise. Doesn't that mean anything to you?"

"I did not love him, nor did he love me. We are both better off this way. Besides, he'll no doubt find some other unlucky girl to raise his brats."

Hannah shook her head in disgust. "Why on earth did you agree to marry him in the first place if that's the way you felt?"

"Because if I could not have Stephen, I didn't care who I married!" Phoebe's glare turned to a satisfied smile. "But then Stephen came back and everything changed."

Hannah knew her sister was truly in love with Stephen Cole and had been for years. She ought to be glad that Phoebe had been able to marry the love of her life, just as Hannah had. Yet something grated. Was it the knowledge that, up until a few weeks ago, Stephen had seemed to take absolutely no interest in Phoebe? And now they were man and wife. What had changed his mind?

Hannah sat down next to Phoebe and

draped a quilt over both their shoulders. Phoebe seemed surprised by the intimacy, and Hannah reminded herself to act more loving toward her sister. Perhaps all she needed was a chance to prove herself a caring and worthwhile person, and marriage to a fine man like Stephen Cole was certainly a step in the right direction.

"Tell me how it happened . . . how Stephen came back and proposed to you," she urged.

"Well" — Phoebe snuggled closer — "he came back just after you and Temple had left. Mother Cole told me he was quite surprised and not a little upset, at first, that you had left without him. He immediately announced that he intended to follow the two of you here. Mister Cole was none too happy about that, I hear. He said that with Temple gone, and him getting on in years, he needed Stephen to stay close to look after the family interests. But Stephen would not change his mind. They had words." Phoebe looked uncomfortable. "I am afraid they did not part on good terms."

"I am sorry to hear that," Hannah said. "But how is it that you and Stephen came together?"

Phoebe's eyes brightened. "Mother Cole said Stephen came to her and asked about me. She told him that I was engaged to Mister Major, so, of course, he did not press his case. But the very next day Mother Cole saw Rhoda at Missus Patterson's quilting bee and told her about Stephen and how he had mentioned me. Well, when Rhoda told me that, I knew I had to do something. I could not marry a man I didn't love when the man I do love wanted me."

It seemed to Hannah that her sister might have been leaping to conclusions about Stephen's intentions, but she kept her thoughts to herself.

"So I asked Rhoda to take him a message from me," Phoebe went on, enjoying her tale more and more. "I told him to meet me at Boiling Spring, that we needed to talk. Oh, Hannah, I was so scared! What if he didn't come, or what if my courage failed me so that I could not tell him I loved him?"

"It appears neither of those things happened," said Hannah, grinning.

Phoebe blushed. "No. He was there waiting for me. And before he could say a word, I told him I loved him, that I had loved him since the first time I saw him at your wedding, and that, if he wanted to marry me, I would break my engagement to Mister Major and follow him anywhere!"

"My goodness, Phoebe! Weren't you afraid

135

such forthrightness would overwhelm the man?"

Tears filled Phoebe's eyes. "I reckoned this was my one chance. If he left for Kentucky without me, I knew I would never see him again."

Hannah gave her sister a playful nudge. "And then what? Did he take you in his arms and declare his undying love for you?"

"Not exactly." Phoebe looked a bit sheepish. "He was quite formal actually. I am sure he was as nervous as I. He . . . he said that he needed a helpmate to start a new life in Kentucky and would I do him the honor of becoming his wife."

"I see," said Hannah, wishing for Phoebe's sake he could have managed a bit more fervor in his proposal. "What did Ma and Pa think of your news?"

Phoebe dropped her eyes and picked at the quilt. "They weren't very happy. Pa is a friend of Mister Major's, you know. They do business together. He thought it was a slap in the face to break our engagement. And Ma, well, she didn't think Stephen's prospects were as good as Mister Major's. I don't understand either of them! They were pleased as could be when you married Temple, so why isn't his brother good enough for me?"

"You forget that Temple already owned his land and had built a cabin before we were even married," said Hannah. "Stephen has nothing to offer a wife, other than a strong arm and a good heart."

"And those are enough for me!"

"Of course they are. But parents want to know their daughter will be well provided for. You can't blame them." Little Holbert stirred in his sleep. Hannah rose to tuck in his blanket. "How did you finally convince them to let you marry Stephen?"

Phoebe bit her lip, refusing to make eye contact.

"Phoebe, Ma and Pa did finally come around, didn't they?"

"I am sure they will . . . once they get used to the idea."

Hannah knelt and grabbed her sister by the shoulders. "What are you telling me? Did you and Stephen marry against their wishes?"

Phoebe gave her a defiant look. "Yes! We were married by the circuit judge at the courthouse. Ma and Pa weren't even there . . . nor were Stephen's parents. We don't care, neither of us! We have each other, and now we are with you and Temple. That's all we need!"

"Oh, how could you be so rash? If you

had just waited a little while, they probably would have come around to your point of view. As it is, you have broken their hearts."

Phoebe pushed her sister away. "What about my heart? Nobody cared that my heart was breaking over Stephen! I am a grown woman. I have a right to make my own decisions!"

Hannah stared at her sister in disbelief. "Of course you do. But you didn't need to hurt Ma and Pa. You and Stephen could have waited for the right time. Frankly this kind of thoughtless behavior is just what I would expect from you, but not from Stephen. How in the devil did you talk him into this?"

"How dare you say that to me? I will have you know, it was Stephen's wish to marry quickly. He was in a hurry to find you, though I can't imagine for the life of me why he should care so much about you and Temple, or why he wants to live in this godforsaken wilderness!"

As Phoebe broke down in tears, the men, hearing the commotion, wandered over. Hannah hoped Stephen had not heard Phoebe's last little speech, but by the dark look on his face she feared he had.

"What's all this?" asked Temple.

"My dear little sister was just telling me

138

about her hasty marriage to your dear little brother," said Hannah. "It seems the two of them have left some unhappy people back in Virginia."

"Phoebe, stop your crying," Stephen commanded, looking miserable. "Come, it's time for bed."

Silently Phoebe followed him as he strode away.

Temple watched them go. "They only just got here, my dear," he said with a wry smile. "Must you stir the pot already?"

"Did he tell you, Temple? Did he tell you how they married without the blessing of our parents?"

Temple ducked into the lean-to and deposited his long frame on the pallet next to her. "It is not as bad as it seems. He made it up a bit with Pa before starting out."

"Even so, what about my parents? I am not sure they will ever forgive them for running off to marry."

Temple took her hand. "I pray that they do someday. But if they don't, is that a burden Stephen and Phoebe should carry for the rest of their days? Or you? Come now, my dear, what have they done wrong? They are two grown people who love each other and got married. There is not a thing wrong with that."

"They should not have gone behind Ma's and Pa's backs," Hannah insisted.

"Reckon not. But time heals many wounds. Your parents will come to see their union as a good thing one of these days, I'm bound. In the meantime, here they are. Our only kin within three hundred miles, and I, for one, am happy to see them. I hope we have not started off on the wrong foot."

Temple's words made sense, she had to admit. She glanced over, feeling contrite. "You are right. I should apologize."

"In the morning," said Temple, kissing her hand.

"No, now. I don't want anybody to spend the night fretting over hard feelings." Hannah leaned over and kissed Temple on the cheek. "Thank you, dearest. You are my true compass."

As she started to rise, Temple pulled her back and kissed her soundly. "Don't be gone too long," he growled.

Moonlight lit the path as Hannah made her way to the temporary shelter Stephen had erected for him and his bride. The crackling of fallen leaves announced her approach. Stephen was on his feet and reaching for his gun when she came into view. Relaxing, he set aside the weapon.

"I came to apologize," Hannah announced. "I should not have upset Phoebe like that. Where is she?"

"Down by the stream."

Hannah turned, but Stephen held out his hand to forestall her. "She'll be back directly," he said.

"I fear I left you both with the impression that I disapprove of your marriage, but nothing could be further from the truth. I am so happy for both of you, and delighted that you have come to Kentucky." She paused, suddenly aware of the intensity of his gaze.

"Hannah, I don't know what Phoebe told you, but I want you to know I would never have married her over your parents' objections if I had known. When I arrived at the courthouse, she told me your father had fallen ill and your mother had stayed home to nurse him, but that they sent their blessing. I didn't find out the truth until later."

Hannah dropped her head, ashamed for her wily and manipulative sister. "I am so sorry," she whispered.

Stephen stepped closer and took her hand. She felt his long, lean fingers, the roughness of his palm. "It doesn't matter," he said. "I am where I want to be. In Kentucky, with you . . . and Temple."

Hannah looked up. "And Phoebe?"

Stephen shrugged. "She is my wife now. Reckon I'll learn to live with that. Reckon she'll learn to live in this godforsaken wilderness whether she likes it or not."

Annoyed at Stephen's cavalier attitude, Hannah tried to back away. He gripped her hand tighter. Hannah's heart skipped a beat. A small breeze came up, rustling the tops of the trees. His other hand found the small of her back and he exerted just enough pressure to push her pregnant belly against him. For one second, Hannah let herself be held in his arms. Then she put her hand on his chest and gently pushed away.

"Phoebe loves you, Stephen," she admonished. "She wants nothing more than to make you happy. I hope you will do the same for her."

He resisted letting her go a moment longer, a struggle of some sort playing out on his face. Finally he released her.

Phoebe came up from the stream, patting her damp face with her apron. "What are you doing here?" she said, looking back and forth between her sister and her husband.

"I came to apologize," said Hannah too quickly. "I overreacted about Ma and Pa. I am sure everything will be fine, and I . . . I just want you to know how happy I am for you and Stephen."

Phoebe eyes narrowed. "Thank you," she said grudgingly.

"Well, you two are tired, and there is much to do tomorrow. Sleep well." Picking up her skirts, Hannah retreated to her own lean-to where Temple lay half asleep.

As she undressed and laid down next to him, he rolled over and pulled her into his warm embrace. Sighing, she took comfort in molding herself to the well-known contours of his body. Her mind replayed the scene with Stephen. Why had he held her like that, and why had she let him, even for an instant? Why did the touch of his hand send her into a dither when the only man she had ever loved, and ever would love, lay next to her now, cradling her belly that carried the child they had made together? Too tired to puzzle over it for long, Hannah decided to turn the worry over to God. She could not change the way people were. All she could do was stay true to her own sense of right and wrong. As she fell into an exhausted sleep, she knew in the deepest part of her heart that, no matter how Stephen Cole made her feel, Temple Cole was the man she loved.

Dear Cousin Dolley,

You have been much in my thoughts of late. Of course, the news is full of Mr. Jefferson's Presidency, and of your husband's appointment as his Secretary of State. This has necessitated your full-time residency in our new capital city where, as I read in the *Kentucky Gazette,* whenever Temple manages to bring home a copy, you are serving as hostess for the President.

My, how happy I am for you! To have risen from the depths of your sorrow to fashion a life at the very center of power . . . well, it is almost too much for a simple farm wife like me to comprehend.

Your days must be so different from mine. Where I rise with the cock's crow and step outside my humble log house into the fresh air of the country, you no doubt rise whenever your fancy strikes, or whenever the noise from the busy city streets invades your shuttered windows. While I am pulling on my plain calico dress, you stand before an armoire stuffed with frocks of silk, debating which to wear. As I milk the cow and slop the hogs, you entertain at an elegant tea party, dazzling all of official Washington with your clever wit. In short, dear Dolley, where once I thought our lives were on similar paths, I now see that nothing could be further from the truth. And yet, perhaps in the end we are not so different. I know you would tell me that your first duty is seeing to the welfare of your dear husband and son, as is mine. This is the universal task of women, is it not? To nurture our families above all else.

When Temple announced our move to Kentucky, I must admit I feared for the well-being of my family. I was wrong. Kentucky is everything Temple said it would be, and more. If ever there was a paradise on earth, it must surely be here in Kentucky. How things grow in this place! Our first year here we cleared seventy-five bushels of corn per acre! The next year even more, allowing us to ship a good portion downriver to market. And you should see the vegetables in my garden: turnips, squash, beans, pumpkins. Have you ever tasted milk from cows fed on pumpkins? It is sweeter than a baby's breath!

The game is plentiful as well. Turkeys so fat their skin practically bursts when shot, not to mention the deer, elk, and bear. Most everyone keeps a small herd of cattle as the grazing is so fine.

People seem to grow in Kentucky, too! James and Holbert have a new little brother, Stephen, and will soon welcome another brother or sister. Luckily Temple built us a large house so we do not need to add on as yet. It is a two-story dogtrot with two large rooms in front and up-stairs, and a shed all the way across the back for the kitchen and dining room. Last year, Temple added a porch in front where we sit on hot nights and watch the sun set over the river. Oh, Dolley, it is a fine home, one I would be proud to show even a fine lady like you!

Settlements are popping up all over, which is a fine thing, if you ask me. At the mercantile in Fleming's Station I am able to barter furs and skins for shoes, petticoats, even coffee. And the boys now attend school with the neighbor children in town when they are not too busy helping their father.

Speaking of neighbors, they are rather plentiful these days. I daresay there is not a single parcel of unsettled land between our place here on the Licking and Limestone. That is all to the good, in my view. I like having people about, and this land seems healthy enough to provide for an endless number of folks. Of course, Stephen grumbles about all the people moving here, but then I sometimes think he would only be happy if God had made him Adam and never bothered with Eve! After all the fuss he made about moving to Kentucky, would you believe he is now hinting at going even farther west?

It is all the fault of those Boones. No sooner had we arrived than we got word that Colonel Boone and most of his family was moving to the Missouri country. I wish I could have had a word with the old man before he had made up his mind. I would have politely asked him to keep his boots planted so that my kin would not eternally be following him to the ends of the earth!

The Boones are a fine family, in spite of their wandering ways. Temple and I were so pleased to have a visit from Colonel Boone's youngest, Nathan, and his new bride, Olive, last fall. It seems Nathan, who is a mere lad of seventeen, had accompanied his family on their journey west as far as Limestone when he decided he could go no farther without Olive by his side. So he retraced his steps, married the plucky young lady, and embarked on an arduous honeymoon trip to meet up again with his family. Their route took them by our place. I was amazed at how little they carried with them in the way of provisions. Olive's trousseau was packed on one horse; otherwise, it appeared they were surviving on parched corn and whatever game Nathan could bring down. I fed them a hearty meal, though I am not sure they took much notice of it. They seemed to find all the sustenance they needed in each other's eyes. Ah, young love! So consuming, so fleeting. Yet once those raging fires have died down, it is the embers and coals that burn the hottest and last the longest.

Thus, my dear Dolley, rest assured the Coles are thriving in Kentucky. At least, the William Temple Coles are. As for the Stephen Coles, well, they are having a hard go of it. I mentioned Stephen's unrest which may find its cause, at least partly, in his inability to secure a homestead. Unlike Temple and myself, Stephen came here with no warrants or certificates of any kind. For a while, he squatted on a parcel just to the west of us, but, when someone else came along with a proved-up claim, he was forced out. Now he and Phoebe are living at Fort Boonesborough, or, I should say, Phoebe is. Stephen is off hunting and trapping most of the time. Poor Phoebe is desperately unhappy, and the unsanitary conditions at the fort are playing havoc with her health. I have offered numerous times to let them live with us, but pride seems to prevent them from accepting our hospitality. I can only hope that Stephen comes to his senses and renews his efforts to find a place of his own, difficult though that may be.

The land business here in Kentucky is so complicated that it frequently takes years to secure one's claim. Did I mention that Temple has found it necessary to hire a lawyer in an effort to authenticate his warrants? He assures me there is no cause for worry, and I trust that is so.

I would be remiss in not confessing the one dark cloud that occasionally rains on my happiness, namely the apparent estrangement between my parents and myself and Phoebe. They have never forgiven her for breaking off her engagement to their friend and then marrying Stephen without their blessing. And, despite all my denials, they seem to think Temple and I encouraged Stephen and Phoebe's perfidy. I can understand why they were hurt by the deception (which, by the way, was solely on Phoebe's part), but I should think by now they would be reconciled. After all, Phoebe is married to a fine man. A bit stand-offish, to be sure, a bit stubborn, maybe even a bit selfish, but a fine man nonetheless.

Oh, how I wish I could hear your wise counsel on this subject of torn familial relations. When you married Mister Madison, a non-Quaker, I understand you were shunned by the rest of your immediate family. That must have been heart wrenching for you. Yet, devotion to one's husband must outweigh all other considerations. I shall remind Phoebe of your example, and we both shall draw strength from it.

I am, as always, your loving cousin,
Hannah Cole

CHAPTER NINE

Hannah's doubts about her childbearing ability proved to be laughably wrong. Her fourth son, Samuel, was born in 1801. Two daughters, Jennie and Mattie, followed in short order, and in the spring of 1806 she found herself once again with child. When she told Temple of this latest pregnancy, he scooped her into his arms with a randy chuckle.

"Perhaps you will want me staying out of your bed from now on what with all these young 'uns popping out."

She gave him a tired smile, fully aware that an entire army regiment could not keep him out of her bed. Nor did she want him to stay away. At thirty-six years of age and after sixteen years of marriage she still found no greater comfort than in the arms of her husband. Besides, she gloried in her offspring, all of whom were healthy, thank God. Childbirth itself had become almost routine, keeping her off her feet for only a few days. With the older children capable of doing most of the chores, and with Lucy always there to help, another baby hardly disrupted her life.

"We've only six, seven if you count the one on the way. I sha'n't kick you out of my bed until you have given me at least two more. After all, the Boones had nine children, and I reckon you are every bit the man Daniel Boone is!" She gave him a teasing pinch at his slightly expanding waistline.

"Madam, I shall be only too happy to prove it to you." His hand strayed down the backside of her skirt, but, just as he leaned closer for a kiss, five-year-old Samuel burst into the room, his shirt torn, his knees bloody.

"What happened to you, Son?" Hannah asked, detaching herself.

Samuel gulped air and sniffled, trying his best not to cry. At that moment, seven-year-old Stephen poked his head in the door, a guilty look on his face.

"Stephen, you were supposed to be watching the young 'uns," said Hannah, calmly wiping Samuel's face. "Can you tell me what happened?"

"Yes, Mother. He got in the pen and spooked the new mare. She knocked him down, but I pulled him out before he got hurt too bad."

"I see. Well, little harm done, it appears. Come, Samuel, let's clean those knees." Hannah took the boy's hand and led him to the kitchen, Stephen trailing behind.

"I'm sorry, Mother," said Stephen, hanging his head. "I only looked away for a minute. I told him not to go anywhere."

"That's all right, Son," said Hannah, wetting a clean cloth and dabbing at Samuel's scuffed knees. "This one is tough to keep track of, I'm bound. Always running off when he shouldn't be. You best go keep an eye on the girls, now."

Stephen obediently fled to the yard as Temple strode into the kitchen, grabbing a piece of johnnycake as he headed outside. "Reckon I'd better see how James and Holbert are doing. I set 'em to pruning the apple trees." He paused at the door. "What would you say, dearest, about a trip to Lexington? I've a load of cider and some other goods to sell. While we're there, I'll pay a visit to that damn' lawyer. Probably ought to see if he's making any progress on my claim."

"Oh, that would be lovely!" gushed Hannah, looking up from her work. "It's been over a year since I was there and I do need

153

more cloth and pins and . . . well, so many things."

"Next week, then," agreed Temple. "We will stop in Boonesborough on the way to see if Stephen and Phoebe want to come."

The following week they loaded a wagon with items to take to market and embarked for Lexington, some fifty miles away. They stopped overnight at Boonesborough where Hannah had a chance to visit with Anne Cooper, still raising her brood at the fort while her husband tended to matters far afield.

Phoebe was ecstatic about a trip to the city. Even Stephen, for once at home with his family, admitted it would be interesting to see what was new in town. They piled their two little ones in the back of Temple's wagon and joined the throng of travelers headed for Kentucky's largest commercial center.

Dropping her horse back to ride abreast of Phoebe, Hannah raised her face to the bright sunshine. "Fine day for a ride, don't you think?"

Phoebe's answer was cut off by a hacking cough.

"That sounds troublesome," said Hannah when the cough had finally subsided. "Are you not feeling any better?"

Phoebe had had a hard time with the birth of her children, James and Rhoda. Always a petite woman, she now appeared almost scrawny and her color was wan.

"Anne says the air at the fort is not good for me," Phoebe admitted, wiping her streaming eyes. "She thinks Stephen ought to take me away. I wish he would. I hate living among all those people, with the stench and the filth."

"With Stephen gone so much, it would be hard on you to be all alone with the children. At least at the fort there's plenty of company."

"Don't want any company except my husband's. Too bad he seems to have little need of mine. I count myself lucky to see him for a month out of the year . . . just long enough to get in the family way again." Phoebe arched her back and rubbed her burgeoning mid-section.

Hannah had no idea Stephen was away that much, and thought it terribly unfortunate for her sister. Yet she felt compelled to defend him. "He is making a living the best way he knows how . . . supplying skins and furs to all the settlements. I am sure he would come home more if he could."

Phoebe shot her a look, but said nothing.

At mid-afternoon they pulled into the bustling city of Lexington. Their first stop was at an inn on High Street. Alighting from her horse, Hannah was surprised to feel a hand guiding her to the ground. She turned to see Stephen, standing close, his hand still grazing her back. He smiled down at her, and Hannah suddenly understood better why her sister was so vexed with him. Who wouldn't resent the absence of such a superb-looking man? Blushing at the thought, she glanced at Phoebe, who glared at them bitterly.

"Husband, help me down, please!"

Stephen complied, the smile wiped from his face.

They engaged rooms, then Temple, Stephen, and the older boys departed to tend to business. After resting for a spell, Hannah and Phoebe left the younger children in Lucy's care while they went out to do their shopping. Hannah had no qualms about leaving Lucy unguarded. Over the years, the slave woman had become much more agreeable. In return, she had been granted more privileges, including the occasional visit to neighboring farms to commune with other slaves. Lucy took good care of the children, even showed them affection. She went about her tasks quietly and efficiently, speaking when spoken to, retiring early every evening to her solitary cabin. Hannah occasionally wondered why Lucy had never found a male companion among the other slaves. Now that she and Temple were doing better financially she would be more than happy to purchase whoever Lucy chose for her "husband". She still felt a little guilty about what had happened with Rufus. But Lucy never said a word about any of that.

Pulling on the dress gloves she wore only when she came to town, Hannah walked smartly along the crowded street. "My goodness, every time I am here there are more people, more shops, more factories . . . where will it all end?"

"It won't end," muttered Phoebe. "Not as long as there are folks like us who aren't satisfied to stay where they are born."

"Oh, look! Here's a new china shop!" Hannah stopped to admire a Limoges place setting displayed in the window. "I have always wanted a set of china. Let's go inside." She pulled Phoebe into the shop and struck up a conversation with the proprietor, but left without placing an order. China was a luxury she could not afford.

The women continued their trek down Lexington's main street, stopping here and there to buy spices, drugs, and cloth. They marveled at the new fabrics on the market, dyed in remarkable new colors. Hannah ordered several bolts, having given up the time-consuming job of spinning her own cloth. Phoebe, with fewer coins in her purse, spent less freely.

At the end of the block they encountered a man handing out flyers to passers-by and directing people into the building behind him. Hannah accepted a flyer that turned out to advertise a wax gallery. "Come inside, ladies, you won't want to miss this extraordinary display," urged the salesman. "See a life-like representation of General Washington leading the troops at Valley Forge!"

Hannah immediately purchased two tickets. The women entered a darkened room, sectioned off with heavy curtains. Behind each curtain was a display of figures from history and literature, including several depicting Mr. Washington from the war and as President. Hannah gasped at the models of Aaron Burr and Alexander Hamilton reënacting their famous duel.

Back outside, blinking in the sudden sunshine, they agreed it was a marvelous exhibition and decided to return the next day with their families.

Shielding her eyes, Phoebe pointed across the street. "Why, there's Stephen!"

Hannah looked over to see her brother-in-law just coming out of the Sheaf of Wheat tavern. Dodging horses, wagons, and all manner of conveyances, they crossed over and greeted him with an account of their exciting afternoon. Stephen reported that he and Temple had completed some successful trades and that Temple had gone off to see his lawyer.

As they stood conversing, a tall, lumbering figure of a man passed them on the cobbled walk and started to enter the tavern. Turning back, he squinted at Stephen.

"Ho, there, is that Stephen Cole?"

"Colonel Cooper!" Stephen extended his hand in greeting. "You're back from the western territories, are you?"

"Aye, just arrived. Stocking up on a few supplies before heading to Boonesborough. Always best to come home to the wife and young 'uns with a few presents in hand." He winked at Stephen, and then, sweeping his broad felt hat off his head, asked to be introduced to the ladies.

Hannah told him how she had appreciated Anne Cooper's hospitality when they had first moved to Kentucky.

"Annie's a good woman," he agreed, smiling through an untended beard and mus-

159

tache. "I am eager to see her and the wee ones again, though they ain't so wee any more. Been gone for nigh on to a year."

"How did you find Louisiana Territory?" asked Stephen.

The older man rested the stock of his flintlock rifle on the ground and leaned against it. "Pert near like Kentucky was twenty-five years ago. Ain't been spoiled yet."

"Is there any word from Captain Lewis's party?" Stephen had been following, as best he could, the journey of Lewis and Clark's Corps of Discovery that had set out from St. Louis two years ago. There had been no word of the expedition since May of 1805 when a keelboat sent from Fort Mandan, where the party had wintered, arrived back in St. Louis carrying the captains' journals, maps, botanical specimens, and other cargo. The nation waited anxiously for the men's return, although many feared they had been lost in the wilderness.

"Not as yet," Cooper answered, "but they'll surely be coming back soon. I myself traveled up the Missouri a ways. Dan'l Boone's boys got a salt lick they're working out there. Must say I liked the look of that country. Plenty of timber, bottom lands a mile wide, space to spread out . . . I'm bound I'll go back and claim me some of it, if Anne will hear of it."

Stephen seemed mesmerized by the colonel's description. They talked some more of the fledgling settlements in the Missouri country — New Madrid along the Mississippi, and St. Charles near where Nathan Boone had built a house. Hannah was pleased to hear that Nathan and Olive were prospering.

"What about the Indians in those parts?" she inquired.

"Seem peaceful, for the most part," Cooper said. "The Sacs and the Pottawatomies stir things up every now and then . . . steal some horses or livestock. To tell the truth, ma'am, we're liable to see more Indian trouble in this neck of the woods than farther west."

"Oh?" A knot started to form in Hannah's stomach.

"I'm afeared it's true. That Injun chief, Tecumseh, he's up to something over there in Indiana Territory. Thousands of redskins are streaming in to his village at Greenville. Lots of white folks are leaving, coming back to Kentucky or Virginia, for fear there's an uprising coming."

Cooper spoke calmly, not displaying any particular concern. Yet Hannah could sense he took this new threat seriously. She glanced at Stephen, who likewise seemed unruffled. Regardless, Hannah wanted to know more.

"What is the government doing about this Tecumseh? Surely they won't allow him to gather all these savages together in one place?"

Aware that she was becoming alarmed, Cooper chose his words carefully. "No, ma'am, reckon Governor Harrison won't allow any such thing. That Tecumseh's a clever one, but Governor Harrison's plenty smart, too. Let me give you an example. Like I said, Tecumseh and his brother, who calls himself the Prophet, have been riling up the Indians, telling 'em to band together and not have anything to do with white folks any more. Well, all these Injuns from all these different tribes ain't so sure they want to give up the white man's whiskey, or the white man's women, pardon me for speaking so plain. A lot of 'em are wondering why they ought to follow Tecumseh and his brother. So to prove they get orders direct from the so-called Great Spirit, the Prophet told this big council of redskins that he'd got word from the Spirit that in fifty days the sun was going to disappear right in the middle of the day."

"An eclipse?" said Stephen.

"Aye. Said that if this eclipse happens like he predicted, then that proves he's right about fighting the white man."

"That's ridiculous," Phoebe chimed in. "No one can predict something like that."

Cooper nodded agreement. "Yes, ma'am. And that's just what Governor Harrison said in a message he sent back to this Indian council. He told 'em this Prophet was a false god and was leading 'em astray. Reckon that'll be proved for good when there ain't no eclipse. Let's see who them redskins believe then."

"The Prophet said the sun would disappear on the fiftieth day?" asked Hannah.

"Yes, ma'am. I've lost track of the date, but if it's going to happen, which it ain't, it should be any day now."

Hannah looked around. Was it just her imagination, fueled by Cooper's story, or did it seem darker? Yes, the light was definitely fading. She glanced skyward, scanning for clouds. There was none. People in the street stopped in their tracks, looking around in confusion. A hush fell over the crowd. Then someone shouted and pointed to the sky. Shielding her eyes, Hannah looked up and saw the moon slipping eerily over the arc of the sun. Slowly, steadily it cut into the sun's light and warmth until it had moved completely over the glowing globe, leaving only an aura of light at the edges. "Oh, Lord," she whispered, frightened not of the phenomenon itself, but of what it might mean for her country. She looked away, the vision still imprinted on her eyes. Beside her, Stephen and Colonel Cooper expressed amazement that the Prophet's prediction had come to pass, while Phoebe clutched her husband's arm uncertainly.

Suddenly strong hands gripped her from behind and turned her around. It was Temple, indistinct in the dim half light. She could feel him shaking. Puzzled that he should be upset by the eclipse, she started to say something, but the look on his face cut her off.

"We have lost it!" he cried. "We have lost our land."

Dear Cousin Dolley,

It is with disappointment beyond imagining that I relate the following news: our dream of building a life in Kentucky is come to naught. The land here on the Licking River that Temple has so diligently tended is not ours, and never will be.

What grief it causes me to write those words. How betrayed I feel to have worked for seven years to create a comfortable and fruitful home here in the wilderness, only to discover that my labor, and Temple's, will benefit a perfect stranger. My children's birthright is as a puff of smoke — blown away by the vagaries of fate.

How could this come to pass? It is a mystery to me, even after all of Temple's explanations.

"What about John Allison's army warrants?" I have asked over and over again, trying to understand what happened. "Why aren't they enough?"

Patiently Temple tries to explain. "Those warrants only entitled me to make an entry on this land. An entry is merely a claim that has to be proved after an official survey. Only after it is proved up is the claimant granted a patent. Unbeknownst to me, or to your cousin, John, there is another survey shingling this tract. . . ."

"Shingling?"

"Overlaying. The court found this other survey to be superior. There is nothing I can do about it. We will have to leave."

So, there it is. Once again we shall pick up stakes and move on. Only this time it is so much harder. This time it was forced upon us, not freely chosen. This time there is none of the excitement and anticipation that accompanied our move to Kentucky, only bitterness and regret.

I told Temple the other day that I almost wished we had never left Virginia. As tired and worn out as that land was, at least it was ours. We never would have had to go through this disgrace. And Phoebe and I would never have lost the regard of our parents, who, it seems, still begrudge our choices in life.

Poor Temple. I regretted immediately having spoken such harsh words, for he is, naturally, taking all of the blame upon himself for what has happened. It is not his fault as I have reassured him again and again. If anyone is to blame, it is the incompetent surveyors who platted this tract years ago. And, Lord knows, we are not the first to fall victim to this kind of thing. They say Daniel Boone himself lost thousands of acres and bundles of money on similar faulty land deals. But none of this makes it any easier to bear.

Dear Cousin, forgive this maudlin self-pity. When faced with adversity, I know you have always endured it with your head held high, never feeling sorry for yourself, but simply making the best of things. I shall strive to do the same. Thus, I turn my back on the past and look ahead to the future.

Temple has already settled on our new destination. It is an area of the Missouri territory that has come to be called Boonslick after a salt lick operated by Colonel Boone's sons. It is reputed to be as welcoming to settlement as the Bluegrass was twenty-five years ago. No doubt you are surprised that I deem a journey of this magnitude, to a place on the very edge of civilization, to be a good thing. But I have decided that if we must leave our home here, it would be far better to go somewhere new and largely unsettled, thus avoiding the kind of land dispute that was our undoing here. As one of the first settlers, surely our claims will be given priority.

The Boonslick appeals as well because of the friendly nature of its Indian population. Colonel Benjamin Cooper, who recently returned from a tour of the area, reports that the Osages are a peace-loving tribe, bearing no particular animosity toward the white man. Contrast this with the Shawnees whose leaders are exciting tribes throughout the North-west Territories to rise up against civilized people. Rumor has it that after the Prophet's prediction of an eclipse came true, the threat is worse than ever. Though Temple assures me the Kentucky settlements are too well protected to be in real danger, I confess I am uneasy for myself and my family and would prefer the safe shores of the Missouri River over the treacherous ones of the Ohio.

We are indeed fortunate that Colonel Cooper and his family will be traveling with us to the Missouri country. Not only has he previously reconnoitered the area, but he and his brother, Sarshall, are frontiersmen of the first order, fully capable of leading a party on such an ambitious journey. Another brother, Braxton, will be joining us as well. Altogether, there will be twenty-odd Coopers and, God willing that Phoebe and I both deliver healthy babies, fourteen Coles.

Did I mention that Stephen and Phoebe are coming as well? Hardly surprising, you are no doubt thinking. Indeed, even as Temple was still getting over the shock of losing everything, it was Stephen who came up with the idea of the Boonslick. Though a stranger to it himself, he was quite taken with Colonel Cooper's description.

That is Stephen, of course, always in search of a new frontier. Once, Kentucky was the Promised Land, but he was never able to gain a firm foothold here. Now, he places all of his hopes on the Far West. Ah, well, I hear the Missouri country is well suited to "men with the bark on", as they say, which is certainly a fair description of Stephen Cole.

As for Phoebe, she is of two minds about our upcoming journey. She despises Boonesborough and will be extremely pleased to be shut of the place, yet she is apprehensive about upper

Louisiana. I have suggested to her that she will be far happier in a new setting where she can raise her children outside of the confines of a fort. In truth, I am not sure Phoebe can be happy anywhere, at least anywhere near me.

Which leads me, dear Cousin, to a confession that I am able to make only to God and to you through the pages of this journal. I fear that Stephen Cole favors me over his wife, my sister. Why, you may ask, am I confessing a sin that is his, not mine? Because, God forgive me, I fear I may have contributed to this intolerable state of affairs.

Since we first met, at my wedding, I have felt an odd connection to Stephen, quite different from how most women feel about their husband's brother, I am sure. It is not a romantic or a physical attraction that I feel for him. No, those sentiments are reserved solely for my dearest Temple. Rather, it is a sense of comfort when Stephen is about, a sense that all is well, that my world is complete.

Perhaps he has misinterpreted my welcoming attitude to mean something it does not. And perhaps I am simply misreading the attentions of a well-meaning brother-in-law. I pray that that is the case. And yet, when we catch each other's eye across a room, something is communicated between us. Something I cannot name.

Worse yet, I believe Phoebe is aware of this affinity between Stephen and myself. She has begun taking great pains to ensure that we are never left alone together, and, though she has never been what one would call a jolly person, she has become even more sullen and withdrawn. I am certain that, given her druthers, she would choose to stay in Kentucky, thus placing several hundred miles between me and Stephen.

I have considered having it out with her, that is, simply telling her that my feelings for Stephen do not go beyond sisterly affection. But I fear that acknowledging her concern will only make it seem more real to her. Besides, while I might be successful in reassuring her that my own feelings are harmless, there is still the matter of what Stephen feels for me. On that account, she may indeed have reason to worry.

Thankfully Temple seems not to have noticed anything awry. Certainly I shall not mention it, firstly, because there is nothing of true significance to tell, and, secondly, because it would grieve me to be the cause of friction between him and his brother. No, I have determined to act as if nothing is amiss, and to humor Phoebe by avoiding Stephen when at all possible. It is a pity it has come to this for, next to my husband, it is Stephen whose company I most enjoy. But I must endeavor to erect a barrier between myself and this man who you once described, my dear Dolley, as so appealing. God help me, God help us all, if I fail.

I am, as always, your loving cousin,
Hannah

■ ■ ■ ■

PART III
MISSOURI,
1807–1843

■ ■ ■ ■

Chapter Ten

A flat, gray sky hung heavily over the late spring countryside. The last of the dogwood blossoms, seemingly discouraged by the dreary weather, dropped like creamy pink snowflakes into the trickling waters of Frene Creek. They floated on for a little way before gathering in a snag of brush. One or two escaped to continue their trek toward the mighty Missouri.

Hannah stared into the creek, not really seeing. Shivering, she pulled her shawl close. It seemed unseasonably cold, but perhaps spring was always like this in Louisiana Territory — cold and wet. It had rained almost every day since they left St. Louis, a sharp and hustling city.

Lewis and Clark had returned triumphant from their march to the Pacific, and were now installed in the capital city — Lewis as Governor of the Territory and Clark as Superintendent of Indian Affairs. Temple was, by and large, pleased that such experienced men were in charge, although they were both rumored to be soft on the Indian question, influenced, no doubt, by their close association with them during their two-year expedition.

Confounded by the combustible mix of French, Spanish, and Anglos, all jockeying to advance themselves in the new, freshly charted territory, Hannah had gratefully watched the docks of St. Louis disappear around a bend in the river. Continuing on, the women and children riding in *pirogues* with the supplies, the men driving the horses, cattle, and hogs on shore, they had passed St. Charles and made a brief landing at the mouth of Femme Osage Creek to pay their respects to the Boone family. Nathan and Olive had begun building a magnificent home on a hill a few miles up the creek. Colonel Boone and Rebecca were living in a small cabin on the property. The old man looked frail, but seemed in good spirits.

Yet tragedy had once again struck the Boone family. Nathan and Tice Vanbibber, Olive's brother, had been on a hunt far to the west when a warring band of Kansa Indians stripped them of all their possessions. Through bitter cold and snow, Nathan and Tice followed the Missouri River, on foot, for 200 miles, arriving back home frostbitten and nearly starved. Tice never recovered from the ordeal and died two years later from the effects of exposure. Olive had nursed Nathan back to health, although he had lost much of his bulk. Irrepressible Olive seemed undaunted by her husband's trials, joking that for every pound Nathan had lost, she had gained two.

Later, Hannah had taken Olive aside and asked if what she had heard about the friendly nature of the Indians around here were not true.

"I wouldn't exactly call 'em friendly," Olive had replied in her straightforward way, "but some is more reasonable than others. My advice is, watch yer back."

A noise in the brush startled Hannah out of her reverie. She spun around, but it was only an opossum nosing along the bank of the creek. Chiding herself for being a nervous Nellie, she hurried back to the cabin. Baby Nancy Ann, who everyone called Dykie, had woken from her nap and was loudly signaling her hunger.

Scooping the baby from her crib, Hannah settled on a bench and put Dykie to her breast, covering them both with her shawl. On this cold, damp day she had kept all of her younger children inside while Temple and the older boys were out hunting. Jennie and Mattie played quietly before the fire with their corn-shuck dolls. Samuel had been put to work scraping a hide, but he showed little interest in the job, preferring to bother his sisters at their play.

"Go away!" screamed Jennie, giving Samuel a shove as he tried to grab her doll from her.

He retreated, only to sneak up a moment later behind Mattie. This time he was successful. Laughing, he held the doll just out of little Mattie's reach, goading her into sobs of fury.

"Samuel, stop that this instant!" Hannah demanded.

Reluctantly he handed the doll back, then went to stand by the door, kicking at a bucket.

"You have not finished with that hide," warned Hannah.

"No'm," he muttered, making no move to pick it up.

Lucy, stirring a pot of hominy at the hearth, put down the spoon. Grabbing Samuel by the upper arm, she marched him across the room, sat him down on the floor, and handed him the hide. "Git to work!" she ordered.

"Thank you, Lucy," said Hannah, switching Dykie to the other breast. "I don't know what it has come to when a boy won't obey his mother." She glanced around the tiny cabin, a far cry from the home they had left in Kentucky. This cabin had only one room, with not even a loft overhead. It was only meant to be temporary, their shelter only until the territorial government would allow them to continue west to the Boonslick. And that would not happen until Captain Clark had come to an agreement with the Osages on land cession. Until then, they were stuck here, at the Loutre Island settlement, with several other families, including Stephen and Phoebe and the Coopers.

The baby had drifted back to sleep, her tiny mouth still attached to the nipple. Gently Hannah slid a practiced finger between the infant's lips and her skin, breaking the suction without waking the child. Laying her back in the crib, she informed Lucy she was going to go check on Phoebe who had been feeling poorly ever since they arrived at Loutre Island. Wrapping her shawl around her shoulders, she stepped outside. Lucy followed right behind.

Hannah turned in surprise. "What is it, Lucy?"

"I gots sumpin' to tell ya," Lucy said, her

179

hands twisted in her apron.

"Yes?"

"I . . . I'm gonna have a baby."

"Oh, my!" Hannah's gaze instinctively went to Lucy's stomach that, as yet, showed no signs of pregnancy. "How . . . when . . . ?"

"Musta happened right befoh we lef'. I'd been keepin' comp'ny wid a boy b'long to Mastuh Wintuhs. Din't know 'bout de baby till we's already heah." Lucy appeared neither happy nor sad about her condition. Nor did she appear contrite.

"I see. Well, naturally we shall welcome your child." Hannah offered a congratulatory smile. It seemed odd that Lucy had been carrying on with someone at the neighbor's place without her knowledge, but then, ever since the business with Rufus, Lucy had kept quiet about her liaisons. In any event, Temple would be pleased to hear that he would shortly own another slave, and with no extra money out of pocket other than what it took to feed and clothe it.

Lucy shifted back and forth on her feet.

"Is there something else?" Hannah asked.

"De fathuh . . . I'd lak him to know 'bout it."

"Oh." Hannah thought for a moment. "Is that wise, do you think? After all, he is all

180

the way back in Kentucky. Wouldn't it just grieve him to know you were going to have a baby?"

Lucy looked up, her black eyes showing a momentary flash that reminded Hannah of the way she used to be. "It's his chil'," she murmured. "He gots a right to know."

Hannah was tempted to correct her. This black buck, whoever he was, might well be the father, but he had no rights to anything. The child would never be his . . . it would belong to Temple. Nevertheless, she felt some sympathy for Lucy, torn from her home like the rest of them, missing the old and familiar.

"Very well. I shall write Mister Winters at the first opportunity, though I can't guarantee he will tell . . . what is this boy's name?"

"Dooley."

"I can't promise he will tell Dooley." Hannah raised the shawl to cover her head, a slight drizzle having started as they talked.

"Miz Hannah, he'd hafta tell Dooley iffen you was to buy him for yo'self."

Hannah snorted in surprise. "Buy him! What on earth gave you the idea that Mister Cole would consider anything of the kind?"

"He a real good worker, ain't no trouble a-tall."

Lucy's eyes were fixed on the ground, but

181

Hannah could still see them glistening with tears. She sighed. "I am sure that is true, but you know quite well that we are in no position to buy Dooley. We lost everything in Kentucky except what we could carry with us here. We've not a penny to spare. Now, on second thought, I do not think I shall write Mister Winters with this news. It would only lead to grief and unrest. I am sure you understand."

Hannah put her hand on Lucy's shoulder, trying to offer a measure of kindness. Lucy flinched at her touch, turned, and disappeared into the cabin.

Exasperated, Hannah saddled up one of the horses and pointed it in the direction of Stephen's and Phoebe's place, just a mile or so down the creek. Imagine Lucy thinking they would scrape together enough money to buy some darkie merely because she had had the bad sense to get herself with child. And now that Hannah had set her straight, she would probably sulk for days.

At the top of a bluff, the river came into view, muddy and turgid from all the rain. It was so different from the rivers she was used to — the New back in Virginia, and the Licking in Kentucky. Although its current was not as swift, the Missouri seemed somehow more threatening, full of unseen snags and deep pools that could swallow a person before she knew it. The rushes lining the banks, sharp as razors, acted like sentries guarding against unwanted encroachment. Like all rivers, it was a highway, but one that could be expected to exact a heavy toll.

Riding through the settlement, Hannah passed by the homes of several families she knew. Most folks were inside on this chilly day, but, as she passed, she waved to Mrs. Patton who was out searching for dry kindling. Like themselves, the Loutre Island settlers were mostly waiting to move on to more permanent quarters. Colonel Cooper, vexed at not being able to reach the Boonslick, was already talking about scouting a different area, perhaps near New Madrid farther south. Certainly they were all unhappy with the state of limbo forced upon them.

Phoebe's cabin came into view, a slap-dash affair much like her own. Even accounting for the inclement weather it seemed unusually deserted — no stock in the yard, no smoke rising from the chimney.

Without bothering to knock, she pushed open the ill-fitting door, calling Phoebe's name. Five-year-old James and three-year-old Rhoda instantly were upon her, clamoring for attention. She bent to give them a hug, noting their dirty faces and runny noses. Over in the corner the baby cried weakly. She crossed to the bed where Phoebe lay huddled under a thin blanket.

"Phoebe?" Hannah touched her shoulder. "Phoebe, the babe needs feeding."

Phoebe looked at the squalling infant with bleary eyes. "Too tired," she mumbled.

"None of that, now," Hannah said gently. "Your son is hungry. You must feed him."

James and Rhoda came to stand by the bed, looking at their mother with solemn eyes. "She's sick," explained James, as though that fact were not obvious.

"Yes, dear, I know." Hannah felt her sister's forehead. "Let's see if we can make her feel better. You can help me. Can you stoke the fire, please?"

Hannah helped Phoebe rearrange herself so she could nurse the baby, then set about preparing a meal. Pickings were slim, but she found some pemmican, and some dry corn that she put on to boil for hominy. After a steaming cup of sassafras tea and some food, Phoebe looked much better. James and Rhoda wolfed down the leftovers.

The baby sated and once more asleep, Hannah lifted him into his crib. Fixing herself a cup of tea, she sat on the bed next to her sister. "Where is Stephen?" she asked.

184

"Hunting."

"How long has he been gone?"

Phoebe shrugged. "A few days."

"Were you ill when he left?"

"Not so much. I know what you are thinking. He would not have left if he thought I was too sick to care for the children."

"Of course not. Now, listen. I am going to send Lucy over here, later today, with more vittles. One of us will check on you and the children every day until Stephen returns. How does that sound?"

"We don't need your charity," Phoebe snapped.

Hannah pursed her lips, holding back a sharp retort. "Not our charity, perhaps, but you do need our help until you get to feeling better. You would do the same for me."

At that, Phoebe's face crumpled. Tears rolled down her sharp-boned cheeks. "Oh, Hannah, forgive me. I don't mean to be disagreeable. It's just . . . I look at you, so strong and healthy and beautiful, and I wish I could be more like you."

Hannah looked at her in amazement. "Beautiful? Me? What a silly notion. Why, I am not half as attractive as you, my dear."

"It's not just the way you look," Phoebe sniffed, wiping her eyes with a corner of the bed sheet. "It's the way you are. Always

185

cheerful, always so sure of yourself. Never disheartened by life. It's no wonder. . . ."

"Yes?"

Phoebe looked away, suddenly embarrassed. "Never mind. I'm running on at the mouth."

Hannah sat for a moment, not certain whether it would help matters to explain that she was as full of doubts as the next person. In the end, she simply gave Phoebe's hand a squeeze. It was ice cold. She rose to fetch another blanket.

"I didn't want to come here," Phoebe whimpered. "Why does Stephen always have to go where Temple goes? Why couldn't we have stayed in Kentucky?"

"Hush, now. It does no good talking like that. Besides, you have got it backwards. Stephen was the one who convinced Temple to come here. I reckon you are just feeling gloomy from all this rain, and being sick to boot. Just wait, you will be back on your feet in no time and things won't seem so bad."

Phoebe rolled away, her face to the wall.

Sighing, Hannah covered her with the extra blanket. "That's right. Try to get some rest. I will take James and Rhoda with me and send Lucy back later today. Now, don't worry, dear. Everything will be all right."

Hannah set the children on the horse and led it home. As she walked, the sun started to break through the cloud cover, lifting her spirits despite everything. "Thank you, Lord," she whispered. "We could use a little sunshine."

CHAPTER ELEVEN

The sun came out, the crops grew, the mosquitoes bit, and still there was no indication of when Governor Lewis would allow settlers into the Boonslick.

By the time of the first frost, both Hannah and Phoebe found themselves pregnant again. Phoebe had recovered enough to get out of bed, and the fresh, clean air put the color back in her cheeks. But her mood enjoyed no similar improvement. She moved through the days in a constant state of gloom, snapping at the children and even making life unpleasant for Stephen on his rare visits home. It was no wonder, Hannah thought, that Stephen stayed away as much as he did, either hunting or on sorties with the local militia. Who wouldn't prefer the company of jaunty fellow frontiersmen to that of a shrewish wife?

Although Hannah lamented her sister's unhappy state of mind, she at least took comfort in the knowledge that it did not have jealousy as its root cause. True to her intentions, Hannah had taken great care to distance herself from Stephen. It was not hard to do, given Stephen's frequent absences from the settlement. Still, if he happened to ride by while she was in the yard, she kept their conversations short and superficial. He seemed puzzled, at first, by her stand-offishness, but soon he responded in kind. It hurt Hannah to treat him so, and to be treated the same way by him. Nevertheless, it was better this way.

Once, after she had acted particularly reserved, Temple asked if Stephen had done something to anger her.

"Not at all," she replied. "Why would you think that?"

"Because, my dear, you have barely a word to say to the poor fellow these days. The two of you used to get along like a bear and honey."

"I really don't know what you are talking about," Hannah said, concentrating on her spinning, a chore she had taken up again as there were no stores in Loutre Island supplying fabric.

Temple came up behind her and placed his hands on her shoulders. "I think you do," he said.

Her mind raced as fast as the spinning wheel, wondering if Temple had noticed the same things Phoebe had. Before she could say anything, he walked out the door, leaving her to ponder the matter.

In December, Lucy had her baby, a fine, healthy boy she named Isaac. She had never again brought up the subject of purchasing Dooley, and, with the baby's birth, she seemed determined to put the past behind her. She doted on Isaac, fashioning a sling so she could carry him about, Indian style, while she worked. When he was not in Lucy's arms, he was most likely being tended by Jennie who had taken a particular shine to him. Hannah saw no reason to admonish the little girl — babies were babies, black or white, and, if Jennie wanted to practice mothering on Isaac, what harm was there in that?

As winter drizzled into spring, Colonel Cooper finally got tired of waiting for permission to settle the Boonslick. He packed up Anne and their children and moved west, claiming a spot in the rich bottom lands not too far from the salt lick that had given the area its name. By summer they were back, ordered to return to Loutre Island because the government could not guarantee their protection in the Far West.

"It's outrageous!" fumed Cooper, seated at the Cole's sawbuck table. "Nobody's asking for protection. I can protect my own family, I'm bound. If you want to know what I think . . . that fine gentleman, Meriwether Lewis, wants to keep settlers out so he and his fur trader cronies can have it all to themselves!"

"It figures poorly," Temple nodded in agreement. "We've no more protection here than our own militia, yet no one's telling us to leave Loutre Island."

Hannah, hugely pregnant, refilled the men's cups of grog before retreating to a corner with her sewing. This talk of "protection" unnerved her. Indian raids on Loutre Island and other settlements along the Missouri had increased of late, and it had her worried. Although the raids mostly involved the theft of livestock, every now and then a settler would get killed trying to protect his property. Rumor had it the British were supplying guns and liquor to the redskins, urging them to resist American encroachment. Why, she wondered, had she ever thought Louisiana Territory would be safer than Kentucky?

Hannah's eighth child, who they named after his father, was born during their second summer on Loutre Island. As it had been with all but her first delivery, it was over quickly and easily. Hannah gave thanks to God that all of her children were strong and healthy, especially since barely a family she knew had escaped the tragic death of an infant or child.

Shortly after little William's birth, Phoebe was delivered of her fourth child, a girl named Nellie. Tiny and weak, this baby struggled to survive. Phoebe herself was too sickly to tend to the infant, so Hannah took over the care of them both. For several days, Hannah never left their bedside. With a newborn of her own to care for, she was almost overwhelmed and so exhausted that she often found herself dozing off whenever she had a moment to sit.

She could not have done it without Stephen's help. Every day he rose early to stoke the fire before heading out to do the chores that normally fell to Phoebe — milking the cow, feeding the chickens, gathering eggs. Then, while Hannah prepared breakfast, he took his turn at his wife's bedside, talking softly with her if she was awake or simply holding her hand if she slept. Later, he would take charge of the other children, making sure they stayed out of the way while Hannah tended her patients.

Both of them were so tired they lacked the energy to speak much beyond the necessities. But the shared smiles and easy familiarity between them was back. Hannah had not realized until now how much she had missed Stephen's companionship. With a happy heart, she decided she would no longer have to avoid her brother-in-law since whatever untoward feelings he may have once harbored for her appeared to have vanished. How pleased Phoebe would be to know that she had been wrong about her husband — that, in truth, he loved his wife and felt nothing but friendly affection for her sister.

After two weeks of around-the-clock nursing, Phoebe and Nellie were well enough so that Hannah could return to her own brood. Before leaving, she sat next to her sister for a private talk.

"Phoebe, this is not easy, but I must discuss something with you."

Her patient sat up straighter in bed, baby Nellie in the crook of her arm. "Out with it, then."

Hannah shifted, searching for the right words. "You know this birth was hard on you. For a while there we were not sure you or the baby would make it."

"Aye." Phoebe stroked the underside of

Nellie's tiny chin. "Reckon I've got God and you to thank for pulling us through."

"Well, God played the larger part. What I am getting at is that I don't think you ought to do this again. You are so small, and each time it gets harder and harder for you. I don't know if God could work a miracle the next time."

Phoebe's eyes widened. "Are you saying I shouldn't have any more babies?"

"I am saying you would be taking a big risk if you did. It is something you and Stephen should talk about."

Phoebe looked away, her cheeks reddening. "I could never . . . we don't . . . that's not possible."

Hannah reached for her hand. "It is your life we're talking about. He will understand."

"No, he won't." Phoebe drew back her hand. "We are not like you and Temple. We don't . . . share things like the two of you do. If I denied him the one thing . . . I can't do it."

"Nonsense. You don't think much of the man you married if you think he would be so selfish as to . . ."

"Of course he wouldn't. But don't you see? If we don't have that together, we have nothing."

The look of anguish on Phoebe's face cut Hannah deeply. Gently she reached over and brushed the hair from her sister's forehead. "You poor thing. All this time you have been thinking your husband doesn't care for you. But he does, so very much. I have seen it clearly these past two weeks, the way he sat by your side praying for you to get better."

"What you saw was his sense of duty, nothing more," said Phoebe, her voice cracking with misery. "Now, this discussion is over, and I will thank you to keep it to yourself."

Hannah looked at her hands folded in her lap. Could she have mistaken Stephen's attentiveness to Phoebe as a sign of something more deeply felt? It seemed unlikely. And yet, perhaps she had been striving to see something she wanted to see, something that would absolve her own feelings of guilt.

"I shall not breathe a word of it to anyone," she sighed. "But you must promise me, for your own sake, that you will speak to Stephen."

Phoebe glowered at her. "What Stephen and I discuss is not for you to know."

"Promise me!"

The two women locked eyes. Finally Phoebe looked away. "I promise."

While Hannah had been off tending the sick, the men on Loutre Island had been celebrating some good news. General Clark had signed a treaty with the Osages that was highly favorable to the Americans. In return for protection from their enemies and the right to maintain certain hunting grounds, the Osages ceded almost all of their land in Missouri to the government. Clark was preparing to establish a fort on the river west of the Boonslick that would house a regular army garrison and a trading post. With this treaty guaranteeing friendlier relations with the Indians, and the fort providing protection, surely the lands to the west would very soon be opened to settlement.

Immediately Temple, Stephen, Ben Cooper, and many of the other men began to make plans. Cooper was the only one of them to have actually seen the Boonslick, and, while his descriptions were no doubt accurate, several men decided they wanted a first-hand view of the area before moving their families and goods. They would make it a hunting trip as well as a scouting trip, and come home loaded with food for the winter and visions of the Promised Land to last until spring.

Hannah spent the month of Temple's absence burrowed in their tiny cabin, like a mole in its den. She and Lucy kept busy with cold weather chores like spinning yarn from nettles and pouring candles. In free moments, she drew her children around her and conducted a makeshift school, determined that they would grow up with at least a passing familiarity with their letters. The three older boys sat dutifully for these lessons, although James at first argued that at sixteen he was too old for school. Samuel, now seven, was perhaps the smartest of her children, but her worst student. Like a wild horse, he fought the bit, unable to sit still long enough to learn anything. Finally Hannah gave up, letting him run free so he would not bother the others while they studied. Mindful of her own upbringing, Hannah encouraged Jennie to join the class, but the little girl, just turned six, was far more interested in playing with Isaac, Mattie, and Dykie than in any sort of school work.

Temple returned with enough meat to last through the winter and beaver pelts aplenty. He held them rapt with descriptions of what he had observed: land that sloped gently down to numerous springs and creeks, fertile soil, abundant forests, teeming game, and, of course, the highway known as the Missouri River flowing through it all, linking the Boonslick to the rest of the world. Just as Ben Cooper had said, it was like Kentucky must have been thirty years ago. Furthermore, he had spent a month in the woods and had not run into a single redskin. Not that he had ever doubted, but he was doubly sure of it now — the Cole family would prosper in the Boonslick.

That night, snuggled beneath a heavy buffalo robe, he and Hannah whispered their plans and dreams to each other. Hannah was so happy she felt her heart had taken wing. Her man was home, safely in her arms. What's more, he had come back to her with an enthusiasm for their future that had been missing for far too long.

Temple told her that he and Stephen had both picked out plots of land that they intended to claim. "Cooper and the others favor the bottom lands on the north side of the river, but, to my mind, the bluffs on the south side are the place to be. Once it is cleared, that land's going to be mighty fine. It's up high, so it won't flood, and the bugs are not half as bad when you get away from the shallows." He pulled Hannah closer and kissed the top of her head. "It is what I have been looking for my whole life, my love, just this one spot on God's earth. And now I have found it."

CHAPTER TWELVE

The waiting continued. Trappers and traders moved freely up the river, many of them
headed for Fort Osage, yet permanent
settlement of the Boonslick was denied. Day
after day, the men of Loutre Island rose,
praying that this day would bring good news
from St. Louis, and night after night they
fell into bed disappointed. The uncertainty
was the cruelest thing of all. A man was
faced with impossible choices. Should he
clear and plant more land for cash crops, or
would his labor be wasted if the ban were
lifted? Should he add on that extra room to
his cramped cottage, or would he be abandoning it tomorrow?

For the women, waiting was not as hard.
Although their "temporary" lodging might
be smaller than what they were used to,
there were still meals to be fixed, clothes to
be sewn, children to be raised. Many of
them shared their husbands' dreams of

200

owning a plot of land in the paradise known as the Boonslick, but none thought achieving this dream would significantly change their lives. So while the men gathered together to complain over mugs of whiskey, or sent emissaries downriver to learn the latest news, the women squared their shoulders and went on about their business.

One glorious late summer morning Hannah busied herself grinding corn at the hominy block. It was that time of year when the sun still gives out a soothing warmth yet the air is crisp and dry. Cool nights had vanquished the mosquitoes and the flies buzzed with a sluggish energy.

Hannah paused in her work, relishing a rare moment of quiet. Temple had taken the four older boys on a fishing expedition, and Lucy, toting Isaac on her back, had Jennie and Mattie off gathering nettles. Only Dykie and William remained at home, napping in the cabin.

Warmed by the sun and her exertions, Hannah loosened the kerchief tied around her neck and used it to wipe her face. Stretching out the tight muscles in her back and shoulders, she stooped for a cool dipper of water. Refreshed, she stood for a moment with hands on hips, her face turned to the sun. The unaccustomed silence surrounded her like a warm, wet fog. Only the hushed and muted sounds of Nature — Frene Creek's quiet trickle, a woodpecker's insistent tapping — interrupted the stillness.

I should be using this quiet time to write in my journal, she thought. Three years had elapsed since she had last opened it. Since that time, Cousin Dolley's husband had ascended to the Presidency of the United States. Yes, hard as it was to believe, the diminutive Quaker lady who had befriended her so many years ago was now the First Lady of the land. Something about this exalted status intimidated Hannah, for she was finding it hard to address herself to the wife of the President. It was one thing to confide in your cousin, entirely another to unburden yourself to the First Lady. Silly, she realized, since her journal entries were nothing but private thoughts that she never intended Dolley, or anyone else, actually to read.

Hannah poured more kernels onto the block and resumed her grinding. Thinking of Dolley brought to mind her other Virginia relatives. She maintained a fitful correspondence with Rhoda and her other brothers and sisters, but her father had not answered any of the many letters she had sent. It was as though he had completely erased her and Phoebe from his life. Rhoda wrote that their mother was more inclined toward forgiveness, but that Holbert Allison forbade her from contacting her wayward daughters. Hannah was stunned by the depth of her father's anger. He must have been much closer to Phoebe's jilted fiancé than anyone knew. Yet, why would he hold a grudge for so long, and why would he blame Hannah for what happened? Likely she would never know the answers to these questions, and, as time went by, she puzzled over them less. As Temple reminded her, it was a waste of time to fret over a situation she could not change.

Immersed in her thoughts, Hannah was startled when Stephen galloped into the yard, his horse sleek with sweat.

"Hannah," he cried, "you must come with me! I need your help!"

She took in his dirt-encrusted breeches, loose-hanging shirt, and sweat-stained buckskins. Her throat constricted in fear. Could Temple be hurt, or one of the boys? Was Phoebe ill again?

Stephen gripped her arm, and then she saw it in his face — not the frantic concern that comes with the injury to a loved one, but the pure rush of adrenaline that accompanies intrigue and adventure.

"There's a woman," he panted, "in a cave over on the Gasconade. She's demented, or near abouts. I don't know, she barely made sense. She wouldn't come with me, so I thought maybe if another woman. . . ."

"Slow down," Hannah said. "I don't understand. What are you talking about?"

Stephen let go of her arm. Sweeping his hat from his head, he ran his hand through his grimy hair. "I was looking for saltpeter in the caves over on the Gasconade River. I stepped into one, and this woman leaped out at me, screeching like a banshee! Scared the hell out of me! She pert near scratched my eyes out, till I got her calmed down and more or less convinced I wasn't going to do her no harm. I left her part of a deer carcass I had with me, but that won't last long. We have got to find her and help her!"

"Why can't her own people help her?"

Stephen's agitation increased. "We are her people. She's a white woman, Hannah, though she's in such bad shape it took me a while to see it. She's filthy, and her clothes are in rags. Reckon she's been lost in the woods for some time. We must help her!"

"Why didn't you say that in the first place?" Hannah said, rushing toward the cabin. "Saddle up the mare for me while I gather some food . . . oh, wait a minute . . . Dykie and William are here. I can't leave them alone."

"Bring them with us."

"Take a three-year-old and a baby into that redskin-infested wilderness? I think not. Ride down the road and see if Missus Patton can watch them until Lucy returns."

Thirty minutes later Stephen returned with the Pattons' slave girl. Hannah tossed him a bundle of provisions and tied another bag, containing her spare dress, a woolen cloak, and a two-point trade blanket, on the back of her saddle. She started to lead her horse to a stump she used for easy mounting, but Stephen impatiently lifted her into the saddle. She thought to protest this unnecessary assistance, but he was already trotting down the road.

They headed toward the river, turning away from Frene Creek just before reaching Stephen's and Phoebe's cabin. It seemed as though Stephen purposely avoided going by his own house. For the first time, Hannah wondered why Stephen had come to her for help, instead of his wife. She posed the question; he answered with a look that seemed to say: *You and I both know Phoebe would be of no help in a situation like this.*

Riding swiftly, they followed the river for

about seven miles to its intersection with the Gasconade. Here, Stephen paused to let the horses rest. This was the farthest west Hannah had ever been. Far from being worried about venturing into unknown territory, she felt energized. Perhaps this was the pull of the wild that men folk always seemed to hanker for. She glanced over at Stephen and laughed. He looked just like a little boy, eager to show his mother his latest exciting discovery.

He smiled back, his dark blue eyes sending a message that was decidedly not one a son sends his mother. "Thank you for coming," he said. Behind his words, she could hear what he really meant to say: *Thank you for not letting propriety, or how I feel about you, prevent you from being here with me.*

"The way gets a bit rougher from here on," he explained. "The banks of the Gasconade are mostly rocky, and it will get hillier as we head south. We may have to get off and lead the horses in a place or two."

Hannah nodded for him to lead on. By now the sun was high in the sky. She could feel it burning her chest and neck, and wished she had her kerchief with her. In the confusion of leaving, it had been left draped across the hominy block. Occasionally Stephen led them away from the river, back into the woods where she welcomed the shade.

"Who is this woman, do you think?" she asked after a while. "How did she come to be here?"

"Hard to say. Could be the redskins stole her, maybe even when she was a little girl, and now she's lost. She spoke some English, but it was all nonsense. I couldn't make heads or tails of it."

"Poor, poor thing," Hannah said. "Imagine being ripped from your family and enslaved by murderous heathens. No wonder she has gone crazy." She shuddered, remembering her own encounter with a hostile Indian. What if she had been kidnapped, stolen away, and forced to endure unspeakable atrocities?

The path they followed, no more than a game trail, veered back toward the river. They came to a place where huge slabs of moss-speckled rock blocked their way. Stephen reached up to help her dismount. "We'll have to walk from here. It's not much farther."

They untied the bundles of food and clothing. Carrying his rifle easily in the crook of his arm, Stephen hopped up nimbly on the first rock and held out his hand.

Hoisting her skirts with one hand and

holding a bag in the other, Hannah had no way to grab hold. "Wait a minute," she said. Dropping her bundle, she reached between her legs, pulled up the back hem of her skirt, and tucked it in at the waist. This arrangement revealed an indecent length of her legs, but at least it left her a free hand. Retrieving the bag, she grasped Stephen's hand and let him pull her beside him onto the rock.

"It's down there a ways, then we'll have to climb back up the hill," he said, still holding her hand. "Can you make it?"

Hannah sniffed the air. "I smell meat roasting."

"She must be fixing that haunch I left her. Come on!"

Over slippery rocks and through dense underbrush he led her, holding tightly to her hand. At first, his touch made her uncomfortable, but soon she realized it was wholly necessary. Several times she would have tripped over tangled roots or loose stones had he not held her up. More than once, the bank became impassable so they were forced to wade into the river.

"Watch for snakes," he warned. Finally he turned and pointed up the slope. "The cave I found her in is up there."

Hannah could see nothing but more rocks

and prickly undergrowth, but she gamely followed as he picked his way upward, pausing to give her a hand as needed. Before long her bodice was drenched with sweat, as wet as the hem of her skirts that had trailed in the water. Stephen did his best to clear a path, but every now and then a branch would snap back, sometimes catching her in the arms or face. Soon, she was covered with tiny scratches.

At last, Stephen came to a halt. Peering around his back, Hannah saw, ten feet away, the entrance to a good-size cave. In front of it, on a ledge the size of a small cot, a fire smoldered. Bones from the deer carcass were scattered here and there. But there was no sign of the woman.

Stephen put his mouth close to Hannah's ear. "I'm going to call out. If she is still here, I don't fancy startling her like I did before."

Hannah nodded her understanding.

"Madam!" Stephen called in a non-threatening voice. "I have come back as I promised. I have brought more food and clothing for you, as well as a lady who would like to help you."

For several minutes nothing happened. Then a shuffling noise came from inside the cave. As Hannah watched in fascination, the woman slowly emerged, keeping her back to the cave's wall and clutching a hefty stick to her chest. She was, as Stephen had said, in a wretched state. Her dark hair was matted with dried leaves and her dress hung in tatters. She was barefoot, and her skin was so dirty it was indeed difficult to identify her heritage. Hannah stared at the woman's features — short, upturned nose and round, blue eyes — and knew that Stephen was right. The creature before them was a white woman.

Hannah took a couple of steps closer. The woman shrieked and shrank back into the cave. "It is all right," Hannah said, holding the bag of clothes out in front of her. "I won't hurt you. Look, here are some clothes for you, and a warm blanket."

The woman's shriek subsided into a low moan that repeated over and over like the cry of a tired baby. She remained hunched inside the cave, the stick held ready to strike.

"See? I will just put them right here," Hannah said, laying the bag on the ground. "Here is some food for you, too." Stephen handed her the second bundle that she placed beside the first. She backed away and stood next to Stephen, waiting to see what would happen.

Slowly the woman's moans died away. Laying aside the stick, she crawled to the lip of the cave and peeked out. When she caught sight of her would-be benefactors, she scuttled back inside.

Hannah started to call out to her, but Stephen hushed her with a finger to his lips, then signed that they should simply wait quietly.

Fifteen minutes passed before the woman showed herself again. This time, she paused at the cave entrance. Satisfied that her visitors were not going to attack, she crawled on all fours to the bundles. Grabbing the one containing food, she dragged it with her back into the recesses of the cave.

Stephen and Hannah looked at each other, wondering what to do next. "She must be starved if she ate that entire haunch and is still hungry," Hannah whispered.

"Why don't you try to talk to her," Stephen urged. "I don't reckon she's dangerous, but I'll be right behind you if she proves me wrong."

Hannah did not fancy getting close to a maniac, but she had to agree the creature would likely feel less threatened by her than by a big, strapping man like Stephen. Taking a few tentative steps at a time, she approached the cave entrance. Stephen followed a few paces behind.

"I am coming to talk with you," she announced. "Don't be frightened." Taking a deep breath, she eased herself into the cave. The woman crouched just a few feet away, gnawing on a piece of pemmican. She looked up at Hannah, then went back to her chewing. Very slowly Hannah crouched down herself, giving the woman time to get used to her. After a while, she stopped eating and regarded Hannah with strange, watery eyes. They glistened, although not with tears. It was probably just smoke from the fire that made them shine, but the effect was eerie.

"What is your name?" asked Hannah gently.

The woman stared, no sign of comprehension on her slack face. But then she shook her head as though remembering something. "No name," she mumbled, wiping her mouth on her tattered sleeve.

Although Hannah had barely heard the response, she was certain it had been in English. Perhaps she would be able to help this strange creature after all. Going to her hands and knees, she edged a little closer. "Where are your people?"

The woman's eyes clouded over and she uttered some kind of gibberish. Her head started to shake, almost as though palsied.

By this time, Hannah was close enough to

touch her. Hoping to calm the poor, demented thing, she reached out and laid a light hand on the woman's bony shoulder. "Come with me," she cajoled. "Let me take you to a safe, warm place. Perhaps we can find your people."

The creature's shaking gradually subsided. She stared at the hand on her shoulder as though she had never before experienced the touch of another human being. Slowly her eyes traveled to Hannah's face. Deep in their glistening depths, Hannah saw fear. Unexpectedly the woman dropped her head back and began moaning, louder and more insistently than before. Hannah tried to pull her into an embrace, but she pushed away. Suddenly the moaning ceased. She raised a shaking finger, the nail cracked and encrusted with dirt, and pointed it at Hannah.

"Dead. Man dead."

Hannah shook her head, not certain she had understood.

"Man dead," the woman repeated, punching the air with her claw-like finger. "Your man."

"My man dead? I don't know what you mean." Hannah decided she had had about enough of this. She did not like this clammy cave, nor this raving lunatic with the devilish-looking eyes. She would make one last attempt to help the woman, and if that was rejected, then so be it. "Please come with me now. I promise we will take care of you." As she spoke, she took hold of the woman's arm and tried to get her to stand.

Gasping in panic, the creature shoved Hannah with the strength of a bear. Hannah toppled backwards, striking her head on the wall of the cave. The woman took off running. Stephen grabbed for her, but she eluded him and disappeared into the dense forest.

Ducking into the cave, Stephen knelt by Hannah. She was conscious, but dazed. "Sweet Jesus," he whispered, cradling her head in his lap. "What did that deranged wench do to you?"

Hannah could not answer. She lay still, aware only of the pain in her head, a ringing in her ears, and Stephen's cool fingers stroking her brow. After a while, she forced herself to sit up. The room spun and a wave of nausea overtook her. She swallowed, fighting it back.

Stephen probed the back of her head, causing her to wince with pain. His hand came away bloody.

"We've got to get you out of here," he said. "That wound needs tending." Throwing off his vest and shirt, he tore a strip from the latter and wrapped it around her head. He slipped the vest back on and bent to help Hannah to her feet. Dizzy and sick, her knees buckled. "Ah, God," he groaned, clutching her against his bare chest. "I should never have brought you here."

"I am all right," she insisted, although she knew it was far from the truth. Her head pounded like a blacksmith's hammer.

"Always the brave one, ain't you?" he whispered into her ear. "Always caring for everyone else. Well, my darlin', right now you need someone to take care of you, and, seeing as there ain't a whole lot of candidates for the job at hand, reckon that someone will have to be me."

She closed her eyes, savoring the pungent smell of his skin against her cheek, the feel of his muscled arms wrapped around her so tightly. How lovely it would be to rest here for the night, safe under the watchful eye of her brother-in-law. *Her brother-in-law.* Temple's brother. Phoebe's husband. And what, exactly, to her? No more than a friend, surely, but how to explain that to her jealous sister? Or to Temple, for that matter, who lately had seemed to suspect something awry between his wife and his brother. There was nothing untoward between them, of course, at least not as far as she was concerned. Nevertheless, she would not relish having to explain an overnight absence spent in Stephen's company. Besides, her babies needed her.

Gathering herself, she pushed away from Stephen. "We must go back. Now. You know it as well as I do."

Stephen's face fell. "That bump on your head looks bad. You should rest here till morning."

She fixed him with a haggard gaze. "Now, Stephen. While there is still light left."

He dropped his head to his chest, fighting something internal. "All right," he said, giving in. "We'll see if you can make it to the horses. But if you can't, I'm bringing you back here for the night. That crazy witch knew a good shelter when she saw it."

Leaving the provisions they had brought in case the mysterious woman came back, they headed down the steep slope, Hannah leaning heavily on Stephen's arm. She had to stop frequently to fight dizzy spells, and, when they reached the river, Stephen picked her up and carried her through it, but they eventually made it back to the horses.

Mounted up, she started to feel a little better, although the knot on her head still throbbed like a bullfrog's throat. Stephen kept the horses at a slow walk. She knew he did it for her comfort, but wished they could go faster. By now, with the sun sinking in the late afternoon sky, folks at home would be starting to worry.

As they sauntered along, her thoughts turned to the demented woman. What had she meant by her garbled words: *Your man dead?* She was a complete stranger to Hannah so could not possibly know anything about her man, and, in any case, he certainly was not dead. Surely it was just the rambling of a lunatic.

But what if the crazed thing was some kind of soothsayer? Hannah had heard about people like that. People with the uncanny ability to predict the future. Like that Shawnee leader, the Prophet. Perhaps this woman's unnatural powers had branded her as some kind of witch, so the people around her had shunned her, abandoning her to a life of wandering. Hannah put a brake on her thoughts, realizing they were careening out of control. Still, she was left with an uneasy feeling.

As the sun dipped below the bluffs at their back, she became chilled and started to shiver. Stephen, who had not taken his eyes off her for longer than a minute, removed his vest and draped it over her shoulders. She tried to protest, as this generosity left him bare-chested in the cool air, but he would not hear of it. Secretly she was glad. The buttery soft garment, warmed by his body heat, felt wonderful.

It was fully dark when they finally rode into the yard. The tiny, ramshackle cabin had never looked so appealing.

Temple heard them coming and was out the door before Stephen could dismount. Taking in the amazing scene — Stephen shirtless, Hannah with a bloody rag tied about her head and scratches all over her arms and face — his face went white. "What the hell have you done to my wife?" he demanded.

"I can explain," Stephen said.

"No doubt. It had better be good."

Suddenly Hannah felt faint. She slumped forward. Strong arms lifted her from her horse.

As Temple carried her to their cabin, he glanced back at his brother. "Here's a piece of advice. Go home to your wife."

Hannah's Journal
May, 1810, Loutre Island, Louisiana Territory

Dear Cousin Dolley,

It seems a mite disrespectful to address the wife of the President in such familiar terms. Still, I remind myself that long before you were First Lady, you were simply Dolley Payne, my dear Temple's cousin. I trust that you believe, as I do, that the bonds of family are stronger than position or class, and that you would be pleased to still be referred to simply as "Cousin".

When last I visited these pages, I wrote of our anticipated move to the Boonslick in Louisiana Territory. Three and one half years later, little has changed. True, we are closer to our destination, but, like fish swimming upriver, the closer we get, the farther away it seems. The last few years have been like running a raging river — one moment perched atop a swelling crest, the next dashed into a deep trough.

Our hopes were raised with the signing of the treaty with the Osages. Yet months passed with no word from St. Louis lifting the ban on westward movement. Then, when Governor Lewis died last fall, everything was thrown into chaos. I do grieve for the poor man, cut down so young in life. Nevertheless, his careless handling of certain administrative affairs of the Territory seems to have left his successors collectively scratching their heads. It is Temple's hope that the new governor, Benjamin Howard, will arrive soon to put things in order. Perhaps he will finally authorize opening the Boonslick to white settlers.

Now, a confession. Though Temple, Stephen, Colonel Cooper, and most of the men on Loutre Island fairly itch to be gone, I cannot say that I share their agitation. While the Osage treaty solidified friendly relations with that tribe, it angered many of the others. The Pottawatomies, Sacs, and Foxes, to name a few, now see the white man as being in league with their mortal enemies, the Osages. These tribes have reacted by increasing their attacks on the Osage and white settlements alike.

Your husband, our esteemed Commander-in-Chief, himself issued an order directing all volunteer companies to equip themselves with good horses and weapons to prepare for a possible

Indian uprising along the Mississippi and Missouri Rivers. As captain of the Loutre Island militia, Stephen was charged with carrying out that order, but it is a fact that many of our men lack rifles, swords, or other means of defense. His company consists of a mismatched crew of farmers, some armed with only a hunting knife or broad-axe.

Temple believes the Boonslick would be safer as it is deep in the heart of friendly Osage country. He has a point, and I must defer to his judgment in these matters. Still, I cannot see how we would be safer living on the very edge of civilization, far removed from any other white settlement. It would seem to be inviting trouble.

Ah, well, in the end it is God alone who holds our fate in His hands. He has seen fit to bless me with eight healthy children (soon to be nine!), a loving husband, a warm hearth, and a full larder. I would do well to thank Him for these blessings, and trust Him to continue to provide.

Would it be impertinent of me to ask for your prayers, and those of your cherished husband? I think I should sleep sounder at night knowing the

President of the United States and his lady were petitioning the Lord on my behalf! And please keep Phoebe in your prayers, as well. She, too, is expecting another child, contrary to my advice. I could throttle Stephen for placing her in such a precarious position. Though husbands have their rights, I am, quite frankly, shocked that in a matter of life and death he has not chosen to be a gentleman. You were right about him when you said, all those years ago, that it would take a woman of fortitude to tame him. Our little Phoebe is not up to the task.

Were it not for Temple's restraining hand, I would march right over there and give Stephen Cole a piece of my mind. Temple argues it is not my place to interfere. Perhaps not. But life is so precious, as you well know, my dear Dolley. It must be carefully guarded, like a priceless gem. I cannot respect someone who would treat it so carelessly.

Your loving cousin,
Hannah Cole

CHAPTER THIRTEEN

Hannah bolted upright in bed. Sweat soaked her nightdress, pooling in the space between her breasts and rounded belly. The violence of her awakening roused Temple at her side.

"What is it?" he whispered, smoothing the long, dark braid that stuck damply to her back.

"A dream," she answered, forcing herself to take deep breaths to calm her galloping heart. "Just a dream."

"Again?" Temple propped up on an elbow. "Hannah, you haven't slept through the night in weeks. What is wrong?"

"It must be the baby, "she said, lying back in the crook of his arm. "He must have some kind of powerful magic in him that comes out in my dreams."

Temple chuckled, rubbing her stomach lightly. "I am not much of a believer in such things. Are you sure there is nothing troubling you? You have not seemed yourself lately."

Hannah bit her lip. Part of her wanted to tell him what had been haunting her dreams, while the other part was afraid to.

He found her hand and laced his fingers through hers. "Tell me, dearest."

"It is always the same dream," she said, looking into his strong face for reassurance. "The woman in the cave, the lunatic woman Stephen found . . . she appears suddenly, as though stepping out of a dense fog, and starts toward me. She is saying something, mouthing words of some sort, but I can't hear them. She comes closer, shakes me, tries to make me understand. Then I wake up."

"Is that all? That is what has been robbing you of your sleep?"

Hannah turned her head away, reluctant to say more. She had never told Temple of the strange words uttered by the maniac that day: *Your man dead.* How could she tell him that she was sure the creature visited her dreams to impart a warning of some sort?

Temple tightened his hold on her. "I can't fathom how it is that old crone scared the starch out of you, but you have got nothing to fear. I will keep you safe."

224

It is not me I am fretting about, she thought. Sighing, she rolled over and nestled against him, spoon-like. His hand once again stroked her belly, around and around in soothing circles. Soon she could feel his arousal against her back. Her body responded with a warmth of its own. She shifted slightly to let him know she recognized his desire and shared it. She wondered if other couples did this — enjoyed each other this way even during pregnancy.

His hand slid lower, and then abruptly stopped. "Did you hear that?" he whispered.

She strained her ears. All she could hear was little William sucking his thumb. "What was it?" she said.

"Something outside. A banging sound . . . there it is again."

This time Hannah heard it, the dull thump of wood striking against wood.

"Reckon I better see what it is," he said, sliding out of bed.

"Hurry back."

"Madam," he grinned, pulling on his boots, "you can count on it."

Lifting the musket from over the fireplace, he checked its load before exiting the cabin. Hannah heard his boots scrunch around the corner, then silence. The silence itself was odd, now that she thought about it. Where were the usual night sounds of tree frogs and crickets? Where was the hoot owl that made his home in the cottonwood tree by the creek?

Temple burst back into the cabin. "The horses are gone," he said, his voice grim.

"What?" Hannah stumbled out of bed, fumbling for her shawl.

"Gone. Stolen, by Indians, I reckon. No one else could have done it so quietly. The noise we heard was the corral gate knocking in the wind."

Despite his deliberately low tones, the older children began to stir.

"What's happening, Pa?" said James from his pallet in the corner.

"Indian raid. They took four horses, near as I can tell. I'd better go warn the others." He moved about the cabin, filling his powder pouch, strapping on his knife.

"I'll go with you!" exclaimed James, leaping up.

"So will I," Holbert chimed in.

"No. I need you to stay and protect your mother and the young 'uns. No telling if those thieving redskins are still about."

"Temple!" Hannah's voice trembled. "What if they are still about? You might be walking into an ambush!"

"I'll watch my backside," he promised.

"Boys, keep a sharp eye out."

Hannah bolted the door behind him, and then dressed, knowing sleep would be impossible for the rest of the night. James and Holbert armed themselves with whatever weapons were at hand. The family owned only one gun, which Temple had taken, so they were forced to resort to a collection of knives and cooking utensils. The prospect of having to defend their home and family from rampaging Indians seemed exciting to sixteen and eighteen-year-old boys. Their mother found it terrifying.

Two hours later, as the sky was just beginning to lighten in the east, Temple returned. He reported that a band of perhaps eight to ten redskins had made off with seven horses, his four and another three belonging to Abraham Patton. Stephen, in his rôle as captain of the militia, was putting together a party to go after them.

"Oh, my Lord." Hannah clasped her hands under her arms to keep them from shaking. The lunatic woman from her dreams danced before her eyes. "Must you go, Temple? What if . . . oh, God, what if something should happen to you? I don't care about the horses, but I can't live without you. I need you, we all need you!"

Temple pulled her into his arms. The

227

burgeoning life they had created together pressed hard against his belly — a reminder of all that was at stake.

"We can't let them get away with it," he said, taking her face into his hands. "If we let them take the horses today, then tomorrow it will be the cattle, and the next day they will be stealing our children. We must take a stand."

Hannah could not hold back the tears. "Promise me you will come back!"

"Madam, you can count on it!" He kissed her quickly, and then was gone.

The morning brought its usual demands — children to be fed, stock to be tended, chores to be done. Hannah moved through it all by rote, like a mule pulling a mill wheel. Finally she could not stand it any longer. She had to know what was going on in the rest of the settlement. Leaving Lucy and James in charge of the children, and taking Holbert with her for protection, she headed down the road for Phoebe's cabin.

On the way, they passed the Cooper place. It stood empty, the family having recently moved to the Boonslick. After years of delay, the territorial government had finally lifted its ban on western settlement. The Coles were within weeks of packing up and moving themselves. The only thing holding them back was Phoebe, who was due to give birth any day. Hannah had convinced the men that her sister was more likely to deliver safely if she did not have to undergo a strenuous move in the late stages of pregnancy.

It was ironic, she thought, that after three years spent on Loutre Island, waiting to leave, they would be delayed at the last minute. Also, that the present crisis would arise just as they were preparing to leave.

Hannah found Phoebe sprawled at the kitchen table, her heavy stomach hanging between outstretched legs. Sweating in the July heat, she listlessly shelled beans. Her children had obviously been running wild. The oldest, eight-year-old James, was nowhere to be seen. Hannah immediately sent Holbert to look for him, and set the others to work cleaning up the cabin. Helping Phoebe to her feet, she led her outside and deposited her under the leafy shade of a sugar maple.

"What is going on?" she asked, arranging herself next to her sister. "Have you heard anything new?"

Phoebe shook her head. "They left at sunup. Six of them."

"Who besides Temple and Stephen?"

"Mister Patton, John Gooch, James Murdock, and Sarshall Brown."

"Which direction?"

"They followed Loutre Creek north. Stephen didn't think the redskins had too much of a jump on them."

Hannah rubbed her cheek nervously. "So it could be over soon."

"P'raps. P'raps not. It's hard to tell with savages. Could be they'll keep running, could be they'll stand and fight. Stephen says they're mighty unpredictable."

Phoebe's attitude was a little too blasé for Hannah's liking. "One would think they are off on a picnic to hear you talk about it," she snapped. "Aren't you at all concerned for your husband's safety?"

"Yes, Hannah, I am deeply concerned. And you have no right to suggest otherwise," Phoebe shot back.

Hannah lowered her head, ashamed of her outburst. "Forgive me. That was out of line. It is just that I am so scared. Aren't you?"

"Yes," Phoebe admitted. She shifted around, trying to find a comfortable position. "I am scared for the men. I am scared this baby will come while Stephen's away. I am scared I won't live to see him again."

"My poor dear." Hannah reached over and brushed strands of hair from her sister's sweaty forehead. "I am most disappointed in Stephen. That he would place his own needs over the health of his wife. . . ."

"Don't blame him," Phoebe rushed to his defense. "You see . . . I never told him what you and I discussed when Nellie was born."

Hannah was aghast. Scolding words started to tumble out of her mouth.

Phoebe held up a hand to silence her. "Don't, please, Hannah. I know what you are going to say, and I reckon you are right, like always. But you might as well know that I will never turn my husband away from my bed, even if it kills me."

"You don't need to do this," Hannah pleaded. "You don't need to sacrifice your life to ensure Stephen's loyalty."

Phoebe's look was so full of resentment that Hannah blanched. "That's easy enough for you to say," she hissed. "You have never doubted Temple, never had to wonder why he married you. You have never felt sick inside because you know your husband despises you, or, worse, just doesn't care. You have never felt your heart shrivel up because you know your husband loves someone else!"

"Stop it!" Hannah shook the distraught woman's shoulders, desperate to silence her before she said something that would poison the rest of their lives. "You don't know what you are saying! Stephen does care for you."

Phoebe did not argue, although it was clear she did not concede the point. The two women sat in silence for a moment. Hannah picked at the grass. It felt like someone needed to apologize, but who?

"The thing is," Phoebe finally said, "nothing bad ever happens to you. Sometimes I wish it would, just so you would know how it feels."

Three days passed while the inhabitants of Loutre Island waited for the party to return. Some of the men who had stayed behind made reconnaissance trips into the surrounding woods to determine if other hostile Indians were in the area. They found nothing, indicating the earlier raid had been an isolated event. The settlement breathed easier, all except for the families of the men who were still in pursuit.

On the fourth day, Phoebe went into labor. Anticipating a long and difficult delivery, both Hannah and Lucy attended her, packing with them a bag full of homemade remedies, although, in the end, all three women knew the outcome was in God's hands.

The afternoon proceeded as slowly as a

watched pot. Phoebe drifted in and out of consciousness, the pains coming infrequently, but with excruciating power.

"Dis gal ain't lak you, Miz Hannah, jus' poppin' out de babies lak co'ks outta de bottle," said Lucy, dabbing at the patient's sweaty brow.

"No, indeed," agreed Hannah. "She should have quit after the last one."

A knock came at the door. Lucy rose to answer it.

"Is Missus Cole here?" Hannah heard a voice she recognized as belonging to one of the neighbors, George Talbot.

"Dey's two Missus Coles heah, but one of 'em ain't in no condition to talk."

"Mister Talbot." Hannah opened the door wider. "What is it? Is there news of the men?"

Talbot looked past her, caught a glimpse of Phoebe on the bed. He motioned Hannah to step outside. "We found Stephen about a mile from here, collapsed by the side of the road. They're bringing him in. I rode ahead to warn Missus Cole."

Hannah's hand flew to her mouth. "Warn her?"

"Yes, ma'am. He's in bad shape."

"The others?"

Talbot shook his head. "No sign of them."

Hannah trembled. Where was her Temple? Lying by a muddy bank with a tomahawk stuck in his brain? The crazy old woman had been trying to warn her, after all. But no, surely he was alive. She would have felt it if he had died. Maybe he and Stephen had gotten separated, and Stephen had had the misfortune of running into the Indian party on his own. She must see Stephen, talk to him. Find out what had happened.

She glanced back at Phoebe, thrashing in the throes of another pain while Lucy stroked her arm. "Take him to my cabin," she instructed Talbot. "My sister is in no condition to see him right now."

Talbot nodded and rushed off to intercept the men bringing in Stephen.

"Lucy," Hannah said, hurriedly throwing her remedies back into the bag, "Mister Cole has been found. I must go to him."

"Marse Temple?"

"No." A knot of emotion made it difficult to get out the next words. "Mister Stephen. They are taking him to our place. You will have to take care of things here."

Lucy's brow knit. "Dis ain't gonna be easy."

"I know." She laid a hand on the black woman's shoulder. "But you have always been a great help to me when it is my time.

There is no one I trust more. Whatever you do, don't say anything about Mister Stephen. I don't want that worry on her mind right now." Then she bent and kissed the top of her sister's head, and slipped out the door, praying that this would not be the last time she would see Phoebe alive.

When she arrived home, the men were just riding in with Stephen. They had managed to get him on a horse, where he slumped, unconscious. They carried him inside and laid him on Hannah's and Temple's bed.

"Good Lord," Hannah breathed. Never had she seen a body so ravaged. It was a wonder he still lived.

Hannah turned to the men who had brought him. "I will do what I can here. Please, you must go look for the others. Perhaps they are somewhere out there, like this, or worse."

The men nodded and traipsed out.

Hannah's children stared at their uncle, wide-eyed and silent. She shooed all but James outside, and then instructed her oldest to cut away Stephen's mud and blood-encrusted buckskins. While he worked, she set water on to boil and prepared poultices of wild geranium and cup weed to staunch the bleeding.

"Ma!" James called, his voice choking.

"Come look at this."

Hannah stepped closer and stared at the naked man on the bed. Blood oozed from knife cuts so numerous they could not begin to be counted. Some were so deep that muscle and bone were exposed. The skin on his hands was shredded and one was so swollen she was sure it was broken. Mixed with the blood and dirt was a dark, pasty substance. She dabbed at it with a finger and brought it to her nose. "Elm bark. Can you imagine? He had the presence of mind to chew elm bark and treat himself with it."

"He's hardly breathing, Ma." James pointed to a wound on Stephen's chest. "This one must've got his lung."

"Pray that it didn't, Son." Hannah poured hot water into a bowl and sat on the edge of the bed. "I am going to clean these wounds and apply poultices for the bleeding, but they are bound to soak through before long. I will need more geranium and cup weed, and quinine for fever. Go find some, and put the other children to work on it as well."

James sprinted out the door, glad to have a task that removed him from the unsettling sight of his battered and bloody uncle.

With her son gone, Hannah felt free to make a more thorough examination of her patient. Most of the wounds were on the upper half of his body, and only half a dozen or so looked deep enough to require stitches. The chest wound James had noted was the most serious. There was no doctor on Loutre Island. One could be sent for from downriver, but, by the time he arrived, it would be too late. Hannah knew Stephen would either live through this night, or die by morning.

Wetting a clean cloth, she began wiping away the blood and grime, beginning with his feet and legs and moving upward. When she had finished with the lower half of his body, she raised the sheet to cover him. Stephen's nakedness did not bother her. She remembered how he had come to her aid in the midst of her first childbirth. He had not been ashamed to see her naked then. She had simply been a human being in need, just as he was now. She covered him to keep him warm, and for propriety's sake should someone else enter the cabin.

The wounds on his arms and chest took longer to clean, and many of them continued to ooze blood. She laid poultices on them and wrapped them with bandages. Throughout all of her doctoring, Stephen had not stirred. He still breathed, but his skin felt cold to the touch.

"Stephen," Hannah whispered, a tear

escaping down her cheek, "don't die. You must not die. Not my dear Stephen, not my dear, strong Stephen."

She poured fresh water and turned her attention to the wounds on his face and neck. "Do you hear me, Stephen? You are too strong to die. Don't you know how we all count on your strength? Phoebe and your young 'uns, Temple . . . me. Yes, it is true, Stephen, me perhaps most of all."

His head moved on the pillow. She paused, her hand holding the cloth on a gash on his forehead. He stirred again, and then opened his eyes. They looked right at her, black and unfocused.

"Stephen?" she breathed.

His eyes rolled back and she thought he had fainted again. Suddenly his body jerked and he uttered a choking sound.

"It is all right," she soothed, pressing on his shoulders to keep him still. "You are safe now, here with me. It is me, Stephen, it is Hannah."

"Hannah . . . my . . . life," he rasped, head tossing back and forth.

She stroked his brow. It had gone from cool to raging hot. Fever had set in. His parched lips formed words she could not make out. "Hush, now. Hush, my dear. Lie still," she crooned.

"Can't . . . get to him," Stephen groaned. "My fault . . . love her . . . too much."

Hannah's breath came short. What was he saying? Can't get to whom? Love who?

"Couldn't . . . help it. Love her . . . with . . . my life. God . . . don't . . . take him. Take me . . . take me." The last words were barely audible as he sank back into unconsciousness.

Frantic, Hannah put her ear to his chest. A weak beating assured her he was still alive. Suppressing a sob, she picked up the cloth and wiped fresh blood from cuts that his thrashing had re-opened. Her head reeled. She could make no sense of his fever-induced ranting.

Oh, God, where was Temple? Where was Temple?

James returned, toting a basket filled with the medicinal plants she had requested. "How is he?" the boy asked.

She shook her head. "Just keep praying." She brewed the quinine into a weak tea and had James hold Stephen's head while she tried to get a few sips down him. Then she instructed the boy to rustle up some sort of dinner for the rest of the children and after that to see if Lucy needed anything for Phoebe.

As she sent James back out into the night,

she realized it must be very late. *If Temple had not come back by now. . . .* But she could not let herself think about that. She must think only about keeping Stephen alive. She dropped to her knees beside the bed, cradled Stephen's raw and broken hand in her own, and prayed like she never had before. She prayed for Stephen, for the other lost men, for Phoebe, and, most of all, she prayed that the baby inside her still had a father, alive and well.

CHAPTER FOURTEEN

Morning sun streamed in through the walls' loose chinking, casting random dots of light on the hard-packed dirt floor. A mouse sniffed its way across the stone hearth. Across the room, Hannah stirred. She had fallen asleep on her knees, her arms sprawled across Stephen. Waking to stiff joints and a fuzzy head, she momentarily wondered what she was doing half on the bed and half off. Then she remembered. Leaning over, her distended belly grazing his side, she put her face close to Stephen's, felt his warm breath on her cheek. Relief that he had lived through the night flooded through her.

Outside, the sun shone in patches through the leafy trees. Her children were scattered here and there. Some slept in the bed of the wagon, others underneath it. Oh, how she wished their father were here to roust them out like he did every morning, dispensing a hug here, a loving pat there. She caught herself before the tears could start and hurried back inside to fix a proper breakfast for them.

While the fire built, she checked Stephen's dressings. Some were soaked through with blood; these she removed, probing the wounds for infection. Although she had tried to be gentle, her ministrations dragged him out of sleep. His eyelids fluttered open.

Hannah took his hand. He turned to look at her, and his eyes filled with a mixture of pain and love that cut right to her heart.

"I could die a happy man, now," he murmured, "knowing the last thing I ever saw was your face."

She closed her eyes, not wanting to hear these words, not wanting to acknowledge the feeling behind them, but knowing that it was the time for truth between them. She clutched his hand tighter. "You will not die, Stephen. I won't let you." She took a deep breath. "Tell me about Temple."

His hand returned the pressure of hers. He looked straight into her eyes. "He is dead, Hannah."

She felt nothing. No pain, no grief, not even emptiness. Her first thought was that Stephen must be lying. "You saw it with your own eyes?" she challenged.

He nodded. "We were ambushed, late at night. Everyone was asleep, everyone but me. I heard 'em coming at the last minute, tried to warn the others, but it was too late. They shot Temple. I saw him go down. Gooch and Brown, too. I fought 'em best I could, but there was maybe a dozen of 'em. Still, I dropped four or five. The rest ran off." He paused, grimacing as some random pain coursed through his body. Hannah waited, still as a stone. "I must've blacked out for a while. When I come to, I crawled over to Temple. I was hoping the gunshot hadn't killed him. I'll never know whether it did or not. He was cut up bad, Hannah. The Injuns must've snuck back and finished the job."

Dry-eyed, she stared at the empty space above the fireplace where the musket usually hung. She imagined some Indian brave strutting around, showing it off, proud of his blood-stained booty. "You are the only one who survived?" she asked.

"Gooch and Brown died where they dropped. Patton managed to crawl off into the woods a ways, but I found him . . . dead. Ain't sure what happened to Murdock. Never did see him, even when they first attacked. Guess he ran off."

She swallowed, tried to summon up an

emotion of any kind. She was dead inside.

Stephen reached up to brush her cheek. She jerked her head away and went to stand at the kitchen table, palms flat on it for support. "How could this happen?" she wondered. "You said you were the only one awake. But you knew you were tracking a large group. Shouldn't there have been another sentinel posted?"

He pursed his lips, refusing to answer.

"You were in charge, Captain Cole," she pointed out, anger flooding in to fill the dead space. "Why did you post only one guard?"

"They wouldn't listen!" he blurted out. "I told 'em we needed another guard, that the danger was still high. They laughed at it. Said the redskins weren't any match for well-armed white men."

"That can't be true. Temple would never have ignored such danger. He promised me he would be careful."

Once again, Stephen resorted to exasperated silence.

"What are you keeping from me?" she demanded.

"Nothing."

She stood over him, her fists balled. "My husband is dead! I have a right to know what happened."

"He wouldn't listen because he was angry with me," he finally admitted. "We'd argued. Over you."

"What?"

"Temple accused me of . . . having unusual feelings for you." He looked away, his jaw clenching. "I denied it. He wouldn't believe me. Said he'd known it for years, ever since I followed you to Kentucky. Said he didn't want me near you any longer, that I wasn't to go with you to the Boonslick. I told him he would never make it there without me, that he wasn't fit to protect a family in that wild, Indian-infested country. I wish now I'd never said such a thing."

Hannah's knees gave out. She sank onto the edge of the bed, her anger spent. "But it is true, isn't it? Temple was a farmer, not a fighter."

"No, it ain't true. He was a strong and brave man, and I'll spend the rest of my life trying to make up for the wrong I done him." Stephen's voice choked. "He was right, you know. I do love you, Hannah. God forgive me, I do. Since the day I first laid eyes on you."

She looked at him in sorrow, wondering how a man's love could feel like a curse and a blessing at the same time. "What about Phoebe?" she said softly. "Why did you marry her?"

"I couldn't have you. She was the next best thing." His face colored in shame. "I am the worst kind of sinner, and now God's paid me back. He's taken Temple, and I reckon He will send you away from me as well."

Gently she took his hand and stroked the swollen, battered fingers. "What I have to say, I will say only once, and then we shall never speak of this again. If God took Temple as some sort of punishment for sins, then I am as much to blame as you. I loved my husband truly, but not with my whole heart. There has always been a small piece of it that belongs to you." She drew his hand over to her rounded belly and held it there with both of hers. "But this child belongs to Temple, and Phoebe, at this very moment, is struggling, maybe dying, to give life to your child. So, I must honor Temple's memory, and you must honor Phoebe, in life or death, and we can never forget that. Do you hear me, Stephen? We can never forget."

A week after Stephen's miraculous return to Loutre Island, James and Holbert Cole set out to retrieve their father's body. Stephen insisted on going with them to show them the way, although he was still so weak the two boys had to ride on either side of him to hold him upright. They returned empty-handed, the men's remains so ravaged by wolves that there was nothing left to bury. Empty-handed, that is, but for a tiny wreath made from human hair, braided with a bit of blue ribbon, that they found clutched in what remained of Temple Cole's hand.

Dear Dolley,

The leaves are so beautiful this year, brilliant shades of red and orange, so vivid they almost sear the eye, like looking directly at the sun. We have not yet had a frost. My garden boasts so many vegetables even this late in the season that I cannot keep up with it. I have been sending one of the boys every day with a fresh supply for Phoebe as she was unable to plant much of a garden herself this year. The poor thing has still not regained her strength though it has been nigh on to three months since her little girl, Polly, was born.

My own daughter, who I named Elenor, entered this world a month ago. She is a dear thing, apple-cheeked and round as a pumpkin. I cannot help but smile when I hold her to my breast. It is at night, when I lay her next to me in the spot that used to be Temple's, that the tears come.

I cry for a little girl who will never know her father, for her brothers and sisters who will never again feel his gentle hand on their heads, or hear his hearty laugh. I cry for myself, robbed of a husband, partner, and friend — the one man who knew me through and through and loved me even with all of my flaws.

Most of all, I cry for Temple. Well-wishers have tried to comfort me by saying that he is in a better place now, and I believe that is true. But he was not yet ready to go to that place; he had far too much left to do here. He had moved his family across an entire country, searching for that one perfect place that he could call his, and he had found it, he told me, found the very spot where he would sink his roots and live out the rest of his days. But like a dark cloud that promises rain and then dissipates in the wind, his dream has vanished.

What a cruel joke! Made even crueler because his death did not have to be. We should not even have been on Loutre Island when those Indians came raiding. We should have gone with the Coopers to the Boonslick back in the spring. That is what Temple wanted to do. But I made him wait so that I could help Phoebe in childbirth. Yet Phoebe should never have been in that condition, and I should have obeyed my husband, instead of fretting over my foolish sister, and Stephen should never have loved me, and Temple and Stephen should not have argued, and a second guard should have been posted, and . . . oh, God, the "should haves" and "should nevers" go 'round and 'round in my head at night, and the worst thing is, I can change nothing. Death is beyond our power to change.

Perhaps by now word of the massacre has reached even the august halls of the President's house. Certainly it has created a stir in St. Louis. People tell me the newspaper is reporting that the Pottawatomies are responsible for this murderous crime, and that General Clark continues to seek the actual perpetrators in hopes of bringing them to trial.

For my part, I care not whether my husband's murderers are punished. I do not seek revenge, for what purpose would it serve? Would it deter future crimes against whites? I do not think so, for I have come to believe that the white man and the Indian are like grease and water — they do not mix, and never shall.

If Temple were here, I know what he would say. He would tell me the best revenge is to take a stand — to hold fast to our dreams and not be deterred by obstacles thrown in our path. But, oh, Dolley, how do I stand on my own? How do I keep on that path without Temple to guide me?

It would be so much easier to turn the other direction, to go back to Virginia. There, at least, we have family to support us. It has been years since I have communicated with my parents, but I cannot believe that, under the circumstances, they would not gladly welcome our return. My children would receive an education there, would grow up to be ladies and gentlemen of culture and refinement.

And yet, that is not how Temple wanted them to grow up. He wanted them to be free and independent, not beholden to anyone. He wanted them to be men and women of action, not parlor-sitting palaverers. He wanted them to have a piece of land they could call their own.

To add to my dilemma, James, my oldest, has told me he will not leave Missouri, that he intends to stay here no matter what I and the rest of the children do. He is eighteen years old, a man already, with a right to decide his own fate. I cannot force him to go with us.

So, do I return to Virginia for the sake of safety and stability, thereby leaving behind a son who I likely would never see again? Or do I set my sights to the West, to the land of Temple's dreams, as difficult and dangerous as that may be?

This is not a decision I can make on my own. I have not had much truck with God since he took my Temple, but today I shall lay down my pen and pray to Him for guidance.

Yours,
Hannah

CHAPTER FIFTEEN

"Lucy, mark my words." Hannah placed the last of her pewter dishes in a trunk and closed the lid. "This is the third time I have packed up and moved my entire household, and there shall not be a fourth."

"No'm, I reckon not." Ever the stoic, Lucy grabbed the handle at one end of the trunk while Hannah took the other. Carrying it outside, they hoisted it into the back of the wagon.

A brisk wind snapped their skirts around their ankles. Hannah looked up, evaluating the chunky clouds skidding across the sky. It would be bad luck if weather were to set in just as they got under way. The winter had been mild so far, prompting their decision to move now rather than wait for spring. After nearly four years of waiting, they were tired of it. The Boonslick beckoned and, finally, they would heed its call.

"Ma, Ma, are we 'bout ready to go?"

Nine-year-old Samuel sprinted up, his bare feet and lower legs sticking out from a shabby pair of breeches he had long since outgrown. Already practically as tall as his older brother Stephen, Samuel was the wild child of the family, more at home in the woods and on the river than within the four walls of their cabin.

"Soon's you find your moccasins," she said, giving his filthy toes a pointed stare.

"Don't need no moccasins," he scoffed.

"Suit yourself. Just don't come crying to me when your feet give out. There's no room in this wagon for a strong lad like yourself. Now, go see if James needs help with the stock."

"Yes'm." With a grin he was off, his untucked shirt flapping in his wake.

Thank God for the resilience of youth, thought Hannah. Most of her children seemed to be coping with the death of their father as well as could be expected. James and Holbert, impressed with the responsibility of becoming the men in the family, shouldered their grief in strong silence. Free-spirited Samuel missed his father fiercely, but, nevertheless, could not contain his excitement about their move West. The girls, Jennie and Mattie, cried their hearts out, and then threw themselves into being their mother's little helpers. Dykie, William, and baby Elenor were too young to appreciate what had happened.

Only Stephen, eleven years old, worried her. A shy, quiet boy to begin with, he seemed to have retreated into himself even more since Temple's death. Although he had always been keen to keep up with his older brothers, he no longer asked to be included in any of their adventures, preferring to stick close to home. Hannah supposed it was natural for the boy to be fearful of the unknown given what had happened to his father, so she said nothing. In fact, it was rather nice to have at least one son who favored the company of his mother and sisters. Still, she kept a close eye on him.

Rubbing her hands together vigorously to get the blood flowing, Hannah headed back to the cabin for a final load just as the older Stephen loped into the yard. He sat tall in the saddle, his strong body having staged an amazingly speedy recovery. The wounds of battle still marked him, and always would, but his constitution was as healthy today as it had been before the attack.

Not so poor Phoebe. Even now, seven months after giving birth, it was a struggle for her to get out of bed. Too weak to produce milk, she had been forced to feed her baby Polly goat's milk that left her colicky. Hannah knew that life for her sister's family had been hell. Even in her own distress, she had tried to help out there when she could. During one especially nerve-wracking session, as she paced the floor with a screaming baby on her shoulder, she had broken her promise to Phoebe, and told Stephen that another baby would likely kill his wife. He had given her a look that seemed to say making a baby was the furthest thing from his mind. Other than a few conferences to discuss the move, that had been the extent of their conversation together since the day Stephen had lain in her bed, grievously wounded, and told her he loved her. Neither one had ever again mentioned what had passed between them. There was nothing to be said.

It had occurred to Hannah that in returning to Virginia she could escape this tangled relationship with Stephen. But running away was not the answer. Now that Temple was gone, Stephen was the closest thing to a father her children had. And he seemed aware of that as well, making a point to include the boys on his hunting and fishing trips, helping Samuel carve a bow and arrows. He had even been solicitous of the girls, setting them on his knee and listening patiently while they prattled on, as girls do. Hannah knew he was acting like this not so much because of his feelings for her, but because he still felt somewhat responsible for Temple's death. Whatever the reason, she would not consider removing her children from his kindly influence.

He smiled down at her, the scar on his forehead making him look a bit piratical. "Are you ready?"

"Pert near. The boys are rounding up the stock, then we can get under way."

"I'll give 'em a hand."

Hannah stepped into the empty cabin. She gave it one final look. These were the last walls that Temple had ever known, walls that had surrounded and protected his family, walls that had seen sorrow, but mostly joy. Now his family was moving beyond these walls, just as he had done.

"Oh, Temple," she whispered, feeling his presence as she did so often. "I do this for you. Be with us, my darling, every step of the way."

"That's it, right there." Stephen pointed to a bluff across the river. "That's the spot."

Hannah set the wagon brake and let the reins go loose in her hands. She stared at the place Stephen indicated. From here, it

257

did not seem particularly noteworthy, but, if it was anything like the country they had just passed through, it was clear why Temple had chosen it.

The road west had been treacherous, studded with deep holes that swallowed wagon wheels, and thick woods as tangled as a rat's nest, but it had also passed through some of the most stupendous country Hannah had ever seen — prairie grasses growing as high as a man's shoulder and clear streams running with water as sweet as mother's milk. They had feasted on elk that were so unaccustomed to human beings they did not know to run. She had seen her first buffalo, a magnificent animal so stunning in its size and power that all she could do was stare, mouth agape.

For the first time since Temple's death she had felt her spirits lift. Perhaps she had done the right thing in coming to the Boonslick, and in keeping the family all together. Temple's vision of raising his children in this bountiful paradise had been so sharp, and now it was clear to her, too.

The other wagon rolled up beside her, James at the helm and Phoebe next to him on the plank seat. Bundled up in two layers of blankets to ward off the chill from her emaciated body, Phoebe stared disconsolately at the muddy water. "I still don't see why we have to cross the river," she complained. "If this side is good enough for the Coopers and the others, why isn't it good enough for us?"

"Quiet, woman. We'll do as I say."

Hannah seconded Stephen's reprimand with a disapproving look at her sister. Everybody knew the men had chosen the south side for solid reasons. And even if that were not so, it was not a wife's place to disagree with her husband, especially not in public.

"It's early yet," Stephen said, gauging the position of the sun. It sat low in the winter sky, a glaring, but ineffectual heat source, like a weak fire that warms only the facing surface. "There's still plenty of time to make a crossing today."

"That would please me greatly," Hannah announced. "I would like to sleep tonight at the site of my new home."

"Looks like bad weather could be moving in." James nodded in the direction of some clouds building in the west.

Stephen took their measure. "Should hold off long enough for us to cross, but let's not tarry. We'll have to make two trips. James, you and I will take everyone across, then come back for the stock and supplies."

As the men set to work unleashing the *pirogues* from the sides of the wagons, Hannah climbed down from her seat and retrieved Elenor from her crib. Walking off a way, she found a private spot protected by a thicket of willows and sat down to nurse.

Soon all was ready. There were nineteen of them, and two *pirogues*.

Phoebe regarded their transports with a dubious look. "How will we all fit?"

"They'll ride low in the water, but we'll make it," Stephen assured her. "Hannah, James will steer your family across. I'll take mine, and Lucy and Isaac."

One by one, Hannah handed her children into the hollowed-out log, making sure Holbert had a firm grasp on little William. Clutching Elenor to her breast, she stepped in carefully, her skirts trailing in the murky water. James pushed them out and swung into the back. Glancing behind her, Hannah saw everyone take their places in the second *pirogue*. Everyone but Lucy who hung back, her arms wrapped around three-year-old Isaac. Even from a distance Hannah could make out the terror on Lucy's face. Stephen beckoned impatiently, but she stood rooted to the spot. He grabbed her arm and forced her into the shallow water. Awkwardly, one arm still holding Isaac, the other braced on the lip of the *pirogue,* she half stepped, half fell inside, causing the boat to rock violently. Phoebe shrieked in alarm. With a practiced smoothness, Stephen slid into the rear and headed them out.

By this time, James had steered his boat well into the middle of the river. The current was much stronger here. Logs and débris floated by at a fast clip. Choppy waves smacked the side of the *pirogue.*

"A bit rougher than it looked from shore, isn't it?" Hannah called over her shoulder.

James grunted a response, his strong young arms pulling the oars in deep, sweeping strokes. Their progress was uneven as he attempted to steer them around snags and eddies while the mighty river moved them inexorably downstream.

They had lost the sun underneath a bank of roiling clouds and the wind was constant now, whipping spray over the edge of the *pirogue.* Wrapping her baby in her half-soaked shawl, Hannah leaned to the right to compensate for the wind's pressure.

In the front of the boat, Holbert, his little brother clutched between his knees, pointed frantically at the water ahead of them and shouted a warning. Too late, James saw the snag sticking up out of the water, directly in their path. Rowing with all his might, he tried to cut to its upstream side, but it grazed the stern as they passed, swinging them around horizontal to the shore.

James fought for control, manipulating his oar with thrusts and parries like a master swordsman. Finally the bow swung back. They were close now but downstream from the clearing where they had intended to land. Here, the shallows and shore were lined with tall stalks of cane as forbidding as the bars of a prison cell. The bow slid into the razor-sharp cane, miring them in what looked to be four or five feet of water.

"Holbert, pull us in!" James called.

Before Hannah could protest, Holbert eased himself over the side and hauled the *pirogue* through the treacherous cane. He pulled the bow onto shore and turned to help his family alight. Hannah almost wept at the sight of his scratched and bloody arms.

Cold, wet, but delighted to be on *terra firma,* Hannah looked back to the river. Stephen's *pirogue* was mid-current and moving rapidly downstream. The wind was now at gale force, tipping the boat so far on its side that water trickled over its edge. Tiny beads of ice blasted its passengers like shotgun pellets. Screaming in terror, the women and children tried to duck for cover from the ice assault, their movements only rocking the boat more. Stephen shouted something, his words carried away in the wind. Rowing for all he was worth, he managed to steer them into shore. James and Holbert dashed down the bank, ready to grab the hull and pull them in.

Suddenly little Isaac tugged free from his mother's grasp and toddled forward in the *pirogue.* Terrified, Lucy lunged for him. The boat tipped and Isaac plunged into the frigid water. Lucy screamed and would have jumped in after him, but Stephen held her back. Unable to abandon the rest of his passengers until his craft was safely on shore, he had no choice but to let Isaac go.

Holbert watched the child stream past him, arms and legs flailing. Batting aside the knife-like cane, he leaped, wrapping a bloody hand around Isaac's foot. But now he, too, was swallowed by the water, unable to get his feet back under him.

James tacked back to shallower water and splashed downstream, trying to stay abreast of the two struggling boys. Coming up for air, Holbert was not sure how much longer he could hold onto Isaac. His hand was frozen stiff; his grip on the child's foot loosened. Suddenly something grabbed at his shirt. Gasping, James hauled him into shore, still holding onto little Isaac.

Back upstream, Stephen had managed to beach his *pirogue* and get everyone safely on land. Fighting through willow thickets and the dastardly cane, he made his way to the three boys. He found them exhausted, frozen, and scratched like pieces of red ribbon, but otherwise unhurt.

Rejoining the others, he handed Lucy her crying son. "We'll never make it back to the other side for the supplies!" he shouted, his voice barely audible over the whistling wind. "We'll build a fire and dry out, wait for the weather to pass."

Shouldering the youngsters, the group struggled inland, searching for a spot that would provide protection from the wind and ice. Once on top of the bluff, the land became heavily wooded. Stephen found a rock overhang that would serve as a partial shelter. Phoebe immediately collapsed beneath it, shivering so violently her teeth chattered.

Soon they had a fire going, started with powder and a flint that Stephen had tucked away. Aside from those two items, a hunting knife, and the clothes on their backs, they had nothing. Sleet continued to pelt them, hissing in the fire and plopping on the dead leaves. Hannah made James and Holbert strip down, laying their wet clothing on rocks before the fire to dry. Lucy had long since removed Isaac's clothing. She sat with him in her lap, wrapped in Hannah's shawl, rubbing and blowing on his cold hands and feet.

The day waned and the weather worsened. Huddled around the fire, the adults and older children held the young ones close, trying to warm them with their own diminishing body heat. Every now and then, Stephen would rise and walk to the edge of the bluff, peering across the river as though trying to make out their wagons and stock on the opposite shore. On one of these trips, Hannah joined him.

"Don't be fretting now about decisions already made," she said, guessing the tack his thoughts were taking.

He grimaced. "It was damn' foolish, thinking we could make it across before the weather set in. Even James could see it coming, but I was so sure we'd beat it."

"We did. We are all safely ashore."

"Only by the grace of God and the courage of your sons. And now we have to get through this night out in the open with no tents, no blankets, no food." He sighed in exasperation. "I even left my gun over there."

She laid a comforting hand on his arm. He covered it with his own, then lifted it and felt each icy finger.

"You're so cold," he said, as though this state of affairs was his fault. Without a word, he drew her into his arms, rubbing his hands over her back in an attempt to warm her. She considered pulling away, knowing that this embrace was improper given all that had passed between them. But — he was so incredibly warm. Somehow, despite the wind and sleet and freezing water, Stephen had retained every last degree of his body heat and was now generously sharing it with her. It was like curling up beside a blacksmith's forge. She stood immobile, hands at her side, soaking up the warmth.

"What's this, then?"

Hannah stumbled backwards, found herself looking into the furious face of her sister.

"She's cold. I was warming her." Stephen spoke without a trace of shame in his voice.

"You've a wife and five young 'uns need warming. What about us?"

"Reckon there's enough to go around." With a touch of a smile, he reached for Phoebe intending to hold her as he had her sister. Jerking her arm free, she stalked away.

"Oh, dear," Hannah sighed.

"Never mind her." Stephen dismissed his wife with a shrug. "Come, let's see what we can do to rig a shelter."

Stephen managed to weave together some heavy rushes that he found down by the river and stake them with some fallen poles of timber to form a semblance of a wind-break, but it did nothing to cut the cold. Somehow they made it through the night, taking turns with the blankets and Hannah's shawl, piling wood on the fire to keep it at a life-preserving level.

The morning brought no relief from the bitter cold and icy rain. Stephen returned from inspecting the river with a grim face. "It's running fast and full of ice. If an ice floe struck the *pirogue* it would tear a hole in it and sink it faster than you can say Jack Robinson. We can't risk a crossing."

"Mama, I'm hungry," little Mattie whined, the tip of her nose as red as a berry.

"I reckon you are, darlin'. Seeing as we are not going to get back over to the wagons for a while, we'd best see what we can rustle up around here. James, you take a group in that direction. I will take the others this way. Look for nuts, berries, anything we can eat. Don't go far and stay together." Hannah

267

made her voice sound as cheery as she could, but she knew their situation was dire. There was little chance of finding edible berries this time of year, and without a gun no way to bring down game.

An hour later, the two groups converged around the fire. Their take was pathetically small — a few acorns and some slippery elm bark that Hannah tried to mash with a rock. While the children nibbled on the niggardly meal, Hannah put Elenor to her breast, thankful she could at least keep one of her offspring satisfied. Across the fire, Phoebe vainly tried to push a pinch of elm bark into Polly's tiny mouth. The baby screamed and spit out the pulpy mess. When Elenor had drained one side, Hannah handed her over to Jennie and went to her sister, her arms extended.

"Let me," she said.

Phoebe looked at her with eyes dulled from failure.

"Please," Hannah said, still reaching for the squalling infant. "Let me feed her."

Reluctantly Phoebe lifted Polly into her aunt's arms. Cooing words of comfort, Hannah put Stephen's daughter to her breast. Phoebe watched with red-rimmed eyes as the infant latched onto Hannah's nut-brown nipple, watched her splotchy face grow calm with contentment. She leaned over to cough, found she could not stop. Clutching at her chest, she staggered away from the fire, her body bent with spasms.

Stephen rose to help her, Hannah thought. Instead, he paused and squatted before Hannah, his eyes transfixed on the nursing child in her arms. Slowly he reached out and stroked his daughter's downy head. Over and over he brushed the silky curls, his hand pausing with each stroke to cup the perfect roundness.

Hannah watched in fascination — the baby's perfect pink mouth tugging at her nipple in a rhythm that matched her own heartbeat, Stephen's scar-nicked hand cupping the round little head so close to the curve of her breast. She could not speak, dared not raise her head to look into Stephen's eyes.

In a moment, he rose and went to attend to Phoebe. Hannah kept her head down, trying to ignore the terrible pleasure that Stephen's closeness had brought. Every nerve in her body was liquid, her face flushed with molten heat. Sated and lulled into a half sleep, Polly's mouth slipped from the glistening nipple. Lifting the baby to her shoulder, Hannah glanced across the fire and saw James cut his eyes away from her.

His face was a mask of hurt and confusion.

Words of explanation — no, excuse — rose to Hannah's lips, but before she could utter them Samuel burst out of the underbrush, gleefully holding aloft a wild turkey.

"Found us some supper!" he crowed.

James used the interruption to disappear into the woods.

The hungry family engulfed Samuel, shouting their gratitude and begging for the story of how he captured the bird. Lucy immediately began dressing it out while Holbert set to work fashioning a roasting spit.

Hannah held back. Her shame over the spectacle she and Stephen had made of themselves prevented her from sharing in the excitement. That her son should have witnessed such a tender scene was too much to bear. Still cradling little Polly, she paced to the edge of the bluff. Below, the ice-clogged river raged. Above, the gloomy sky spit frozen rain. Somewhere nearby the man whose very nearness brought fire to her senses was tending to his sickly wife. And behind her, her children huddled around a paltry fire for a few pathetic scraps of food.

"Oh, God," she whispered, her freezing lips barely able to fashion the words, "what have I done?"

CHAPTER SIXTEEN

The baby was crying, a frantic mewling born of pain and hunger. Dragged from a fitful sleep, Hannah reached for her, tried to shush her with soft words and gentle strokes. But Elenor could not be comforted. She needed to be fed. Hannah was not sure she had the strength to lift the babe to her breast — or that, even if she did, her body would produce any milk. By her count, this was the eleventh day that they had been stranded on the south side of the river. Eleven days spent out in the open with no shelter to speak of and no food besides the one turkey Samuel had caught, and a pitiful collection of acorns and elm bark. They were all starving, but Hannah, who was eating for herself and two nursing babies, was the hungriest of all. Still, despite Stephen's urging, she could not bring herself to take a larger portion of their meager offerings. She could not take food out of the mouths of her children.

Slowly, painfully she rolled over to her hands and knees. She let her head hang between her shoulders for a moment until it cleared, then picked up Elenor and carried her away from the clearing so her fussing would not wake the others. As she did, she caught Stephen's eye. He was the only other one awake. In fact, she was not sure he ever slept. Squatting by the fire, he fed kindling into it, his face haggard, his eyes tortured. Silently he watched her go.

When she was finished, she staggered back to the fire and laid Elenor between Samuel and Jennie, hoping their bodies would expend enough heat to keep the baby alive until morning. Her own limbs shook with cold and fatigue. She started to lie back down, but once again she caught Stephen looking at her. This time he rose and nodded his head, beckoning her to follow. She sighed, reluctant to leave the fire's warmth. Nevertheless, she walked with him behind an outcropping of rock, and sank to the ground, hugging herself to stop shivering.

Stephen knelt next to her, removed his buckskin coat, and draped it over her shoulders.

"No, no," she protested.

"Take it," he insisted. "You need it more

than I do."

She relented, hunching into its luxurious warmth. A slight breeze came up, rustling the fallen leaves around them.

"Feel that?" Stephen murmured. "It's from the south . . . downright balmy."

Hannah rubbed her cheek against the soft skin of Stephen's coat. The wind did not seem balmy to her. Maybe she had been cold for so long she had forgotten what balmy felt like. Tiredly she asked Stephen why he had summoned her for this midnight conference.

"Tomorrow I'm going to cross over for our supplies," he announced.

She stared. "But the ice . . . it is still too dangerous."

"I've no choice. We can't hold out here any longer without food and shelter. I will not watch my family starve to death while there's any chance of getting across. Besides, it's been warmer the last couple of days, the ice has melted some. And the stars are out." He raised his head to survey the flickering sky. "We will see the sun tomorrow."

A surge of emotion swelled Hannah's breast. Stephen was willing to risk his life for their well-being. Of course, he was right. Without some relief, they would all die.

"You can't go alone," she bit her lip. "You

will take James and Holbert with you?"

"Stephen, too," he said.

"What? He is too little!"

"He is a strong lad, Hannah. Built like his father. Besides, each *pirogue* requires two oarsmen. I need him. I swear to you I won't let anything happen to him."

"You should not make promises you cannot keep."

Stephen reached for her hand and held it lightly in both of his. "I will not take him if you say no. But I make you this promise, and it is one I can keep . . . I shall do everything in my power to bring all three of your boys safely back to you."

Once again, Hannah felt secure in the strong hands of Stephen Cole. "Very well, take him then. But be prepared to deal with Samuel. He will not fancy being left behind."

"Don't worry." Stephen chuckled. "I can handle that hot-headed son of yours. I shall tell him he is the man in charge while I am gone."

They smiled at each other. Something about the curve of Stephen's lip, so like Temple's, caught at Hannah's heart. She pulled her hand free and wiped at a tear threatening to escape.

"Dearest," he said in a ragged whisper,

"don't cry. I count on your strength to keep me going."

"I am trying to be strong," the words burst out of her. "I am trying so hard. But it is not easy when I look at you and see. . . ." She broke off.

"See what?"

Hannah buried her face in her hands. After a moment she wiped her eyes and continued, not able to meet Stephen's gaze. "I see a man who is kind and strong, who would be so easy to rely upon. But that would be a mistake. I think, Stephen, that we must separate. For the sake of our two families."

Stephen's face turned dark. "What do you mean?"

"I mean that I think it would be best for you and Phoebe to settle some distance away from me."

"Impossible!" Stephen leapt to his feet. "These woods are crawling with redskins! Do you think I would leave you to fend for yourself? I made a vow, when Temple died, to protect you and your children, Hannah, and I intend to do just that!"

"That is just what I mean! It has been so easy to let you take over as the head of my family, and you have filled that rôle self-lessly, there can be no doubt. But I have come to see danger down that road. Not only because of what you and I may feel for each other, but because of what it is doing to Phoebe, and perhaps James as well. Phoebe needs you, all of you, not just whatever portion is left after you have cared for me. And James, well, he is a man now. He is fully capable of filling Temple's shoes, and he must be given that chance." Hannah paused for breath. "I am not suggesting a great distance, you understand. We will still want to look in on each other, and help each other. But we must have independent households. Surely you see that."

"You ask too much, Hannah. If something should happen to you. . . ."

"It would not be on your shoulders. This is my choice. Please accept it."

Stephen gave her a dark look and strode deeper into the woods.

Hannah's stomach wrenched, from hunger or sorrow, or perhaps both. She stumbled back to the fire where she removed Stephen's coat from her shoulders and placed it gently over the sleeping Phoebe.

In the morning, the sun did indeed rise, bright and shining. Its very presence lifted everyone's spirits. Everyone but Phoebe who was too weak to rouse from her spot by the fire. Stephen's plan to try a crossing was met with enthusiasm. As soon as the sun was up, he and Hannah's three oldest sons made their way through the sharp cane and pushed off. The current carried them far downstream, but they made shore safely, portaged upstream to the wagons and stock, which had survived quite well on the abundant forage, and managed to bring everything back across with no mishaps.

That night, the men and boys rested from their exertions, but with full bellies and wrapped in warm blankets. The next day, they crossed again to tear apart the wagons and load them in pieces to the other side. Upon their return, they feasted on roast venison and boiled hominy.

After a few days of decent nourishment, almost everyone was fully recovered. That was when Stephen announced that he and Phoebe would be moving on to a site he had scouted about a mile away.

None of the children seemed pleased that the two families were splitting up. None, that is, except James who looked curiously at his mother and uncle, although he said not a word. Phoebe, likewise, had little to say about the plan. With her dull eyes and croupy cough, she shouldered her baby and followed silently as Stephen led them away.

Hannah refused to watch them go. Instead, she turned to James and asked him to get to work building them a cabin. A smile played across the young man's lips as he prepared to do her bidding.

Hannah's Journal
December 17, 1811, Boonslick

Dear Dolley,

An event most strange and frightening has occurred. Last night I was literally shaken from my bed as the ground rolled and heaved beneath our cabin. As I crouched there on the floor, listening to the earth groan and being tossed about like a ship on rough seas, I felt that the world had gone completely mad! Or perhaps, I thought, I was no longer in the world as I know it. Perhaps I had been spirited away to a place where the sun rises in the west and the ground moves beneath one's feet!

Soon, of course, I came to my senses and realized that I was experiencing an earthquake. James was already herding the children outside for fear the walls would collapse. They did not, thankfully, though they are slightly askew. A few stones fell from the fireplace, but, all in all, our sturdy little home survived quite well. James and the other boys have already begun repairs.

I thank the Lord for Temple's foresight in choosing a site well up on the bluffs. The quake tumbled the river far out of its banks, but we stayed high and dry. I fear the Coopers and their neighbors who live on the bottom lands across the river may not have fared as well. I shall send one of the boys to check on them shortly.

Stephen came by this morning to see how we were. His cabin, too, sustained only minor damage. He told a perplexing story — one that has perhaps reached the ears of you and your husband, although it is so strange as to be nearly unbelievable. He reminded me that one month ago, another of Nature's oddities took place — this one a bright, greenish-white light that flashed across the night sky leaving a trail of fire in its wake. Of course, I remembered it, but I did not understand what it had to do with yesterday's event. Stephen then related the following.

The Indian leader, Tecumseh, a name I am sure your husband is well acquainted with, had predicted this flash in the sky. Furthermore, he stated that exactly one month following, the earth would shake from ocean to mountains. And that is exactly what happened. How is this possible, for a human being to predict natural calamities over which no man has control? What kind of power does this Tecumseh possess?

Stephen dismisses both predictions as lucky guesses, which to my mind is difficult to reconcile. But lucky guess or not, he is worried that Tecumseh's reputation as a visionary will be enhanced, thus encouraging Indians from across the country to rally around him. We are just now receiving word of another great battle — somewhere called Tippecanoe — in which the redskins were soundly defeated by American troops. While this seems like a matter for rejoicing, Stephen fears the British will use this battle as an opportunity finally to woo the Indians over to their side.

What does all this mean for the Boonslick, I wonder? The Indians around here are friendly, for the most part. Why, my boy Samuel has even gone hunting and fishing with them from time to time (without my approval, but then Samuel is not one to ask permission). But will they turn against us if they fall under Tecumseh's influence, or if we go to war with the British?

It is a troubling question, but I take comfort in the knowledge that our President must surely have matters well in hand. I would expect no less from the husband of Dolley Payne Todd Madison!

We have enjoyed such a peaceful existence here in the Boonslick that it is hard to imagine a life of conflict. For the first few months, the Coles were the only settlers south of the Missouri. Such isolation was occasionally vexing to me, but more often than not I found it pleasant to be only in the company of my dear children, and now and again Stephen and Phoebe and their brood. That is changing, however, for several families have recently joined us in our little settlement. They are good people and I welcome them, for there is plenty of everything to go around.

We do not want for meat as the woods are brimming with game of all description. Indeed, the wildlife is so abundant that I have given up trying to plant a proper garden; the squirrels and other creatures ravage all the new shoots despite our best efforts to keep them out. I do have a small corn crop going, which provides for our bread. And the berries, nuts, and wild plants surround us like a veritable Garden of Eden. Never have I lived in a place where it was easier to put a meal on the table!

Oh, how I wish Temple were here to share in this good fortune. God must have taken him for a reason, which I confess is yet a mystery to me. But we are following the path he set for us. Daily, I see James and all my boys growing up to be men like their father. I am so proud of them.

You perhaps noted that I wrote of seeing Stephen and Phoebe only now and then. I thought it best for us to maintain separate households, and the arrangement has indeed benefited my family. As for Stephen's family, I cannot say. Phoebe is frequently under the weather, so I have sent Lucy to help. Lucy reports that theirs is not a happy home. Stephen, true to form, is away much of the time, and, when he is there, he and Phoebe have little to say to each other. Their children suffer from a lack of discipline, though they are well fed and clothed.

Their plight hangs heavily on my heart. I had hoped that sending them off on their own would signal a new beginning for my sister and brother-in-law. A chance to fashion a harmonious life together away from my constant presence. Perhaps it will simply take time. Time, I have discovered, is a marvelous healer.

Affectionately,

Hannah

CHAPTER SEVENTEEN

Hannah secured the last of their provisions on the back of the already over-laden pack horse and turned to Lucy with a sigh. "Didn't I once say that I would never again pack up and leave my home?"

"Yes'm."

"Then why am I doing exactly that?"

"So's you won't git yer head bashed in with a tommyhawk, I reckon."

"Balderdash! I have yet to see a hostile Indian in these parts. More likely to see one down on the bank, tossing in a line with Samuel. Forting up will only give these heathens notions, I'm bound. If we act frightened, they will likely give us something to be frightened about."

Lucy's only answer was to pick up toddler Elenor and grab Isaac's hand. She stood waiting.

"Oh, all right. Let's get going, then." Hannah signaled Samuel to lead the pack animals forward. It would have been much easier to tote their belongings in the wagon, but the path to Cole's Fort, as Stephen's place was now called, was too rugged for wagons. With four-year-old William in tow, she took her place at the rear of the procession, prodding the milk cow with a stick if she threatened to stray. Jennie, Mattie, and Dykie skipped along after Lucy, excited about going to see their cousins. Her oldest boys, James, Holbert, and Stephen, were already at their uncle's place where they had spent the last week helping to build the fort.

Hannah sniffed the spring air. It smelled of damp earth and blooming redbud. A shame she would not get in a corn crop this year. Of course, they would probably plant a truck patch near the fort, but that would not be the same as tending her own plot. No, her own poor garden would go to weed, and her modest, but cozy cabin would fill with dust and vermin. Yet it was all in the name of safety, so why did she resist so heartily the necessity of forting up? After all, she could not really argue with Stephen and the other men's reasoning. Although there had not been any serious attacks on the Boonslick settlers, in recent days the petty raiding — a cow here, a horse there — had increased. And the news from back

East all pointed toward war, which would undoubtedly mean Indians on the rampage throughout the Territory. In all likelihood, Stephen's caution in suggesting the families south of the river fort up at his place was duly warranted.

But still — she did not want to leave her home, did not want to crowd into a fort with ten other families. She liked to do things her way, liked to be in charge, although she was careful to give James his due as the man in the family. How likely was it that the men at the fort would listen to her, would value her opinion? Well, Stephen might, but he would not want to appear to take her advice. Oh, damn men and their wars, anyway!

Despite her resentful frame of mind, Hannah had to admit she was impressed when the fort came into sight. A dozen cabins flanked the rectangular walls that were a good twelve feet high and looked sturdy enough to repel the most determined invaders. She turned her stock into the pen outside the walls, guarded by two well-armed men, and led her family inside.

The first thing she saw as they entered the gates was Stephen, standing tall in his buckskins, his hand on Muke Box's shoulder as he issued a directive of some sort. To her surprise, her heart gave a little flutter. What was this? Hadn't she tamed her feelings toward Stephen over this past year? Although separated, they had seen each other on numerous occasions and she had felt no overwhelming attraction. But here, in the fort that bore his name, leading this tiny group of settlers who had banded together for protection, he seemed so in his element. Hannah knew at this moment she beheld the essential Stephen Cole, and that was a man she had never been able to resist.

Stephen caught sight of them and bounded over. "So, you're here at last. James said you would put it off until the last minute." He chided her with a smile on his sun-browned face.

"Yes, well, we are here now." Hannah spoke with more starch in her voice than she intended. She allowed herself to relax. "You have outdone yourself, Stephen. The fort seems quite commodious. I reckon we will be comfortable, under the circumstances."

"More importantly you'll be safe. Come now, let's stow your things. This will be your cabin over here." He showed them to their temporary — at least Hannah hoped they would be temporary — quarters: a one room edifice much like the home she had just left, but smaller. New and clean, no soot yet darkened the hearth, and the compact room smelled of freshly hewn logs.

She left Lucy and the children in charge of unpacking and sought out Phoebe who, once again, was ailing. She found her sister mixing up a stew for dinner.

"Good afternoon, dear. You are looking much better!"

Phoebe turned her head into her shoulder to muffle a phlegmy cough. "Is that so? Can't say as I feel any better."

Hannah patted her sister's back. She could feel each rib beneath the linsey-woolsey blouse. "I am sorry to hear that. But the warm weather is almost upon us. I am sure you will start to improve. It is good to see you up and about."

Phoebe shifted away from Hannah's touch. Four-year-old Nellie skipped over and yanked on her mother's skirts. "Bite, Mama?"

"No, indeed!" Phoebe slapped away the child's hand. "If I let you have a bite, then your brothers and sisters will want one and before you can say Jack Sprat there will be no meat left for your pa."

"Please, Mama, I'm hungry," the little girl whined.

"I said no!" Phoebe turned and gave her a

hardy swat. Nellie screeched and ran out the door, holding her smarting behind. " 'Bout time someone taught that child manners," Phoebe muttered, turning to hang the stew kettle over the fire. "Her pa don't bother to do it."

"Well, most men don't bother about such things. They count on us womenfolk to instill the finer sentiments in their children."

Phoebe snorted. "I might have guessed you would stick up for him."

"I am doing no such thing! I am simply suggesting he is a typical man."

Sighing, Phoebe flopped down on a stool, rested her elbows on the table, and buried her head in her hands. "I only wish he was," she moaned.

"What's that?"

"I wish he was a typical man."

"What on earth can you mean?" Hannah rolled up her sleeves and began chopping herbs to add to the stew.

"Seems like a typical man would want to bed his wife."

The knife slipped from Hannah's hand, nearly slicing her thumb. She thought back to that night, years ago, when she had told Stephen, contrary to Phoebe's wishes, that another baby could be the death of his wife. Evidently he had taken the warning to heart. Unless there was another reason for his stand-offishness. "Stephen is a gentleman," she said, resuming her chopping. "He does not want to place you in danger."

"There's more to it than that. I could see it if he just didn't want to get me with child. But he won't even come near me, won't touch me, and won't let me touch him. When he's home, which is none too often, he throws his bedroll in the corner . . . says I need my rest to get well and he doesn't want to disturb me." Phoebe rubbed her wet eyes and nose with the back of her hand.

Hannah cleared her throat. "I am sure there is some truth to that. After all, Stephen is a very . . . robust man. Perhaps he is afraid that being close to you would be too much of a temptation. You see, he loves you too much to take even the smallest chance he might hurt you."

Phoebe shook her head; her shoulders sank in despair.

Gathering the chopped herbs, Hannah knelt by the hearth and stirred them into the pot. She longed to be able to go back and make things right for everybody. But when had things first started to go wrong? When Phoebe lied about her fiancé to get Stephen to marry her? When Stephen asked her to become his wife knowing he loved another? Or was it even before that, when Hannah had sent Temple away from her birthing bed and called for Stephen, or the very night of her wedding when she had taught the rough young man to dance? So many moments over the years — some large, some small, some meaningful, some trivial — and they had all led her here, to this one moment of guilt and shame for whatever rôle she had played in her sister's unhappiness.

Holbert, now a strapping young man of seventeen, peered into the cabin. "Ma, Uncle Stephen's about to speak. Reckon you'll want to hear him."

"Yes, indeed." Hannah came to her feet and rolled down her sleeves. "Phoebe, shall you come with us?"

"I'm so tired. Reckon I'll lie down for a bit."

"All right, dear. I'll send Lucy along later to see if you need any help." Grabbing her bonnet, she followed Holbert out into the yard where Stephen had mounted a tree stump to speak to the fort's assembled population. He swept off his hat and Hannah thought he looked quite dashing with his long hair pulled back in a queue, his high forehead with its Blackbeard-like scar, and his confident blue eyes. A quick look around confirmed that she was not the only woman who appreciated the overall effect.

"Well, friends, now that we are all finally here" — he gave Hannah a pointed look — "it is time to lay down a few rules to ensure the safety and comfort of all. Reckon I don't need to remind you why we are here. Indian attacks north of the river have caused Colonel Cooper and his men to get everyone there forted up. Some of you don't feel there is much of a threat around here as yet, but I reckon it's only a matter of time till the redskins get bold on the south side. I thank you all for joining in to get this fort built."

"I ain't got no quarrel with forting up," came a voice from the crowd. "What I want to know is . . . where's the reg'lar Army? Why ain't they out here doing something 'bout these damn' Injuns?"

Stephen swerved to address the speaker. "That is a fair question, Walter. Earlier this month I met with Captain Boone. As many of you know, he has put together a company of rangers that has been assisting the regulars in building forts. He told me Governor Howard thinks the biggest threat right now is to those settlements along the Mississippi, so that is where they're putting the manpower. Boone is well aware we got Injun troubles in the Boonslick. What we ain't got is the numbers. The Army can't spare men to protect just a few families when there are thousands of people who are in worse danger. For now, at least, we're on our own."

Hannah knew the man Stephen referred to was Nathan Boone, their old friend. He was now one of the most respected men in the Territory.

"For everyone's safety," Stephen continued, "the gates are to be kept barred at all times. No one is to go outside the walls, unless he's on a hunting detail, or tending the stock or crops."

A discontented rumble moved through the crowd.

"Reckon that sounds harsh" — Stephen quieted them down — "but there's no point to forting up if we let folks wander free. Redskins are sneaky varmints . . . they'll wait till we drop our guard and then attack. So we ain't going to drop our guard. Everyone clear on that?"

The adults all nodded agreement — all but Hannah. She cast dejected eyes around the crowd. She knew all these people — the Savages, Walter and David Burress, Joseph Jolly and his family, and all the rest of them. They were her friends and neighbors. Yet could she stand being cooped up with them for days, weeks, perhaps months? Not that she discounted the danger. After all, she, more than any of them, was familiar with the depredations Indians could inflict.

As the crowd dispersed, Walter Burress approached Hannah, hat in hand. He was a short, wiry fellow with a full beard and bulbous nose. His wife and child had died back in Kentucky, so he had followed his brother West to start anew.

"Afternoon, Miz Cole." His nervous smile displayed tobacco-stained teeth.

"Mister Burress." Hannah nodded.

"Jist wanted to tell ye that, if there's anything I mought could do for ye, ye jist holler."

"Why, that is awfully kind of you," Hannah replied. "Thankfully I have four strong sons to rely upon. I am sure we will be fine."

"Yes, ma'am, them is fine boys ye got. Ye done raised 'em well. Still, sometimes it's hard for a widder woman. Ye jist keep me in mind."

"Thank you, I will."

Grinning broadly, Walter Burress slapped his hat on his head and left her to contemplate his meaning. Had he been offering more than assistance with the occasional chore? Would she find herself having to fend off an unwanted suitor?

Dismayed, Hannah realized she had been at Cole's Fort for no more than a couple of hours and already felt the walls closing in on her.

The days lengthened, the nights became warmer, and life took on a certain routine. Hannah kept busy caring for her family, looking in on Phoebe, and doing her share of chores around the fort. She lived for the days when it was her turn to venture outside the walls and work in the communal garden. Only then could she shake the pall of confinement.

Hoeing in the corn rows one morning, Hannah looked up to see Stephen galloping across the fields. A member of Sarshall Cooper's recently formed band of rangers, he made frequent scouting trips about the country. Hannah envied him his freedom although she knew his frequent absences pained Phoebe. As he neared, he waved an arm, and shouted. "Back to the fort! Hurry, everyone inside!"

Dropping their hoes and rakes, the women dashed for the gates. Stephen followed them, leaping from his horse to close and bar the heavy doors. Calling the men to join him, he made for the fort's center yard, directing four of their number to stand as look-outs. Hannah trailed close behind.

"Captain Cole," cried one distraught wife, "it ain't my Joseph, is it? He's out with a hunting party and ain't come back yet. It ain't my Joseph them redskins got?"

"No, ma'am, not as I could tell." Stephen paused for breath, brushing sweat-streaked hair from his forehead. His brows drew together like the point of an arrowhead. "They've killed some other poor souls."

A hush fell over the crowd. Hannah felt the cold of a deep dread fill her veins. Unconsciously she reached for her daughter Jennie and held her close.

"I was over on the north side of the river," Stephen continued, "on the road near Prairie Creek when I come across two men, dead only a few hours by the looks of it. Seems like they'd fought hard, maybe killed a few redskins, though them Injuns didn't leave any of their own behind. The white men had been butchered. I won't say any more, not in front of the women and children."

"Who were they?" several voices asked.

Stephen passed his hand over his eyes. "I couldn't rightly tell. Nobody from the south side or I would have recognized their kit. One of them might have been that new fellow by the name of Todd, but I can't be sure."

As Stephen's meaning became clear — that the men had been mutilated to the point of non-recognition — moans and cries passed through the crowd. Mothers pulled their children close and fathers' eyes turned flinty.

"I need volunteers to help me go back for the bodies," Stephen said.

Several men immediately stepped forward. One woman grabbed her husband's arm. "Don't do it, Gil. What if those Injuns are still about?"

"I understand your concern, Missus Rupe," Stephen said, "but decency requires that we bring these men back, or at least bury their bodies. I would have done it myself, but I wanted to warn the fort first."

Stephen had no trouble enlisting a party of ten men to retrieve the bodies. Although James and Holbert both volunteered, Stephen directed them to remain at the fort to help protect the women and children. Hannah silently blessed him.

Arming themselves with rifles, muskets, knives, clubs, and whatever else was at hand, the group rode out. James was instructed to make his way to Cooper's Fort for help if they had not returned by night-fall.

Shortly after they left, the fort's hunting party returned. The women busied themselves with dressing out the game, while the few men on hand herded the livestock inside the walls. People spoke in hushed tones, keeping an eye on the slowly moving sun.

As the day inched along, Hannah prayed the men would return before dark. She did not want James to venture beyond the safety of the fort's walls. All day long, her oldest son avoided her, afraid that she would try to prevent him from leaving, if that proved necessary. She would not do that, would not ask him to ignore Stephen's directive, would not emasculate him in front of the others. But it would kill her to stay silent.

Dinner finished, Hannah stepped out onto the cabin's stoop and settled her back against the rough wall. She watched with growing uneasiness as the first stars flickered to brightness in the dusky sky. James followed her out and paused to look up as well. She noticed he was wearing his powder pouch and carried his hat.

"It won't be full dark for another hour," she said.

James smiled down at her. "Ma, you needn't. . . ."

His words were cut off by a volley of gunfire.

CHAPTER EIGHTEEN

James sprinted for the blockhouse, Hannah close behind. They climbed the stairs to find Muke Box squinting through the narrow window.

"Can you see anything?" James asked.

Box shook his head. "Too dark and too far away. But it come from the north. Could be our boys."

James waited impatiently for the older man to step aside. When he finally moved away, Hannah peered over her son's shoulder. She, too, could see nothing.

"I'm going out there," James announced. "They might be in trouble."

"No!" Hannah cried. "What if it is a trick to lure the rest of the men from the fort? You might ride right into an ambush!"

"Reckon she's right," Box agreed.

James sighed with frustration and turned again to the window. "Wait! I think I see something. Over there, a light flickering on and off, like a rider carrying a lantern."

Box started down the stairs. "I'll tell 'em to open the gates."

"Better make sure it is really them," Hannah warned.

"It is. I can see them now. Uncle Stephen and. . . ." James paused to count. "Yes, they're all there!"

The three of them dashed into the yard with the news. The gates were swung open to admit the returning horsemen. Two of them carried canvas-wrapped bundles over the front of their saddles. The men dismounted to cheers and embraces. Phoebe stepped forward and touched Stephen's arm. He turned his back as though he had not even felt her touch. His eyes, reflecting the lanterns' glow, landed on Hannah. She ducked her head, afraid he would see the tears of gratitude in her own. Or worse, that Phoebe would.

"Who fired the shots?" Muke Box shouted above the din.

"We did!" exclaimed Gil Rupe, grinning with pride. "Shot us a redskin!"

"Was you attacked?"

"No, he was alone. Must've been sent to spy on us," Stephen said. "We captured him, but he broke free. Would've been better to bring him in alive to get information out of him, but he was too fast. We had to shoot him."

"I say well done!" declared Mrs. Rupe. "One less filthy savage to worry about."

"This one might've been acting alone. We'll never know." Stephen looked at the two bodies draped over the horses. "We'll bury these unlucky souls tomorrow. Muke, set the guards for the night. We'll make our plans in the morning."

Weary, yet relieved, people straggled back to their cabins. Stephen tossed his reins to his young son, directing him to make sure the animal was bedded down for the night. He turned to Hannah and spoke under his breath. "Meet me in the blockhouse. I need to talk to you about something."

Before she could ask his purpose, he strode off, his eyes searching the crowd. Hannah returned to her cabin to make sure her children were settled for the night, then, carrying a candle, made her way though the dark to the blockhouse. The first level of the two-story building was used for storage. There, amid the boxes, barrels, and bags, she found Stephen, James, and another young man about her son's age also named James, last name of Davis. Davis had arrived in the Boonslick the previous winter, all alone, and, although he spoke little of his past, he had proved himself to be a hard worker with a quick mind. Hannah could not imagine why she had been asked to join this meeting.

Stephen rose as she entered and offered her the trunk he had been sitting on. She perched gingerly. "What happened today," Stephen began, "may have been the first shot across the bow, or it may mean nothing. Those two men maybe just came across some Indians feeling feisty, or their killing might be the first sign that we are at war. Judging from the way they were killed, I'm bound it was the last."

"How bad was it?" Davis asked.

Stephen glanced at Hannah, weighing whether to tell her. "Reckon you'll hear soon enough anyway. Their hearts were cut out and their heads were stuck on poles right by the side of the road. Seems to me them Injuns were sending us a message."

Hannah's stomach turned. "Savages," she whispered. "Do you think they will try to attack us here at the fort, or are they too cowardly for that?"

"Right now, I couldn't say what their intentions are, but we dang' sure better find out. That's what I wanted to talk to you about. We need to send out scouts to take the lay of the land. Nobody on either side of the river knows how many bands are out there, nor where they are exactly, nor if they got a plan of attack. I'd like to send out these young bucks to see what they can scare up."

Young Cole and Davis exchanged excited glances.

Hannah took a deep breath. "You are asking them to do a very dangerous thing. Is it really necessary?"

"I think it is. If we find out the redskins are more interested in fighting the white man than each other, we got a real problem. We'll have to notify Captain Boone and the Army about the situation. I know it is hard for you to let your son go, Hannah, but he knows these woods better than anybody, except me. And now that the redskins look to be on the warpath, I can't afford to be roaming around the country . . . I got to stick close to the fort, in case of an attack."

Hannah nodded. "When will they leave?"

"Tonight."

A week passed, a very long week for all the fort's residents, before the two young men returned to Cole's Fort — dirty, disheveled, and tired. The tale they told was both thrilling and sobering.

"For days we seen nothing," reported the

Davis boy as he sat at Hannah's table with a welcome cup of grog. "We covered the country north to south and didn't see no sign of redskins. We was ready to come back and report that them savages must've cleared out all the way to Ioway when we realized there was about a hundred of 'em on our tails."

"We was down on Moniteau Creek, near the trading post there, the one called Johnson's Factory," jumped in the younger Cole. "The Injuns was between us and the fort, and we knew, if we tried to break through them in the open woods, they'd've had our scalps. So we holed up at the post. They surrounded us . . . looked like they was going to wait us out."

Davis took a swig from his mug. " 'Course, long as we was at the post, we had plenty of food and ammunition, but we reckoned we better get back to the fort right away to warn everybody. That's when James figgered out how to escape."

"How'd you do it, boys?" asked Stephen.

"Well, sir, late at night we pulled up a plank of the floor, crawled underneath, and slipped through the redskins' camp to the creek," explained his nephew, his chest puffed with the telling of the daring story. "Johnson had told us of a canoe he kept tied up, and sure enough it was there. We floated down to the river, quiet as mice, and just thought we'd gotten clear when one of the paddles struck the side of the canoe. It didn't seem loud enough to carry, but them savages could hear an acorn drop a mile away, I'm bound, 'cause all of a sudden they was everywhere!"

Hannah's heart raced as her boy recounted the dangerous escapade. She reached out and squeezed his shoulder.

"We rowed upriver all the way to Big Lick, but couldn't shake 'em."

"We finally figgered we wasn't gonna outrun 'em," cut in Davis, "so we turned and fired. Both of us nailed an Injun!"

"You killed a man?" Hannah looked at her son in amazement.

"Yes, ma'am. It was me or him."

"I am glad you killed him," she said, and it was not just because doing so may have saved her son's life. Somehow, James's act helped to avenge his father's death.

"Did they keep following you?" Stephen asked.

Davis drained his cup. "Nah. Them cowards turned tail."

"They didn't halt their pursuit because they're cowards, son," Stephen said. "Reckon they was just cutting their losses.

Make no mistake, they'll be back."

Hannah wrapped an arm around her James.

"You did well, boys," Stephen said. "You found out what we needed to know. War may not be officially declared, but we got one nevertheless, right here in the Boonslick."

CHAPTER NINETEEN

Hannah sat on a stool in the shade of her cabin, stitching a new pair of moccasins. With the corner of her apron she dabbed at her moist forehead. The oppressive midsummer heat weighed on her like a heavy yoke. The fort was quiet today except for the buzzing of bluebottles near the livestock pen. Two hunting parties had gone out this morning, and those folks who remained mostly stayed inside their cabins to avoid the burning sun.

Yet, Hannah could not remain indoors. The four walls of her tiny home were dark and confining. She longed to be in the cool woods, perhaps gathering berries by a trickling stream. But that was impossible. Although there had been no further attacks since the Indians had butchered those two white men in the spring, the settlers were remaining vigilant. Particularly now that war between America and Britain was official.

When the residents of Cole's Fort had gotten the news of the war's declaration, Hannah had immediately thought of Dolley. As difficult as life was for people on the frontier, how much more difficult must it be for the wife of the man whose duty it was to conduct the war — the man who must send soldiers into battle, inevitably creating widows and fatherless children? If Hannah knew Dolley, the First Lady was dedicating herself to helping her husband shoulder his immense responsibilities. Of course, Hannah kept these thoughts to herself since most of the settlers were none too pleased with the government in Washington, which they viewed as having hung the western territories out to dry.

As she punched the deerskin and pulled the leather thong through the hole, she looked up to see Lucy coming across the fort's yard, taking her time in the sodden heat. She was returning from helping Phoebe who was once again down with some mysterious ailment.

"How is my sister?" Hannah asked, laying her sewing in her lap.

"I dosed her wid some sass'fras tea. She seemed to perk up a mite."

"I am glad to hear it. Poor thing, the heat always seems to afflict her so."

Lucy dipped her tin cup into a barrel of water and took a long drink. "Reckon I'll go see to gettin' up some dinner," she said, wiping her mouth with the back of her hand.

"Oh, there is plenty of time for that," Hannah said. "Sit here and rest your bones for a while."

Gratefully Lucy obeyed, sinking down on the ground next to her mistress and stretching out her tired legs.

Hannah resumed her sewing. "Was Mister Stephen there?" she asked after a moment.

Lucy gave her a sideways glance. "Yes'm."

Hannah waited, but Lucy did not seem inclined to elaborate. "Well, what was he doing?" she finally asked, trying to keep her voice casual.

"Jawin' wid Mistuh Jolly. Seems we's runnin' low on powduh, and Mistuh Stephen, he wuz aksin' Mistuh Jolly could he make mo', but Mistuh Jolly, he say no cuz it's too dang'rous to mine de saltpetuh, what wid all dem bloodthusty Injuns roamin' 'round."

"I see. And what did Mister Stephen say to that?"

"Nuthin'. Miz Phoebe, she started yellin' how wuz we gonna defen' ourselves 'gainst muh'drous redskins iffen we ain't got no shot powduh, and Mistuh Stephen, he jus' stomps off."

Hannah punched the deerskin with excessive vigor. "That woman! You would think she would realize how hard Stephen is working, night and day, to keep us all safe, and curb her tongue. Particularly in the presence of Mister Jolly."

"Yes'm." Lucy shot her another glance.

"Why do you keep looking at me like that?"

"Lak what?"

"Like . . . I don't know . . . like you disapprove of something."

"I don' dis'prove of nuthin'. I jus' minds mah own bizness." Gathering her legs under her, Lucy retreated into the cabin where Hannah could hear her pulling out pots for dinner.

Sighing, she flipped the moccasin over and began stitching the other side. She knew why Lucy gave her those looks — because she saw through Hannah's carefully constructed façade concerning her feelings for Stephen. She knew Hannah did not ask about him just to pass the time of day, but because she thought about him almost every waking minute, wondered where he was and what he was doing. During their year of separation, Hannah had managed to push

Stephen to the back of her brain, but since coming to the fort — seeing him almost every day, knowing he was only steps away — he had become a constant presence in her mind.

Hannah was certain that her feelings for her brother-in-law were a secret to everyone at the fort. Everyone but Lucy. She could not fool Lucy. Not the woman who belonged to her, who shared so much of her history. Hannah had no doubt that, in spite of Lucy's illiteracy and rough speech, her slave possessed a sharper mind than any of the white women in Cole's Fort. She also knew her secret was safe with Lucy. The black woman's loyalty to her mistress was not in question. So sure was Hannah of Lucy's discretion that she had even considered discussing with her the predicament she found herself in. What a relief it would be to explain to somebody that, although she was drawn to Stephen for his strength and kindness, she would never cross the line by encouraging a romantic relationship. Not just because of Phoebe, but because of Temple, too. She had loved Temple, and would honor him even in death.

But, of course, these were not things that could be discussed, particularly not with one's slave woman. These were things she confessed only in her journal, in the letters she wrote to Dolley. Lucy had seen her writing once or twice, and had asked if she were recording recipes or perhaps keeping accounts. Hannah had laughed and told her that they were things of a much more personal nature.

"When I die," she had joked, although it was not really a joke, "make sure this journal is buried with me."

"Yes'm. Dat's a promise."

Hannah took a final stitch and held up the moccasin to survey her handiwork. Gunshots startled her, the moccasin dropping beside her in the dust. Like a spark touched to dry kindling, the fort came to instant life. Heads poked out of doors, children looked up from their games. Hannah saw Stephen emerge from a cabin and rush toward the blockhouse. He caught sight of her and shouted for her to round up her children. Quickly she took stock. All of the younger ones were taking their midday rest. All but Samuel. She tried to think where she had last seen the boy, but could not. Even in an enclosed fort, Samuel was expert at finding hidey holes.

More shots rang out, closer this time. Hannah picked up her skirts and sprinted to Phoebe's cabin, thinking perhaps Samuel was playing with his cousin. When she got there, she found Phoebe and all five of her children, but not her own son.

"Have you seen Samuel?" she panted.

Phoebe shook her head, but ten-year-old James piped up: "Last I seen him, he was playing jacks with George Jolly in the storeroom beneath the blockhouse."

Hannah whirled, crossing the yard in double time. It took a moment for her eyes to adjust to the dark storeroom, but it soon became clear that Samuel was not there. Voices from the second floor drew her up the stairs.

"My God," she heard Stephen say under his breath. "He can't get up. They've shot him in the gut."

A little gasp of air escaped from Hannah's throat.

"Hannah! What are you doing here?" Stephen looked at her in alarm.

"Looking for Samuel. Have you seen him?"

Stephen stepped aside, revealing her son, his head and shoulders halfway out the narrow window.

"Samuel, step away from there!" she cried.

"It's all right," Stephen said, his voice grim. "They ain't shootin' at us. Not yet, anyways."

"Who are they shooting at, then?" Hannah joined them at the window.

Stephen put his hand on her arm, gently trying to pull her back. "Don't watch this," he said.

But Hannah stood her ground, mesmerized by the scene below. Hundreds of Indians swarmed out of the woods, howling like a thousand packs of wolves. Fifty yards from the fort, two white men struggled on the ground.

"Albert Smith and John Savage," Hannah breathed.

"Yes." Stephen moved his hand to her shoulder. "They were out hunting. Smith has been shot."

Horrified, they watched John Savage pull the wounded man to his feet. After just a few steps, Smith fell to the ground, unable to go farther. Savage crouched beside him, exhorting him to get up, ignoring the lead balls piercing the ground all around them. Smith shook his head, then pressed his rifle into the other man's hands, pointing toward the fort. Savage ducked another shot, looking between the fort and his fallen friend.

"Save yourself, man," Stephen murmured. "It's too late for Smith."

Finally, left no choice by the advancing Indians, Savage tucked the rifle under his

316

arm and dashed for the fort. Stephen clambered down the stairs, rushing to open the gates for him, leaving Hannah and Samuel alone in the blockhouse.

They watched as the Indians surrounded Smith. One of them drew his knife and with two quick slices, removed the injured man's scalp. Smith's scream rose above the unholy din. Hannah cried out. How could this be happening? How could this torture and mutilation be taking place before her son's innocent eyes?

"Samuel, no more, no more!" She tried to pull him away from the window, but, taller and stronger, he shook her off.

"Is this what they did to Pa?" the boy asked, eyes transfixed on the grisly scene.

"No," his mother said, praying she spoke the truth. "No, Son, your father did not die like this."

Below, the butchery continued, although mercifully Smith must have died or lost consciousness, for his screams had stopped.

Samuel reached for a rifle and brought it to his shoulder. "By God, I'm gonna shoot one of them miserable bastards!"

For an instant, Hannah was tempted to urge him on. She took a ragged breath and placed her hand on the gun's barrel. "No, Samuel. Uncle Stephen would have ordered the men to shoot, if that is what he thought best. So far, the savages have not fired directly at the fort. We should not anger them by firing first. That would be foolhardy since they outnumber us by so many."

"I'm gonna do it, Ma," Samuel insisted, his face turning red. "Look what they done to Mister Smith."

Hannah turned her head to the window. The Indians were slowly retreating to the woods, still howling and carrying on. Behind them lay the bloody mess that moments ago had been young Albert Smith. "Oh, dear Lord," she whispered, her gorge rising. She closed her eyes and swallowed. "Patience, Son. If you shoot now, we will have a full-fledged battle on our hands. Besides, there are still two men out hunting. We should give them a chance to return safely."

Samuel lowered the gun, his eyes burning with hate. "Someday I'm gonna kill me an Injun," he promised.

Albert Smith left behind a young wife and baby. Like the Coles, and so many of the Boonslick settlers, they had come to the Missouri Territory from Kentucky, eager to begin anew. Now, in the course of one terrible day, a man was dead, and a young woman, not yet twenty, was left alone to raise her child in a violent, untamed wilderness.

There was no sense to it. Sitting with the distraught Lila Smith, Hannah did not try to make sense of it. She simply wrapped her arms around the sobbing girl and let her cry. More than most, Hannah knew what this young widow and mother was feeling: sorrow, anger, fear, and a sense of loss so profound it was like being swallowed by a bottomless well. She prayed that Lila would find the strength necessary to carry on, just as she had.

Finally the girl fell asleep, her body still trembling from the shock. Hannah left her in the care of others and returned to her cabin. She gave each of her children a mighty embrace, thanking God for these precious gifts who had sustained her in her own time of trial.

"What will Missus Smith do now?" asked eight-year-old Mattie, her eyes wide with concern.

Hannah pulled her daughter close. "She will cry and be very sad for a while, and then she will get on with living."

"Did you cry when Papa died?"

"Oh, yes. Sometimes I still do," Hannah admitted.

"You do?"

"A little bit. I cry because I miss him so . . . but not very often any more, because your pa would not want me to be sad. Or you, either." Hannah gave Mattie a final squeeze, and then set her on her feet. "Now, let's see what we can find for supper."

"Ain' gonna fin' much," said Lucy with a dour look at the bare hearth. "Ain' got no fresh meat. And likely won't for some time, 'less de othuh hunting party makes a safe return. Reckon we will have to make do."

Although their supper of pemmican and johnnycake was barely enough to fill their stomachs, Hannah led her family in a prayer of thanks. When they were finished, she tucked the younger ones into bed and headed for the Smith cabin to see if there was anything to do for Lila.

A commotion at the gate of the fort caught her attention. Gil Rupe and Muke Box stood arguing in stage whispers. Suddenly Rupe held up his hand and put his ear to the heavy door. Box listened as well. A moment later they nodded to each other and pulled open the gates. Two men staggered inside and fell to their knees.

Hannah rushed over, joined by Stephen and several of the other settlers. They surrounded Delany Bolin and Joseph Yarnell, the second hunting party that had gone out that morning. Covered in mud and soaked to the skin, they made a feeble attempt to tell their story, but collapsed from exhaustion before they could finish. Stephen ordered them to be looked after and directed the other men to join him in the storeroom for a meeting.

Although she had not been invited, Hannah followed the men as they marched across the yard and entered the dark storeroom. She sneaked in and stood just inside the door, hoping her presence would not be noticed. Someone lit a lantern and set it on a barrel in the middle of the crowded room. Stephen began talking, pacing back and forth within the circle of dim light. He caught sight of her standing in the shadows and paused for a moment, then resumed his speech. Hannah relaxed. If Stephen did not object to her being there, none of the other men would dare.

"We've no more than a couple of days' food supply," Stephen was saying, "so we must come up with a plan."

"Maybe them Injuns'll get tired of waitin' and just skedaddle," said Walter Burress with more hope in his voice than conviction.

"Not likely." Stephen came to a standstill and crossed his arms over his broad chest.

"There must be four or five hundred of them out there. They wouldn't have gathered a band of that size if all they intended was a quick raid. No, they are planning an attack, I'm bound. And if not that, then they will just starve us out."

"Let 'em attack!" shouted Gil Rupe, shaking his fist in the air. "We'll show 'em what the white man's made of!"

"Only problem with that, Gil, is we're low on ammunition," said Stephen. "Dang' near out of powder."

James stepped into the circle of light, his handsome features and confident voice so like his father's that Hannah's heart skipped a beat. And yet, his resemblance to Stephen was equally striking. "So we can't fend off an attack, and we refuse to surrender," James stated, surveying the men around him. "Our only option, then, is to escape."

"Escape?"

"What are ye sayin', boy?"

"Have ye taken leave of ye're senses?" said Gil Rupe. "The redskins have surrounded us on three sides and the river's on the fourth. What are we goin' to do, swim to safety?"

The room filled with derisive laughter.

"To tell the truth, the lad's on to something," said Stephen, clapping his nephew on the back.

"Is that so?" snorted Rupe. "And just how are ye plannin' to sneak all these people out of here, tell me that?"

Beside Hannah, the storeroom door creaked opened, admitting Delany Bolin and Joseph Yarnell. Cleaned up and fortified with mugs of grog, they looked only a little worse for their ordeal. Stephen invited them to come forward and tell their story.

They had been hunting downriver, they said, until it started to turn dark. As they headed back to the fort, they picked up signs of a large band of Indians in the area, so they proceeded with caution. When the fort came into view, it was clear what had happened. Knowing their only possible approach was from the river, they slipped into the water and floated upstream, keeping almost completely submerged. When dark fell, they climbed the muddy bank and managed to sneak unnoticed to the gates where Rupe and Box heard them scratching at the door.

Stephen congratulated them on their quick thinking and filled them in on the fort's situation. "We've got precious little powder and even less food. Somehow we have got to get across the river and join up with the folks at Fort Kincaid," he concluded.

"What about the *pirogues* we've got hidden in the rushes?" James suggested. "Could we ferry everybody over in them?"

"That'd take at least ten trips over and back," scoffed Rupe. "Do ye think them Injuns wouldn't catch on to that pretty quick?"

Delany Bolin snapped his fingers. "The Frenchmen!" he exclaimed. Joseph Yarnell nodded his head, grinning broadly.

"Come again?" said Stephen.

"Earlier today we spied a flatboat on the river," Bolin explained. "It put in on the south side, right across from Bonne Femme Creek. Looked like they was stopping to make some repairs. Joe and I hid in the bushes, heard some Frenchies jabberin' about heading for Council Bluffs to trade with the Indians. It's a good-size boat. Reckon it'd carry all of us and the stock as well!"

"How do we know they're still there?" questioned Rupe. "They could've made their repairs and be all the way to the Lamine by now."

"Could be," agreed Bolin. "But it's worth checking."

"I agree," said Stephen. "How many men on board?"

"Maybe half a dozen. We could take 'em easy."

"I'd like to see for myself. Do you and Yarnell feel up to leading me there?"

Both men nodded.

"Good. If we leave now, we can see if it's still there and maybe find out how long it'll be beached. The rest of you go back to your families and prepare to leave by nightfall tomorrow. Pack only what you can carry. We'll have to travel light."

"I still don't see how we're gonna sneak all them people and animals past five hundred heathens," muttered Rupe.

"One by one." Stephen smiled.

Talking among themselves, the men filed out of the storeroom. Hannah stayed pressed against the wall, trying to remain unobtrusive. Still, some of them gave her disapproving looks. Well, let them. She had as much right as anybody to know what was going on.

Stephen watched the last man exit. It was well past midnight, and he had hours of dangerous work ahead of him, yet he did not seem at all tired or apprehensive. He gave Hannah a lingering look, as though storing up a vision of her to carry him through the perilous days and nights ahead. Finally he extinguished the lantern and held the door, waiting for her to leave.

"I'm scared, Stephen," she whispered.

"Don't be," he assured her. "I won't let anything happen to you."

She shook her head. "Not for me. For you."

He chuckled. "I'll be fine. The redskins tried to kill me once and failed. Reckon I'm indestructible."

CHAPTER TWENTY

Bolin and Yarnell led Stephen to the boat, which was just where they had last seen it. They sneaked close enough to overhear the captain, whose name they made out to be Coursault, talking to one of his men. The repairs would be completed around noon, he said, but, as long as they were halted, he planned to send out a hunting party to replenish their meat supply. Thus, he was pushing back their departure by a day.

This schedule fit perfectly with the settlers' plans. They would have all day to prepare their escape. Then, when dark fell, the men would overtake the French crew, commandeer the boat, load their families aboard, and make for the relative safety of the river's north shore.

The tricky part, everyone knew, was going to be sneaking all the fort's residents out from under the Indians' very noses. What if a baby cried, or a horse whinnied? What if the inevitable noise of loading people and animals onto a wooden boat carried all the way to the woods where the Indians were encamped? But they had no choice. The last of the meat had been eaten, the last of the corn had been baked into bread. The Frenchmen's boat represented their only hope for survival.

Stephen issued orders. Pack only the bare necessities. No kettles or pots or other items that would clang together, unless they were well wrapped. Mothers, keep your children quiet, and men, muzzle your stock. Wear your darkest clothing and conceal all knives or jewelry that might reflect the moonlight.

Although inwardly torn at having to leave most of her possessions behind to be ransacked or stolen by heathen savages, Hannah put on a brave front. She made a game out of it for the younger children, telling them to pick out one favorite item to bring — a dolly, perhaps, for the girls, a slingshot or hunting knife for the boys — along with one change of clothing. For herself, she decided not to waste precious space packing extra clothing. She would wear two layers of skirts and shirtwaists, and that would have to do. The rest of her necessities — a few kitchen utensils, a sampler made by her mother, the wreath she had given Temple, and her journal — she packed in a basket.

Having organized her own household, she sent Lucy to help Phoebe and went herself to see if Lila Smith needed assistance. She found the young widow beside herself, insisting she would not leave the fort while her husband's mutilated body still lay on the harsh ground where he had fallen. Hannah tried to reason with her, pleaded with her, begged her to think of her child's welfare, to no avail. Still half out of her mind with grief, Lila would not budge until her husband was buried.

Hannah sought out Stephen and told him the problem. Sighing, he ran his fingers through his hair. He had not slept in over twenty-four hours, and rest was nowhere in sight. His chin had sprouted whiskers, and the lines around his eyes were deeper than usual. Still, he radiated an energy that was like a force. Although he had a hundred tasks more important than figuring out what to do about Lila Smith, he drew Hannah to a shady spot and listened patiently as she described the young woman's despair.

"I can't blame her for feeling the way she does," he said, "but there is naught to be done about it. The only way we could get to his body would be under cover of darkness, and even then it's so close to the woods that the redskins would hear us for certain. Besides, I can't spare any men for a burial detail. When night comes, most of us will be heading downriver to take over the boat, and the rest are organizing the departure here at the fort. You will just have to make her understand."

Not wishing to burden him further, Hannah assured him she would find a solution. Still pondering the problem, she crossed the yard to look in on Phoebe. Pushing open the rough plank door, a sour smell assaulted her nose. Phoebe sat sprawled across the kitchen table. Lucy stood beside her, dabbing at her forehead with a damp cloth.

"What's going on?"

"She got into de grog," Lucy explained.

"You mean, she is drunk?"

Lucy shrugged. "See fo' yo'sef."

Brushing Phoebe's stringy hair away from her face, Hannah looked into a pair of unfocused, bloodshot eyes. Like a marionette, Phoebe's head wobbled and fell back to the table when Hannah took her hand away. In a corner of the room, the children, wide-eyed and silent, stared at their stricken mother.

"James," Hannah addressed the oldest, "take your brothers and sisters to my cabin. Help your cousins with their packing."

Without a word, the boy gathered his siblings and left.

Hannah picked up an earthenware jug that lay tipped on its side and held it upside down. Not a single drop fell out. "Do you reckon she drank the whole thing?"

"Mus' have." Lucy shook her head. " 'Nuf to make her mighty sick, anyways. She done los' mos' her stomach."

Hannah pursed her lips in disgust. "Why would she do this? Today of all days when she will need to keep her wits about her . . . why, it is downright shameful!"

"Reckon she scared," Lucy mused.

"That's no excuse. We are all scared, but that doesn't give us the right to abandon our responsibilities. She has five children to look after, for heaven's sake. And it is not as though Stephen can be here to help. He is leading the party to capture the boat. He doesn't have time to deal with a drunken wife!"

"Mebbe tha's why she done it."

"I don't follow."

"Mistuh Stephen, he so busy lookin' aftuh ever'body else, he don' have de time to look aftuh his own fambly. Mebbe she jus' tryin' to git his attenshun."

"A fine way to do it." Hannah paced, hands on hips. "Our lives depend on everybody pulling together, and my selfish sister decides it's a good time to get into the rum. Oh, she will no doubt get his attention . . . and that of a few hundred redskins as well."

Phoebe raised her head and managed a woozy smile. "Time to go?" she drawled. "A boat ride! Won't that be fun!" Her head dropped back to the table.

The two women looked at each other.

"Leas' she ain' scared no mo'," said Lucy.

Suddenly Hannah had an idea. "Is there another jug of that grog?"

Lucy found a jug on the fireplace mantel, uncorked it, and took a whiff. "Sho' 'nuf."

"Give it to me."

"You ain' gonna git drunk, too, is ya?"

"Heavens no. I need it for something else. Now, Lucy, try to get my pathetic little sister sobered up. If it appears she is going to be out for a while, you will have to take charge of getting her and the children ready to go. James is going with the men to take the boat, but Holbert can come over to help. Between the two of you, you ought to be able to manage."

Hoisting the jug, Hannah stepped outside. The evening sun had disappeared behind the tall walls of the fort, casting lengthy shadows across the muddy yard. Very soon the men would be gathering to begin their dangerous trek to capture the French boat. There was not much time to implement her plan for gaining Lila Smith's co-operation.

She found Lila sitting with Mildred Rupe. Still clearly upset, the girl twisted a handkerchief, pressing it now and then to her red, puffy eyes. Mildred rose and lifted her hands in a gesture of defeat.

"Thank you for sitting with her, Mildred," Hannah said, concealing the jug in the folds of her skirt. "I will stay for a while now."

"She's an ornery thing," Mildred whispered as she headed out the door. "Don't see how you'll change her mind."

Hannah smiled. "We'll see." She set the jug on the table and bent over Lila's sleeping baby. She prayed God would forgive her for what she was about to do to the child's mother.

"Lila," Hannah turned, "you have not packed a thing. It will be dark soon. Don't you want to start preparing?"

"I told you, I am not leaving. Not with Albert still out there lying on the ground as though he was nothing better than carrion to be torn apart by wild animals."

"So you did. I will not argue with you, but neither will I leave you and your baby alone to face the redskins. Reckon I will just have to stay with you."

"Stay with me?" Lila sounded confused. "You would let the others leave without you?"

"I would prefer that we all left together, of course. But if you will not go, neither shall I. The two of us shall fight the heathens, or die trying."

"But . . . Missus Cole, I could not ask you to sacrifice yourself on my behalf." Lila twisted her handkerchief into a knot.

"You are not asking, my dear. I am volunteering. You see, I was in your shoes once. I remember feeling that my life was not worth living without my husband. I loved him so, that, in the days after he died, I would have welcomed death myself. You must have loved your Albert just as fiercely, and I honor and respect that love. So I shall not again ask you to leave him. Together, we shall face whatever comes."

Tears flowed freely down Lila's ravaged cheeks as she contemplated Hannah's words. "Oh, Missus Cole, you are just saying that so I will change my mind. You think I will agree to leave so as not to place you in danger."

"Not at all. I fully intend to stay." Hannah drew up a stool and joined Lila at the table. "I will not lie to you, however. The prospect of coming face to face with murderous

Indians has me shaking in my boots. That's why I brought this." She patted the jug of grog. "Nerve tonic. My mother's recipe. A touch of this and we will be able to get through anything." She uncorked the jug and poured two cupfuls.

Lila brought hers to her nose and sniffed. "Smells like rum."

"Well, there might be a touch of spirits in it, but it is good for what ails you. Ma swore by it." Hannah raised her cup and made as if to down all its contents, although she only took a swallow. It burned on the way down and hit her stomach like a lead ball.

Lila followed her example, emptying her cup. "My goodness! That certainly warms a body!"

"Just what the doctor ordered, wouldn't you say? Something to warm our chilly hearts. Now, Lila, tell me all about your family back in Kentucky."

For the next hour, Hannah kept the young woman talking, refilling her cup whenever it came up empty. For her own part, Hannah merely touched the cup to her lips. When she gauged that Lila had had enough to make her more pliable, yet not enough to disable her, she recorked the jug. Reaching across the table, she took Lila's hand.

"Wouldn't you like to see your ma and pa

again, dear? Think how sad they would be to lose not only Albert, but you and your baby."

Lila nodded, her eyes once again welling with tears. But these were tears of remembrance, not anguish. "Yes, they had talked about joining us in Missouri. Now that Albert is gone, I am sure they will come to take care of us."

"Won't it be lovely to see your family again?" Hannah rose and surveyed the cabin. "You will certainly want to take the baby's quilt, and these pretty china cups, I'm bound. Wrap them up carefully so they won't break."

"All right." Lila stood up, holding the edge of the table for balance. "Reckon you and me won't be facing the Indians together after all, eh, Missus Cole?"

"Not today." Hannah smiled. "Now, you gather your things. I will be back when it is time to go."

Slipping out of the cabin, Hannah realized that darkness had descended. Had the men already left to steal the boat? A sense of panic overtook her at the thought of James somewhere out there in the starless night, surrounded by the enemy. But he was a capable young man, and she knew Stephen would protect him with his life.

Her thoughts turned to practicalities. She must gather her children, make sure each had his or her bundle to carry, decide who to put in charge of their horses and cow. With Lucy and Holbert assisting Phoebe, she would have to rely on thirteen-year-old Stephen and the rambunctious Samuel. But then there was Lila, who would also need help. Her mind racing, she was startled when Walter Burress stepped in her path.

"Miz Cole." He doffed his hat. "Seein' as I'm by myself and you got a passel of young 'uns to look after, I was wonderin' do you need my help tonight?"

"Oh, Mister Burress, how kind of you. Indeed I do." Even in the dark, she could make out his wide grin. "Not for myself, exactly. For Missus Smith. She has no man to assist her after yesterday's awful events. Would you be willing to take charge of her and her baby?"

The little man's grin faded. "If that's your biddin', ma'am."

"It is. Poor Missus Smith is half crazy with grief and is not too steady on her feet. I would be most comforted to know she was under the care of a strong, capable man such as yourself."

Burress's shoulders drew back and his smile returned. "It'd be my pleasure,

337

ma'am."

At that moment, the gates to the fort creaked open. A shaft of moonlight emerged from the clouds, striking the imposing figure of Stephen Cole.

CHAPTER TWENTY-ONE

Stephen slipped through the heavy doors and moved with purpose toward Hannah and Walter Burress. A strip of cloth tied around his forehead to keep the sweat from streaming into his eyes made him look almost like one of their enemy. Hannah suddenly imagined him bare-chested, wearing a breechcloth, and was glad the darkness disguised the uncomfortable heat that suffused her body. What kind of woman was she to have such sinful thoughts? *Lord,* she promised, *when this danger is over, I shall take my children and move far away from this temptation.*

"We've taken the boat," Stephen said, the light of pure adrenaline glowing in his eyes. "We floated it upriver, just below the bluff behind the fort. Spread the word . . . everyone is to gather in the yard and prepare to move out."

Silently the settlers congregated, awaiting

their turn to escape. In the hours leading up to this moment, Stephen had given instructions. He would lead each family, one at a time, down to the river. The men holding the boat would see them aboard. Not a word was to be uttered until they were safely ensconced on the opposite shore.

When all was ready, Stephen slipped outside the walls to make sure the coast was clear. Within moments, he was back, gesturing for the Rupe family. As they passed from sight, Hannah strained her ears for sounds of their movement. All she could hear was the high-pitched call of tree frogs, mercifully loud enough on this muggy night to conceal all manner of commotion.

While waiting for Stephen to return for the next group, Hannah made certain her family was ready to go. James, of course, was helping to secure the boat. Holbert had been lent to Phoebe. Her next two, Stephen and Samuel, were in charge of the stock. Ten-year-old Jennie had been given the task of shepherding her little brother, William. Mattie and Dykie were to hold each other's hands as they walked in front of their mother, who would bring up the rear, carrying Elenor. Hannah double-checked her pocket to make sure she still had a bit of sugar for the baby to suck in case she chose the wrong moment to put up a fuss.

Satisfied that they were as prepared as they could be, she scanned the quiet group of her friends and neighbors. To a woman (for most of them were women as the majority of men were holding the French boat) they looked serious and determined. Trepidation showed on a few faces, one or two seemed to be uttering silent prayers, but together they were a hardy bunch. Hannah was proud to be among them. She was especially pleased to see Lila Smith, babe in arms, standing squarely next to Walter Burress. Evidently having thrown off the effects of Hannah's "nerve tonic", the young woman appeared ready to get on with life.

With a shock, Hannah realized that Phoebe and her children were not there. Nor did she see Holbert, Lucy, or Isaac. Could it be that they had not gotten the word that everybody was leaving? Quickly she handed Elenor over to Jennie and whispered that she would be right back. Slipping through the crowd, Hannah pushed open the door of Phoebe's cabin. A distressing sight met her eyes.

On her knees, hunched over a chamber pot, Phoebe choked and gagged, a thin stream of spittle hanging from her bluish lips. Crouched next to her, Lucy held the wretched woman's shoulders. Round-eyed little Isaac hovered near his mother while across the room Holbert tried to quiet Phoebe's whimpering children.

Hannah stepped inside and closed the door. The smell of stale rum and sour bodies nearly made her gag. "How long has she been like this?" she asked, grabbing a rag and wetting it in a bucket of water by the hearth.

"She been pass' out ever since ya lef'. Den, jus' a few minutes ago, she come to and start retchin' lak dis."

"We must get her quieted down. She'll never be able to leave in this condition. Holbert," she said over her shoulder, "take the children out to the yard with the others. Isaac, too."

"I'm not leaving my ma," protested ten-year-old James.

"It's all right, lamb. We will be along directly. Now, be a good lad and go with your cousin."

Holbert ushered the children outside. At the door he glanced back. "Should I fetch Uncle Stephen?"

"No! Lucy and I will handle things. Just keep everyone quiet."

Left alone, the two women continued to minister to Phoebe. Hannah tried to get her to take a sip of water, but the sick woman flailed out and sent the cup flying across the room. Soon, she lost even the strength to hold herself upright, and fell over onto the floor.

"It hurts," she moaned, clutching at her stomach as she doubled up with pain.

"Let's get her on the bed," Hannah said, sweating profusely through her two layers of clothes.

With Hannah at her shoulders and Lucy at her feet, they managed to hoist Phoebe onto the straw tick mattress. Hannah laid her palm on her sister's forehead. It felt cold and clammy. Phoebe tossed and turned, drawing her knees into her stomach.

"Do you reckon this is just from the grog, or is it something more serious?"

"Hard tellin'. She jus' a little bitty thing, and she had herse'f a heapin' dose uh dat drink. Mighta pizen'd her."

"Oh, Lord," Hannah sighed, wondering what to do. There was no way Phoebe could move on her own two feet and yet they had to get her out of there. Maybe they could haul her outside and tie on her on the back of a horse.

"Come on, let's get her up."

Wrapping Phoebe's arms around their shoulders, they lifted her to a standing position. She hung between them, limp as a picked flower. Straining with the effort, they dragged her across the earthen floor.

The cabin door swung open. Stephen entered, eyes blazing out of a sweat-streaked face. "What the hell is going on here?" he demanded.

"She is sick," Hannah explained.

He started forward and came to an abrupt halt. His eyes narrowed. "Damn me if that's not rum I smell. What's been going on?"

Lucy stared at the floor. Hannah met his gaze directly, but said nothing. Her insides churned as she saw comprehension dawn in his ice-blue eyes. Never had she seen Stephen Cole as angry as he was now. His lips grew tight over his teeth, and he breathed through his nose like a mad bull. His body trembled with rage.

"She's drunk," he rasped, barely holding himself in check, "isn't she? Five children to lead to safety and my dear wife chooses to drink herself into a stupor. Wretched woman!"

"Stephen, I think it is more than just the liquor. I think she is truly sick. In any case, now is not the time for laying blame. We must get her out of here. I thought if we could get her on a horse . . ."

"Horse be damned." In one fluid motion

344

Stephen tossed his wife over his shoulder as though she weighed no more than a rag doll.

Phoebe began to cry, blubbering loudly: "Hurts, hurts! Put me down!"

"Dammit! She'll raise every redskin from here to the Kansas." Stephen's gaze fell on the cloth knotted around Hannah's shoulders. "Give me your kerchief," he ordered.

"What?"

"Your kerchief. Now."

Hannah clumsily untied it and handed it over. Stephen dropped Phoebe on the bed and unceremoniously bound her mouth with the kerchief. Hannah stared in disbelief.

"If you can think of a better way to keep her quiet, I would be glad to hear it," he muttered. Once again flinging his wife's writhing body over his shoulder, he stalked out of the cabin, ignoring her muffled moans.

While Hannah and Lucy had been tending Phoebe, Stephen had led the rest of the fort's residents to the boat. Only the two Cole families remained to be evacuated. Stephen had planned to lead them separately, but time was running out. He did not know how much longer the Indians would remain unaware of their activities.

"We will all go together on this last trip," he informed them. "Follow me, single file. Those of you leading the stock bring up the rear. Holbert, can you handle my horses?" The young man nodded. "Good. Step lively, but try not to make a sound. Here we go."

Clutching Elenor to her breast, Hannah took one last look around Cole's Fort. She had hated living here for the last four months, yet now hated to leave it. Lord only knew what awaited them on the other side of the river, if they even made it to the other side. Suddenly what they were about to do seemed like the most foolhardy thing in the world. What made them think they could sneak dozens of people and assorted live-stock past their enemy? No group of that size could move with enough stealth to go unnoticed. Fear gripped Hannah's heart, but it was too late to stop. She must put her trust in God, and Stephen Cole. Just as she had done twenty years ago when Stephen had saved her from an almost certain death by delivering her first-born.

Like the stroke of a gentle hand, a peaceful sense of calm unexpectedly settled Hannah's beleaguered nerves. If anybody could lead them to safety, it was Stephen. He had never let her down. Not even when Indians had attacked and killed Temple. Even then,

346

Stephen had done everything he could to save his brother, nearly dying himself in the effort. There was no braver or more able man in the Boonslick.

The group edged along the outside wall of the fort and came to a momentary halt while Stephen listened for sounds of danger. Hearing none, he raised his arm and beckoned them forward. A few more yards and they reached the bluff that dropped down to the river's edge. Here the way grew steeper and the footing less secure. Holding Elenor in one arm and her basket in the other, Hannah had no way to catch herself if she slipped. Placing one foot carefully in front of the other, she made it to the bottom.

Out of the darkness loomed the French boat. A narrow gangplank enabled them to board without having to wade deeper than their boot tops. In the blackness of the night, and squeezed amongst all the other settlers, Hannah could not see a thing, but she heard a few muffled commands, and then felt the boat move out into the river's current. A feeling of elation gripped her. She buried her face in Elenor's downy curls, repressing her joy until it was certain that the Indians had not followed them.

Breaking through the clouds, moonlight

briefly illuminated the boat's deck. Hannah caught sight of James, gripping the arms of one of the Frenchmen, his hunting knife at the man's throat. Several other Frenchmen had been thrown to the deck, stilled by the guns of the settlers pointing at their hearts.

As the southern shore slipped farther away, a rumble of relief went through the crowd. When the boat hit land, a cheer broke out. They had made it! Congratulating each other and shouting praises to the Lord, the women and children tumbled out onto the blessed ground. The men busied themselves unloading several boxes and kegs.

"What are they doing?" Lila Smith asked.

Hannah stopped James as he set down one of the kegs. "What is all this, Son?"

"Powder kegs!" he replied, full of excitement. "And crates full of balls. Enough to last through the whole damn' war!"

When all the ammunition had been unloaded, Stephen allowed Captain Coursault back on board with this warning: "Back to Saint Louis with you, and, if you ever come this way again with gunpowder for the Injuns, we will hang every last one of you!"

August, 1812, Fort Kincaid

My dear Dolley,

If the words on this page appear splotched and smeared, be assured it is not from tears that have fallen from my tired eyes, but from the perspiration of my hand as it guides an unsteady pen. The night is warm, the air is stifling, and though I lie upon this cot clad in nothing but the ragged remains of my chemise, my entire body is as a dew-covered field. Would that I were as fragrant as such a field. But there is very little water to spare for luxuries like bathing or laundry. My only consolation is that I am no more nor less aromatic than my cabin mates.

We arrived at Fort Kincaid about a month ago, having fled across the river to escape hundreds of angry natives who had surrounded us on three sides, murdering one of our number and two other unknown white men. Happy we were to join our better supplied brethren on the north side. And gracious were the families here to welcome us and share their limited bounty. Still, the addition of our group has strained the fort's capacity, and, occasionally, our hosts' goodwill.

Needless to say, there are not enough cabins to accommodate individual families. As a consequence, the sexes have been segregated, with the women and small children occupying several buildings and the men and older boys in others. A separate cabin has been set aside for slaves, like my Lucy and her little Isaac. Oddly enough, the slave quarters are perhaps the most commodious of any, as the fort's Negro population numbers far fewer than the whites.

On the cot next to me, Phoebe sleeps, though perhaps sleep is too peaceful a word for her current state. Flat on her back, she is barely a bump beneath the quilt pulled to her chin. Always a tiny woman, she has wasted away to almost nothing as the result of some mysterious stomach ailment. She is unable to keep down most solid food, necessitating a constant diet of broth. She rises from her cot only when nature calls, and even then requires assistance. Between caring for her, and keeping the children fed, clothed, and minimally clean, it sometimes seems as though the sun has gone down ere I saw it rise.

Perhaps the most trying circumstance

of our present condition is the lack of privacy. We are like ants swarming an ant hill, constantly bumping into each other. There is no place to be alone. The women are occasionally allowed outside the walls of the fort to work in the garden patch, under heavy guard, but my responsibilities toward Phoebe prevent me from taking my turn. Lately I find myself dreaming of the early days of my marriage when Temple and I lived in blissful solitude on Peak Creek. Did I realize how precious it was just to be able to walk out my door and amble through the grass, all around me silent but for the call of the birds? Alas, no.

But this current state of affairs is only temporary, I remind myself. Temporary and necessary. Already, since we arrived at Fort Kincaid, another white man has been brutally murdered by the Indians, a man by the name of Campbell. I did not know him well as he came from the north side of the river, but his death makes clear the wisdom of forting up. I offer daily prayers that your dear husband will do everything in his power to bring this conflict to a speedy end so that I may soon return to my own beloved home.

We hear little, if any, news of the war's progress. Events far away are not known to us, and yet they seem to have an effect here, in the Boonslick, nonetheless. I hear the men talk. They say America is fighting the British over shipping rights and to resolve the border with Canada. I confess that I do not understand why Indians in Missouri Territory should be concerned with these matters. I suppose, frankly, they are not. What they are concerned about is the white man building homes and plowing fields on land that they have long occupied. But the truth is, Missouri Territory and all the land west to the Rocky Mountains belongs to the United States of America. The white man has a right to settle there, indeed a duty to do so! We shall make the land far more productive than it has ever been under the stewardship of the red man.

Ah, Phoebe is stirring. Let me see if I can make her more comfortable . . . there, I fanned her until she fell back asleep.

I must bring these musings to a close now, dear Cousin. Ink is a precious and very rare commodity. I had to beg Stephen to obtain some for me. He finally traded for an inkwell that was in the possession of Colonel Cooper. Before he would give it to me, however, he wanted to know why I needed it. Of course, I did not mention this journal. I told him I wanted it in order to teach the children their letters. I am not sure he believed me, as there are never enough hours in the day to hold school, but he handed it over with a smile.

Ah, that he would smile that way at his own poor wife. And yet, who is to blame for his unfaithful heart, if not this unworthy scribe? For a man would not look at a woman the way Stephen looks at me unless he saw an answering feeling in that woman's eyes. I have tried, oh, how I have tried, to banish that feeling, or, at the very least, to hide it. I must try harder. No one must ever know of these sinful longings. No one but you, dear Dolley. And you are sworn to a peculiar secrecy in the pages of this journal.

Your troubled cousin,
Hannah

CHAPTER TWENTY-TWO

As winter settled over the Boonslick, hostilities declined. Hunting parties sent out from the fort reported no sign of the redskins. Stephen theorized they had retreated farther south or west to winter camps. Although no one was willing to predict a total end to the fighting, the settlers from Cole's Fort felt confident enough to plan a return to their homes come spring.

Hannah's pleasure at this news was cut short when James came to tell her he would not be returning with his family. The young man had fallen in love with and married another resident of the fort, pretty little Betsey Ashcraft. The couple planned to set up house near her folks on the north side of the river.

"It will be like leaving a piece of my heart behind if you don't come with us," Hannah said, trying not to appear too needy.

"I won't be that far away . . . only a few miles."

"A few miles or a thousand miles, what does it matter? We will still be separated by time, and a mighty river."

James laughed and pulled his mother to him in a hug. "Rivers can be crossed. You can count on me visiting often to make sure Holbert is carrying on as the man of the family. And not only will you have Holbert" — he stepped back and eyed her strangely — "but there is Uncle Stephen, of course. He would never let you down."

Hannah held her head high. "No. He never has."

Over the years she had wondered how much James suspected of the feelings that passed between his mother and his uncle. He had never said a word about the tender scene he had witnessed when Hannah suckled Stephen's child. But, even though he clearly respected his uncle, he had never accepted him as a father figure. Her other boys practically worshipped Stephen, but James had always held himself slightly aloof. For the most part, Hannah attributed his reticence to the fact that he was already grown when he lost his father, and thus had no need of a substitute male figure in his life. But there was something else, too, something Hannah could not quite put her finger on. A hint of suspicion in his manner whenever he saw her and Stephen together.

In the end, Hannah felt she had nothing to apologize for. Unspoken feelings and unrealized passions were all there were to be suspicious about, and she intended to nip those in the bud as soon as this ghastly war was over. With a happy ache in her heart, she gave James her blessing. He was no longer hers. It was the natural way of things. As he strode off, a confident bounce in his gait, she prayed he would have many glorious years with his Betsey.

That spring, the Cole's Fort settlers crossed back over the river and returned to their homes. Families were eager to plant their corn crops in fields that had lain fallow for over a year. As a precaution, however, Stephen advised them to station a guard at each corner of their fields to warn of an approaching enemy. And he cautioned that, in the event of more violence, they would once again be directed to fort up.

Hannah's little cabin, perched on the bluffs overlooking the river, had never looked so inviting despite the layers of dirt that covered it from top to bottom. She and Lucy set to work cleaning out the vermin and scrubbing the walls. Meanwhile, with young Stephen and Samuel posted at watch, Holbert went about clearing, plowing, and planting their abandoned field. In her spare time, Hannah joined him, relishing the freedom of working her own land.

Her house restored to order, her seed in the ground, Hannah began to feel as though the tide had turned. Less than three years ago she had been made a widow whilst living in a strange land far from all that was familiar. She had endured cold and starvation, deadly Indian attacks, and the privations of fort life, and had emerged strong and in tact. More important, her children were all healthy.

Leaning on her hoe, she closed her eyes and spoke to Temple, as she was wont to do in moments of reflection. "Thank you, my love, for giving me such fine children. Thank you for leading us to a place where they can grow strong and free. Forgive me for ever doubting you. Know that whatever happens, you shall always be the guardian of my heart."

"Hannah?"

Her eyes flew open. Stephen towered beside her, looking amused.

"I did not hear you," she said, flustered.

"Daydreaming?" He smiled. "That is not

like you."

"Indeed not. What brings you here?"

He glanced around, taking in Holbert and Lucy who were weeding nearby. Touching her elbow, he steered her away to the shade of a full-leafed cottonwood. Reaching inside his buckskins, he extracted a well-worn letter and handed it to her.

She immediately recognized her brother's handwriting. "Oh, my heavens!" She clasped the letter to her breast. "It's from Virginia! It has been so long since I have heard from them. I was afraid they had forgotten us."

"The mail has not been getting through since the war started," Stephen said. "I just happened to run across a trader going upriver who was carrying this."

"I should save it for tonight, when I can share it with the children. But I can't wait!" Cracking open the seal, she unfolded the single sheet of paper.

"It is dated six months ago. 'Dear Hannah,' " she read. " 'It is with deep sorrow that I must inform you of the passing of our father.' " She drew in her breath, unprepared for the sudden news.

"I am sorry. I was afraid it was something like that," Stephen said.

"Why? I mean, how could you know?"

"Letters in wartime always carry bad

news." He settled his hat on his head. "You'll want to read the rest in private, I'm bound."

"No, don't go. This concerns you and Phoebe as much as myself."

She read the letter silently to the end, her face paling as she proceeded. "It appears to have been a sudden illness. He did not linger and was not in great pain. He kept his faculties about him, enough to have drawn up a will just before he died. My oldest brother, the one who penned this letter, received the farm. My other brothers divided up the remaining landholdings. My mother and sisters each took one of the Negroes, and other odds and ends of the estate."

"And you and Phoebe?"

She sighed. "My father bequeathed us one dollar apiece."

"One dollar! Why, the old . . . forgive me, Hannah, for saying so, but that's mighty stingy for a man of your father's wealth."

"Oh, I have no doubt he could have been more generous had he chosen to be. I think he was sending us a message."

"What kind of message?"

Hannah shook her head. "I am not sure. Perhaps that we wandered too far from home. That we had no right to leave without his blessing."

"You had his blessing. It was Phoebe who ran off without his permission."

Suddenly Hannah's knees gave out. She sank to the ground, crumpling the letter in her hand. "There is no gain to be gotten from laying blame. True, Phoebe should not have done what she did. But what did I do to set things right? Nothing. When she showed up in Kentucky and told me the two of you had eloped, I should have insisted that she return and beg for Pa's forgiveness and blessing."

Stephen knelt beside her. He removed his hat and watched his scarred hands work it around. "It wouldn't have done any good. She couldn't have gone by herself, and wild horses couldn't have dragged me back to Virginia, away from you."

He looked up and their eyes met. "I confess," Hannah whispered, "that I would not have wanted you to go."

A slew of emotions traveled across his face — gratitude that she had given him this affirmation, longing, sorrow. He struggled for control.

Hannah's eyes welled with tears. She tossed the letter away. "I don't care a whit about the money! Let him keep his dollar! All I ever wanted from my father was to know that he still loved me and wished me well. It is too late now. I will never hear those words from him."

As her tears spilled over, Stephen moved in closer and pulled her to him. Although she knew it was only meant to be a comforting embrace, she held back, mindful of how it might appear to onlookers.

"Don't pull away from me, Hannah," he murmured in her ear. "Let me hold you, if only this once. Let me comfort you."

"But . . . the children."

"The children see only their uncle comforting their grieving mother. Only those with guilty minds would see more."

"Then I reckon I am guilty as sin, Stephen. Because I can't be in your arms and keep only innocent thoughts in my head. Please, let me go."

Gently he kissed her forehead. Turning her loose, he rose and started to walk away.

"Wait." She picked up the letter and smoothed it out. "Take this with you. Show it to Phoebe. I don't have the strength right now to tell her myself."

He plucked the letter from her hand, his face grim. "Another reason for her to hate me."

"Hate you?" Hannah gathered her skirts

and got to her feet. "Why should she hate you?"

Stephen sighed like a man tired of struggling out of the quicksand. "Somehow she's twisted everything around in her mind. She thinks the reason for her father's anger is that I forced her to go to Kentucky. I don't think she even remembers how she jilted your pa's friend."

"Perhaps that is so. But I am certain of this . . . Phoebe loves you to distraction."

Stephen shook his head. "If that is true, then there is a mighty fine line between love and hate."

CHAPTER TWENTY-THREE

That fall, the Indians struck again, brutally murdering three more Boonslick settlers in separate attacks. The following spring, Sarshall Cooper, leader of the local militia, was shot while he sat by his fireside, his youngest child on his lap. Concealed by the noise of a fierce thunderstorm, an Indian warrior had crept up to the cabin, chiseled a hole between the logs sufficient to accommodate the muzzle of his gun, and executed Captain Cooper in front of his horrified family.

These attacks angered and sickened everyone in the Boonslick. But they had all occurred on the north side of the river. Furthermore, it was not clear that any of the attacks had been planned in advance or were part of a larger scheme to thwart the white man. The Indians seemed to have given up banding together to wage full-scale warfare. They were content to roam the countryside alone or in small groups, picking off unsuspecting victims one at a time. Thus, although south side settlers increased their vigilance, most opted to stay in their homes, instead of removing to Cole's Fort.

Amidst all this violence, Hannah lived in a constant state of fear. She never let the younger children out of her sight, and, whenever the older boys had to be away, to hunt or fish, her heart was in her mouth until they had safely returned. Sleep eluded her and her appetite disappeared. Lucy fretted at her, warning her if she did not rest or eat she would soon be as frail as Phoebe. But who could relax when, at any time of day or night, death might come visiting?

Stephen urged her to bring her family to the fort for protection. She refused. Abandoning her home and recently reclaimed fields would be an admission of defeat. And, too, she was not sure which was more dangerous — the Indians, or living in close proximity to Stephen.

Two weeks before Christmas, Holbert came to her and asked if she would like to accompany him and a small group of neighbors to cut down a bee tree. Several of her women friends were coming along, so it promised to be a sociable outing. It would do her good, he argued. With much effort, he finally convinced her that the children would be safe left in the care of Lucy and young Stephen who, at fifteen, was fully capable of wielding a steady rifle.

Once under way, she was glad she had come. The sun, warm on her face despite the season, immediately lifted her spirits. So did chatting with Mildred Rupe and the other women as they ambled along on their horses. Their talk was mostly about the infamous confrontation that had recently taken place between General Henry Dodge and their own Benjamin Cooper. Dodge, in command of about 350 rangers including Cooper's Boonslick company, had surrounded a band of hostile Indians, who promptly surrendered. He decided to spare their lives and take them as prisoners of war. Cooper and his men reluctantly agreed. The next day, however, a rifle belonging to one of the murdered Boonslick settlers was found in the Indian camp. Enraged, Cooper confronted Dodge with the evidence that these very savages had killed his friend and demanded that they be executed. When Dodge refused, Cooper and his men loaded their rifles and threatened to do it themselves. Dodge drew his sword and thrust it within six inches of Cooper's breast, daring him to disobey. Blood would have been spilled had Major Nathan Boone not rid-den up and defused the situation, urging Cooper to back down.

"That's Nathan to a tee," Hannah said. "Such a fine man, and very persuasive as his wife, Olive, could tell you!"

"Oh?" Mildred sensed good gossip ahead.

"Didn't I ever tell you how he turned right around on his way to Missouri and back-tracked all the way to Virginia to ask Olive to marry him?"

"Well, this is one time I wish he would've kept his nose out of things," Mildred sniffed. "I'd just as soon our boys would have shot all those redskins. Make an example out of 'em."

"Can't say I disagree with you," Hannah said.

"There it is, just up ahead." Holbert pointed to a gnarled, hollowed-out hickory tree pocked with knotholes.

"That's a big one," Gil Rupe said. "Might be enough honey in that one to last us the winter."

Holbert shinnied up the tree until he was even with a large knothole about ten feet off the ground. "Toss me the bee smoker!" he called.

Rupe threw him a cylindrical device with attached bellows. Bracing himself, Holbert prepared to pump smoke into the knothole to chase away the bees. Suddenly a volley of gunfire erupted. Startled, Holbert lost his balance and fell to the ground.

"Holbert!" Hannah rushed to him, tripping over her skirts in her haste.

More gunfire, then an agonizing scream, too feral to be human. The forest came alive with sounds of crashing underbrush and squawking birds.

"Injuns!" Rupe shouted. "Take cover!"

Frantically the settlers scattered. Some managed to get aboard their nervous horses and flee while others ran farther into the woods, away from the mêlée.

Hannah crawled to her son. He lay flat on his back, his leg turned under him. His eyes darted wildly as he tried to draw breath. Rupe dropped beside them as Holbert finally got his wind back. He rolled to his side, coughing and gasping.

"Are you hurt, Son?" Hannah asked.

"Don't . . . don't reckon so."

"Up you go," Rupe said, hauling the young man to his feet. "Time to skedaddle."

Holbert winced and fell back on one knee. "My ankle!" he cried.

Shouts and eerie, high-pitched cries pierced the air.

"Come, Son, lean on us." Hannah settled her shoulder under Holbert's armpit and

Rupe did the same. The shouts came closer.

"We ain't got much time," Rupe said. "Head for those rocks!"

They limped Holbert over to some large boulders around which thick hawthorn bushes had spread their prickly branches. Crawling between the boulders and the bushes, thorns catching at their clothes, they concealed themselves as best they could.

Hannah's heart thumped a primeval beat. Her blood surged with the adrenaline of fear, but it was not for herself as much as for Holbert. She must get him back to the relative safety of the cabin. Peering out of their cover, she watched as a figure stumbled into view near the bee tree. She clapped her hand over her mouth. It was Samuel Mc-Mahan, a settler from down near the Lamine River. He was bleeding from numerous wounds. Behind him, three savages swarmed, ululating their awful war cry. Mc-Mahan fell to his knees. Like bees on a honey jar, the Indians lit on him. With the butts of their guns, they smashed in his head, and, with long spears, they stabbed him in the back.

Hannah pulled back, shutting her eyes tightly. Holbert took her hand and squeezed hard. Sounds of mutilation — sickening sounds of thudding and ripping — reached their ears. The savages' war cries subsided; at last, they heard rustling in the under-brush, growing fainter. After five minutes of silence, Rupe crawled out from their hiding spot.

"They're gone. Let's get out of here."

Hannah helped Holbert to his feet while Rupe tracked down their horses. Too stunned to speak, they raced back to the settlement to warn the others.

Word of the disturbance had already spread. The settlers rushed to Cole's Fort, clamoring for details of the attack. Hannah and Rupe told them about McMahan.

"How many savages were there?" Stephen asked.

"We saw three, but it sure sounded like a lot more than that," Rupe said.

"I had a feeling something like this would happen," Stephen muttered. "The Army's Indian scouts warned us the redskins would retaliate after Cooper threatened to kill General Dodge's hostages. My guess is those braves you ran into today weren't after McMahan . . . they were waiting to ambush all of you. Butchering a dozen whites, including women, would have shown Colo-nel Cooper a thing or two. McMahan likely wandered into their ambush and got killed for his trouble. Reckon he saved your lives, the poor bloke."

Hannah looked away, the sounds of Mc-Mahan's death coming back to her all too vividly. Tearing a strip of cloth from her petticoat, she began to bind Holbert's swollen ankle, knowing that keeping her hands busy was the only way to distract her troubled mind.

"I'm going across the river for reinforcements," Stephen announced. "If it is as bad as I think, we'll need help."

"We got plenty of guns right here," Rupe argued. "What do we need more men for?"

"For building the new fort."

A ripple went through the crowd.

"You heard me right," Stephen went on. "When the Indians laid siege to us before, it became clear to me this place ain't safe enough. It's too far from the river. Them Injuns could easily have surrounded us on all four sides. And we had to send out parties every day for water."

"Where you suggestin' we build this new fort?" Rupe asked.

Stephen looked directly at Hannah. "Missus Cole's place," he said.

CHAPTER TWENTY-FOUR

They started the very next day. Using Hannah's existing cabin as one of the corner buildings, they constructed a stockade larger than the previous Cole's Fort. Stephen came up with an ingenious method of drawing water: a long log running from the fort to the edge of the bluff with a windlass and rope attached to it. Now they would have a supply of water even during Indian attacks.

While the work proceeded, James, who had come back across the river to help, retrieved Samuel McMahan's battered body. They buried him beneath a linn tree, halting their labors for the shortest possible time to pay their respects. The dead man's widow and children had been brought up to the settlement. Like Lila Smith, they had no idea where they would go or how they would survive. Hannah would have felt rage at another woman widowed, more children rendered fatherless, but she was too tired.

Day after day she crawled out of bed, built up the fire, and put food on the table, although she ate very little of it herself. She helped the men in their labors, too, lifting heavy logs and driving unruly teams. At night she fell back into bed, so sore that each muscle felt like it was under attack. Yet, despite her exhaustion, hours passed before the release of sleep came to her.

During those cold, dark nights she wondered how she had ever thought that the bad times were behind them. How foolish she had been, how naïve! Far from raising her children in the peaceful paradise Temple had promised, she had brought them to a dangerous purgatory where death seemed practically assured. Yet where could they go to be safe? Not back to Virginia. That door had closed. Kentucky? But how? She had no money to buy land, no way to support her family. She tossed and turned deep into the night, the answers eluding her.

On one of these sleepless nights she rose, lit a candle, and pulled out her journal. She opened it to a blank page and inscribed the date: **January 1, 1815. A new year. Usually an occasion for looking ahead, for contemplating new beginnings. Not so this New Year's Day.** All that lay ahead as far as she could see was uncertainty. The only things that seemed inevitable were more work, more violence, more death.

The pen grew heavy in her hand. Snuffing the candle, she threw a shawl over her shoulders and stepped outside. It was snowing. She lifted her ravaged face to the sky, felt the gentle flakes sting her cheeks, melting as they succumbed to the warmth of her skin.

How long she stood there she was not sure. But suddenly she became aware that she was shivering. She turned to go back to the cabin when a strong hand reached out and grabbed her. "What are you doing?"

Stephen's concerned face wavered in front of her. Bundled in a buffalo robe, he seemed huge, like some mythical creature of the Far North. She stared at him, her mind gone blank.

His hand strayed to her cheek, then to the fingers clutching her shawl. "You're cold as ice. How long have you been out here?"

She did not know, and could not have answered anyway. Her lids grew heavy, her knees shook. Were it not for his hand on her arm, she would have fallen to the ground.

Swiftly he removed the buffalo robe and draped it over her. Picking her up, he made for the nearest shelter — a lean-to in the middle of the fort's yard that protected the smithy's forge. A few coals still glowed from the blazing fire that the smith had built up earlier in the day. Pulling a stool close to the warmth, he sat, cradling Hannah in his lap.

Her head fell against his chest. As heat from the fire and the robe soaked into her weary bones, her shivering subsided. But something new racked her body. Sobs, formed in her very core and expelled like buckshot. Wrapped in Stephen's arms, Hannah cried as she had never cried before, cried as though facing the abyss and unable to pull back.

Stephen rocked her, murmuring soft words of comfort as he would to a child. Finally she stilled. Brushing the damp hair away from her face, he looked down at her with what seemed a strange combination of tenderness and fury. His eyes challenged her to look away. *Do it,* she thought. *Look away. Look away or be lost.* But she could not. Her eyes held his.

He bent his head and kissed her, so softly it could have been a feather brushing her lips. The touch held, his mouth so warm, so safe. The fire sighed and the wind blew little piles of snow into the lean-to, and all she wanted was to stay like this the rest of her life.

Yet something called her back. She wrenched away from him. Stumbling to her feet, she flung the robe to the ground and ran. Halfway to her cabin, blackness engulfed her.

My dearest, brave Cousin,

Would that I possessed your courage.

Yesterday I was helping Olive unpack a crate of fine china that had been wrapped in newspaper to prevent breakage. My eye fell upon an article describing the storming of Washington last summer by the British. What horror you must have endured seeing the Capital and your home, the White House, nearly burned to the ground! The newspaper article indicated you were alone with only household staff in attendance when you received word that the enemy was marching on the city. Keeping your head, you directed that important cabinet papers be packed up and carted away. Then, with the British practically at your doorstep, you ordered your valet to remove a portrait of General Washington from the White House walls and sent it off with trusted friends for safekeeping. Only when all this had been accomplished did you look to your own well-being, escaping at the last moment with none of your personal effects, save for the clothes on your back.

My brave Dolley! How I admire you! I can just picture you, perhaps five feet tall if one includes the turban you commonly wear, calmly doing your duty while all around you panic rules. One would almost pity the British commander had he chanced to enter your house before you had departed!

And now, the war is over. You and your husband are overseeing the rebuilding of your home, and Washington, so they say, is returning to normal. Not so the Missouri Territory. Indians around here seem not to comprehend that the signing of a peace treaty between America and Britain means hostilities are over. They are still randomly attacking innocent white people. Major Boone says that General Clark is going around to each of the tribes, presenting them with individual treaties to sign. Perhaps that will finally do the trick, though I myself despair of there ever being permanent peace here on the frontier.

I try not to dwell on these matters as they only distract me in my effort to get well. Yes, dear Dolley, I have been unwell, though it seems to be a malady of the mind and spirit, rather than of the body. I am recuperating at the home of

Nathan and Olive Boone on Femme Osage Creek whence my son, James, delivered me some months ago.

My memory of what happened back then is not clear. We had worked so hard, night and day, to build the new fort. One snowy night Stephen found me in a swoon. They say I simply wore myself out with too much work. That is part of it, no doubt. But not all of it. Something happened that night between me and Stephen. Try as I might I cannot remember the particulars. But in my dreams I am crying and he is holding me. I am wrapped in something soft and warm. His face is close to mine — his features so like Temple's, yet so much his own. Are these visions mere dreams? Figments of my imagination? Or did something happen that night, something that could change everything? God help me, I do not know.

When I was well enough to travel, James insisted I go some place where I would not be tempted to overdo, thus sending myself back to my sickbed. I did not argue, though I knew I was not as physically unwell as he believed. But I needed to be removed from Stephen. I knew I could not think clearly in his presence.

The Boones have been so kind to me. Their house is as grand as any you would see in Washington, with ten fireplaces, beautiful walnut furniture, and soft feather mattresses. Olive is a joy to be around. Her chubby little hands move so fast she seems to be able to do a dozen tasks at once. She senses that there is something troubling me beyond the extreme fatigue that led to my collapse. Graciously she has offered a permanent home to me and my children here on the Boone property. I protested that all those additional mouths to feed would strain even her generous hospitality. She just laughed and said the more the merrier. Like you, dear Dolley, she is capable of handling any eventuality that God throws in her path. Oh, to be such an indomitable woman!

One afternoon I took a walk down toward the river, looking for some herbs Olive said she needed. Who should I encounter but old Colonel Boone, the great man himself. He was sitting by the grave of his wife, Rebecca, who passed on two years ago. They say he has never gotten over his grief at her death. Indeed, he appeared quite feeble, though that is to be expected for a man in his eighties. He left Nathan's commodious home and moved into a tiny cabin belonging to one of his daughters just so he could be closer to his wife's grave.

I thought to pass him by, so as not to disturb his reflections, but his ears, still quite sharp, heard my footsteps. He motioned me over. I sat on the bench next to him and introduced myself, not certain that he remembered who I was.

"Ah, Missus Cole, I heard you were staying up at Nathan's. Come to gather your strength, have you?"

I lowered my head, ashamed to admit I lacked the fortitude his wife had possessed in such abundance. He reached over and patted my knee.

"Come now, nothing to fret about. Reckon it ain't been easy for you, left all alone to raise your children in this wilderness. Many's the time I left my Rebecca, sometimes for a year or more, to go off hunting or exploring. It was hard on her, I see now. If the good Lord allowed us a second chance, reckon I'd try to change my wanderin' ways."

"I have often wished for a second chance, though in the end it is hard to see how one would have done things differently."

He nodded agreement, his deep-set eyes seeming to take my measure. "Your husband was a good man. Too many good men have lost their lives just trying to make homes for their families. Too many."

His eyes strayed back to Rebecca's grave, and I knew he was thinking about the children they had buried on their march into the frontier.

"My husband was a great admirer of yours," I said after a while. "It was you fired his imagination about Kentucky. Then, when he learned you had moved on to Missouri, it put the fire under his feet again."

Colonel Boone chuckled. "You're not the first woman to blame me for their husband's wayfarin'. I say it ain't my fault. I lived my life the only way I knew. If others followed after me, that was their right."

"But was it worth it?" I asked, turning to look at him. "Was it worth all those lives lost, the pain and the sorrow?"

He thought about it, inhaling a deep breath through that hawk-like nose of his. "There's somethin' different about the kind of man wants to settle new ter-

381

ritory. He ain't content to let others go first. He wants to mold the land to his own vision, instead of tryin' to fit in with what's already there. For that kind of man, ma'am, it's always worth it."

We sat for a while longer, spoke of minor matters. I wished him well, placed a spray of sweet clover on Rebecca's grave, and continued on my way.

He has given me much to think about. I confess that I have been considering favorably Olive's proposal to bring my children to Femme Osage Creek. We would be comfortable here, and safer, I believe. But would I be happy living on the charity of even as fine a family as the Boones? If Temple was the kind of man Daniel Boone was talking about, do I owe it to him to see his vision through? If I left the Boonslick, would it only be because I am running away from something that I cannot face?

So many questions, Dolley, and so few answers.

Pray for me,
Hannah

Chapter Twenty-Five

"Olive, you must stop treating me like an invalid. You have your hands full running this household, yet you never allow me to assist. Please, let me do my part." Hannah presented herself to the young matron, determined to earn her keep.

"Very well." Olive laughed. "There's a basket of mending by the hearth in the drawing room. I've been meaning to get to it, but haven't found the time."

"Consider it done!" Taking up the basket, Hannah sorted through it, glad to have something to occupy her. Another month had passed in the company of the Boones, yet she was no nearer a decision on what to do with her future. She had worked it over and over in her mind to the point of total confusion. With the flesh back on her bones and the color restored to her cheeks, she knew there was no reason why she could not return to her home. Part of her longed to do just that — hold little Elenor on her lap and see sweet Mattie's smile. But always in the back of her mind was a vision of Stephen as he appeared to her in her dreams, looming over her in a manner either threatening or protective, she could not say.

A knock came at the door. Hannah waited for the house girl to answer it, but no one came. Setting aside her work, she went into the hall and opened it herself.

"Ma!" A tall young man stared at her, smiling shyly. It took her a second to realize it was her son Stephen. The boy had grown half a foot since she had last seen him. She took his hand and pulled him to her, burying her face in his chest to hide her guilty tears. *What kind of mother leaves her family for so long that she cannot recognize her own son?*

"It's all right, Ma, it's all right," he said, patting her back.

She held him away and took a good look. Yes, taller and more angular now, but still her Stephen with that crooked smile and tender eyes that seemed to take on the whole world's troubles. "I have missed you, Son."

"I've missed you, too, Ma."

"As have I . . . Phoebe and all the rest of the family."

Hannah looked over her son's shoulder to see the other Stephen in her life standing there, hat in hand, looking nervous as a groom. She felt her face breaking into a smile. No matter what, it was always a pleasure to see this man.

"Who have we here? Company?" Olive trundled her portly frame down the hallway, always ready to receive visitors.

"My brother-in-law, Stephen Cole, and his namesake, my son," Hannah said.

"I remember you both, though you, young man, were only yea high last time I saw you." With a twinkle in her eye Olive held her hand at her waist. The lad blushed. "Come, let's get you something to eat."

Herding them downstairs into the spacious kitchen where a bevy of servants were busy preparing dinner, Olive set out some ash pone and honey.

Eager for news, Hannah peppered them with questions. All was well, they said. With the war's end all of the settlers had moved back to their own homes. Occasionally a cow or horse went missing, but no more killings had occurred. New families were coming to the Boonslick on a daily basis. No one mentioned Hannah's illness, other than to say she looked good as new.

Nathan Boone stomped into the kitchen

and greeted the older Stephen heartily. The two repaired to the verandah with their pipes to discuss military matters. Desiring some time alone with her son, Hannah suggested a walk. As they strolled along the creek, arm in arm, she thanked him for coming to visit her.

"I was hoping it would not be just a visit," he admitted, ducking under a low hanging branch. "I was hoping, that is, we were all hoping you would come back home with me."

"Oh, Stephen, I can't tell you how I have missed you and your brothers and sisters. There is nothing I want more than to be with all of you again," she said. "But I don't know if I am ready to come back home." A look of hurt and confusion spread over his face. She rushed on to tell him about the Boones' offer, and how she was considering it. "It is lovely here, as you can see for yourself. So . . . civilized. I think we would be quite content."

Stephen appeared stunned. "What's wrong with our place?" he asked, a note of defiance creeping into his voice. "James and Holbert and me built it with our own hands. It may not be as grand as the Boones' house. . . ."

"Oh, it is a fine home, Son," Hannah assured him. "As tight and well built as any I've seen. Please don't think my head has been turned by living amongst such finery the last few months. I could live in a lean-to and be happy as long as I had my family about me. It is just that life is easier here . . . less worrisome. It may be only a hundred miles from the Boonslick, but it is a world apart. Why, there are mills here to grind corn, and shopkeepers selling all manner of goods. There are schools and churches. By comparison, the Boonslick is so rough and wild."

"We'll have all those things, Ma, quicker than you can shake a stick. Besides, we got something there we don't have here . . . our own land."

The Boonslick had something else unique — his uncle, Stephen Cole — but she kept that thought to herself. "Well, Son, I will ponder it. There is much to consider, and I don't want to make a hasty decision."

"Here you are! Olive said she saw the two of your wander down this way."

Hannah's cheeks began to burn at the sound of the older Stephen's voice. It was uncanny the way he materialized at the precise moment she thought of him.

He stepped over a fallen log and straddled it. "Stephen, the Boone's oldest boy . . .

can't think of his name . . . wants to show you his new pony. You can find him at the barn."

The lad looked to his mother.

"Go on, Son. We will finish our talk later," she said.

He leaned over to buss her cheek and hurried off.

Hannah tucked some stray hair up under her bonnet, eyeing Stephen uncertainly. If only she knew what had passed between them that night! He patted the log next to him, inviting her to sit, but she turned her back and occupied herself with picking wildflowers.

The silence grew, punctuated only by the trickling creek and a meadowlark's tuneful trill. How many hours, Hannah wondered, had the two of them spent in each other's company without feeling the need for words? Yet this silence was different. It fell heavily on her like the weight of a sleeping child on her breast.

He moved, finally, swinging his leg over the log and resting his hands on his buckskin-clad thighs. "When James brought you here to recover, I thought it was a mistake," he said. "Now I see I was wrong. You look wonderful, Hannah. The rose is back in your cheeks."

388

She concentrated on the flowers in her hand, feeling as awkward as a young girl with her first beau. "How is it . . . ?" she stammered. "How is it that Stephen is the one accompanying you . . . my quiet one, my homebody son? I should have thought Samuel would be the one looking for adventure."

"All of the children wanted to come, but that was impossible. I told them to settle on just one, and they chose Stephen. They seem to think he is your favorite."

"I don't have a favorite," she protested, although even as she uttered the words she recognized their untruth. Shy, sensitive Stephen had always held a special place in her heart.

"Reckon not." He smiled. "I am glad he was the one, though. Gave me a chance to see him outside of the shadow of his older brothers, and without the distraction of Samuel cutting didos. He is a fine lad, Hannah. Don't say much, but, when he does, you know it is worth listening to."

"Rather like his namesake."

A shadow passed over Stephen's face. "More like his pa, I'd say."

"You are wrong." Hannah smiled wistfully. "Temple was never at a loss for words. One always knew where one stood with Temple.

Not so with his son." She raised her eyes to Stephen. "Or with his brother."

He met her look. "You know where you stand with me, Hannah. Nothing has changed."

"Is that true? I was not sure."

His hands gripped his thighs a little tighter. "Nothing has changed," he repeated.

Hannah nodded. She understood what he was telling her. No matter what had happened that night, it would never be spoken of between them. He was giving her the gift of his silence. She perched beside him on the log and tossed the wildflowers, one by one, into the creek. They bobbed and swirled like dancers of a slow waltz.

"Perhaps it is time for me to come home, then," she said.

Chapter Twenty-Six

As young Stephen Cole had predicted, civilization found its way to the Boonslick sooner rather than later. Word of the area's lush bottom land soils spread with the war's end. Settlers began arriving in wagons, carriages, *pirogues,* and even on steamers that plied the river's roiling waters. Not far from Hannah's fort some enterprising merchants laid out the city of Boonville. Across the river, the town of Franklin sprang to life. Almost overnight an isolated wilderness gave way to a bustling community sporting taverns, tailors, hat makers, gunsmiths, bakers, doctors, and all manner of commerce.

The Cole family took advantage of all this activity. Hannah bought a license to operate a ferry across the river. At 50¢ per mounted rider, 25¢ per foot passenger, $4 for a loaded wagon, and $3 for an empty one, it did not take long for her to begin accumulating a tidy nest egg.

Stephen, whose leadership during the war had not been forgotten, was appointed commissioner of the newly formed county. His involvement in government affairs kept him away from home much of the time, which seemed to suit him well. Even as he labored to bring civilization to the Boonslick, he remained a bit of an outsider, given to the occasional irreverent outburst or wild antic. He continued to explore far afield, always curious about what lay beyond the next hill, or around the next bend. Months passed without Hannah laying eyes on him. She missed him, but she no longer yearned for him, at least not in a heart-tugging kind of way. When she thought of him now, the warmth that filled her body was not due to passion but to nostalgia for all that he had meant to her and her family.

Now, more than ever, her growing family was the focus of her life. Holbert married and had a son, making her a grandmother at the age of fifty. Stephen and Samuel continued to live at home, spending most of their hours operating the ferry. The older girls were married or had beaus, and the younger children attended the new school in Boonville when they could be spared from their chores. Her "baby", Elenor, the child she had been carrying when Temple was killed, had grown into a joyful, gregarious girl, just like the father she had never known.

Hannah could not believe it had been twelve years since Temple's death. Many of them had been years of hardship and loss. But in the end, his vision had come to pass. Their children were strong and healthy, growing up in a land of freedom and opportunity. It was this more than anything else — the knowledge that she had stayed true to Temple's vision — that filled her with contentment.

These days the only cloud on her horizon was Phoebe. Although younger than Hannah by four years, Phoebe looked like an old woman. Her hair had gone completely gray, her skin hung in limp folds on her rack-like frame, and her shoulders bent like the blade of a scythe. Now that Phoebe's children were old enough to run the household, there was less need for Hannah to look in on them. Nevertheless, she did so with some frequency, although Phoebe's peevish nature made it an increasingly unpleasant duty. Hannah tried to ignore her sister's constant complaining, telling herself that a lifetime of poor health was bound to make a person bitter. Still, she could hardly blame Stephen for absenting himself from such an unhappy home.

By 1822, the Boonslick was no longer on the far edge of the frontier. The previous year, a Franklin businessman by the name of William Becknell had led a group of five men to Santa Fé "for the purpose of trading for Horses & Mules, and catching Wild Animals of every description." The party was successful beyond anyone's imagining, returning with rawhide packages stuffed full of silver dollars. Becknell immediately announced another westward expedition, this one to include wagons. Despite the success of his earlier venture, men were slow to sign on for this trip. It was one thing to travel the treacherous Santa Fé Trail through Indian-infested mountainous terrain on nimble horses. It was quite another to do it using heavy wagons pulled by slow-moving oxen. People started referring to Becknell's expedition as the "Caravan of Death".

Hannah observed the controversy from a distance. She knew that no amount of danger would keep young men from pushing west. The need to explore and tame new territory seemed to run through the blood of most males. Besides, she stood to make money from the treasure seekers who would soon flock to Franklin as the jumping-off point for their western adventure.

None of this was on her mind one blossom-filled spring morning as she wrapped up some pone, cold venison, and pumpkin pie and headed down to the ferry to deliver dinner to young Stephen and Samuel. Last night's rain had filled the creekbeds with rushing water, and she noted the river running swiftly, but she had no worries — both her boys were excellent boatmen.

As the ferry, a simple vessel consisting of a platform over two canoes, neared shore, she was pleased to see the older Stephen standing in the bow. He leaped off the front and helped her boys tie up the ferry and lower the wooden ramp, the broad muscles of his back evident beneath a linsey-woolsey shirt. Almost fifty years old, he stood as tall and moved as quickly as he had in his youth.

Hannah watched with satisfaction as the passengers disembarked, nodding and smiling to her as they passed. Those waiting to board handed their fare over to Samuel, who took a basket of food from his mother before pushing back out into the current for the return trip. Young Stephen stayed on shore, eagerly pawing through Hannah's other basket to see what delights it contained.

"I didn't know you would be on the ferry, Stephen, or I would have brought more food," said Hannah, smiling at her brother-in-law. "Reckon you can share with the two of us."

"I'd be grateful," he said, bending to rinse his hands in the river.

Hannah snatched the basket away from her hungry son, spread a tablecloth on the ground in the shade, and divided the food into three portions, two large ones for the men and a smaller one for herself. They ate slowly, savoring the food and the beautiful day. When they were finished, they lay back on the cloth and watched the clouds trip across the sky, constantly on the move, like the nation itself.

By and by, young Stephen sat up and clasped his hands around his knees. "Ma, we have got something to tell you," he said, glancing at his uncle.

Hannah raised up on her elbows and looked at the pair, not liking their solemn expressions. She sat all the way up and smoothed her skirt. "What is it, then?"

Her son cleared his throat. "Uncle Stephen and me, well, we went into Franklin today and . . . oh, hang it, the long and short of it is we signed up with Becknell's company."

Her shoulders sagged with the weight of this news. "Surely not, Son. Surely this can't be true." She looked to the older Stephen for some sign that it was just a joke, but he offered no solace.

"It is true," he confirmed. "We leave in a couple of weeks."

Why, she wanted to ask — why would they leave their comfortable and secure homes for the danger and uncertainty of the West? But she knew the answer, at least in the case of the older Stephen. He had always been a wanderer at heart, always seeking the new frontier. Now that the Boonslick was just as settled as Virginia or Kentucky, it was time for him to move on. Less clear was why her son wanted to go with him. She could have understood if Samuel had decided to go — Samuel who was always cutting new trail, who was always looking for the next adventure. But Stephen? Her quiet, thoughtful Stephen who, of all her boys, seemed to take Temple's death the hardest? Why would he want to leave his family to traipse halfway across the country? She looked at him with this question in her eyes.

"I've got to go, Ma," he said, his youthful voice coming close to breaking. "I've got to go see what else is out there."

"What about the ferry? I need you here to

help me run it."

"Samuel will do fine, I reckon. And besides, William's pert near old enough to help out. Don't you see, Ma, I just. . . ." He petered out, unable to express his need for independence.

But she did see. She saw perfectly well. Stephen had always existed in the shadow of two older brothers and a younger brother who captured all the attention. This was his chance to break free, to declare who he was as a man. Part of her was proud of him even as her heart was breaking.

"Have you told Phoebe?" she asked the older Stephen.

His face turned hard. "Yes. Reckon she's not too pleased with me, but then she seldom is. I'll thank you to look in on her while we're gone."

"And how long will that be?"

He shook his head, measuring his response. "Hard to say. Becknell's first trip only took four months and that was in the dead of winter, so it could be less than that. But plenty of things could delay us. I wouldn't want you counting on us to return too soon."

Hannah knew him well enough to hear what he was really saying. What he meant was, he might get to Santa Fé and decide to stay for a while or do further exploration rather than return with the company. It could be years before she saw him again. If she saw him again. She looked to her son with anguished eyes.

"Don't worry, Ma," young Stephen assured her with the certainty of youth. "I'll be back soon. And I'll bring home enough silver to buy you a fancy house in town!"

"Just bring yourself home," she pleaded. "Reckon that is enough."

On the day of the wagon train's departure, most of the town of Franklin turned out to see it off. It was a somber crowd, people feeling the impropriety of cheering for men who might be riding to their deaths. Hannah was there with Lucy and some of her children. Phoebe had stayed home.

After the two Stephens had broken the news, Hannah steeled herself to visit Phoebe. Predictably her sister had been full of venom, railing against her husband for "abandoning" her and against Hannah for failing to talk him out of going. Compelled, as usual, to defend Stephen, Hannah pointed out that he had always made a habit of being away from home and that this particular journey might not last any longer than a typical long hunt. Even as she said the words, she felt the weakness of her argument, and, indeed, Phoebe would have none of it.

"He don't care a whit for his family, that's all!" she fumed. "Don't care if he leaves me here to starve long as he gets his adventure!"

Hannah did not bother to point out that with a grown son to provide her with game and a grown daughter to do the cooking and cleaning, Phoebe was in no danger of living in reduced circumstances. Nor did she bring up the fact that Phoebe's own contentious nature might have contributed to Stephen's leaving. Some things were better left unsaid.

As the caravan — she could not bear to think of it as the "Caravan of Death", yet those were the words emblazoned on her brain — creaked along, she put on a brave smile and waved to her son as he passed. He was twenty-three years old, a grown man, yet he seemed so young to her. So full of hope and enthusiasm and excitement for the unknown, just like Temple had been at that age. Just like Temple? For a second her heart constricted at the memory of what Temple's enthusiasm had brought him. But then she pushed the thought away. The son was not the father. History was not destined to repeat itself.

The next wagon rolled by carrying the older Stephen. Since that day on the river-bank, they had spent no time together. They had shared no fond farewells, had not spoken of what each meant to the other. Why should they? Hannah asked herself. That part of their life was over. Yet, as the wheels slowly turned, Stephen searched for her in the crowd, found her, and held her gaze with a look that told her all she needed to know.

Hannah stood there until the last wagon was out of sight, seeing in her mind's eye endless expanses of treeless plains, fortress-like mountains, and white-water rivers. She stayed until the last of the onlookers had wandered away, back to the daily business of their lives. She stayed until Lucy gently touched her elbow and guided her down to the ferry that would take her home.

CHAPTER TWENTY-SEVEN

The Becknell party returned a few months later. Neither Stephen was with it. Nobody knew exactly where they had gone, nor did anyone think it particularly strange that two members of the company were unaccounted for. Every man had joined on as an independent dealer and therefore had no obligation to report their whereabouts. The Cole men had probably decided to explore a bit farther, perhaps following the extended trade route down into Mexico, said Captain Becknell.

Hannah was full of doubts. Not that the pair might have decided to stay longer, but that they would have done so without sending word to their families *via* the return party. For Phoebe and everyone's sake she put up a brave front, predicting their return before the end of the year. Privately she nursed doubts so strong they sometimes left her trembling.

On an icy December morning, the sky as opaque as mother's milk, a knock came at her door. Standing there, hat in hand, was a bear of a man Hannah had never seen before. His grizzled gray hair fell to his shoulders and his chin had not been near a razor in many a month. When he spoke, his voice rumbled like thunder.

"Mornin', ma'am. Ere you Missus Cole?"

Hannah wiped her hands on her apron. "I am. Missus William Temple Cole."

The man looked confused. "Ere you any relation to Stephen Cole?"

"I am related to two such men . . . one is my son and the other my brother-in-law." She knew she ought to invite this stranger in out of the cold, but she was paralyzed like an animal who hopes that by keeping still danger will pass it by.

He nodded, satisfied that he had the right household. "I come with news for you, ma'am. Sad news, I'm afeard."

"They are dead."

He kneaded his hat, thrown off his stride by her flat declaration. "Mebbe this'd be easier over a cup of tea," he suggested.

Hannah stepped aside and let him enter. She was alone this morning, the children at school and Lucy on an errand in town. She motioned him to a chair by the fire, and methodically began brewing tea. Her movements were slow and precise, her face white as a bride's veil.

"My name's James Purcell," the stranger said. His burly voice filled the small cabin.

"Are you acquainted with my son and brother-in-law, Mister Purcell?" She set a cup in front of him, her hand shaking enough to spill a few drops on the table.

"No, ma'am. Never met 'em. But I heard tell of what happened, so I figgered, next time I was back in Missoura, I'd ought to inform the next of kin."

She sank down and clasped her hands in front of her face, waiting to hear the worst.

Purcell picked up the cup and slurped it down in one swallow. He wiped his mouth with the back of his hand and glanced around the neat, homey room as though he were seeing something fine and rare.

"I been trapping out West for nigh on to twenty years now. You might not have heard of me, but I was the first American to ever penetrate the wilds of Louisiana, before Lewis and Clark, before Zeb Pike. Spent a few years in prison in Santa Fé when them Spaniards took a dislike to my gold mine. It's the Spaniards you got to watch out for in that part of the country, don't you know, more'n the Indians. I got plenty of Injun

404

friends. That's how I found out about your kin." Purcell sat a little straighter in his chair and solemnly delivered his news: "I'm sorry to tell you, ma'am, that your son, Stephen Cole, and his uncle, Stephen Cole, were killed by Indians last August. They was down on the Río Grande, 'bout sixty miles from Santa Fé, when a party of Navajos mistook 'em for Spaniards and killed 'em. When they realized it was two Americans they'd shot, they was mighty sorry, but it was too late then."

Hannah's head fell into her hands. She could not breathe. The room seemed to tilt around her and for a minute she thought she would swoon. She would have welcomed the blessed relief of unconsciousness, but it was not to be hers. It seemed that no matter what tragedy God saw fit to burden her with, He had also given her the strength to bear it.

"How can you be sure it was they?" she asked.

Purcell rose and went outside. When he came back, he was carrying a rifle. He laid it on the table. A single tear rolled down Hannah's cheek. The rifle belonged to the older Stephen. She would have known it anywhere.

"The Navajos took his gun. I bought it off

405

'em, knowing it might be the only proof of what happened. Up in Santa Fé some traders identified it as your brother-in-law's. There ain't no possessions of your son that I can show you, but everybody said he was travelin' with his uncle. I went back to the place where the redskins said it happened. There was no sign of the bodies. Most likely wild animals. . . ." He stopped himself, mindful of his audience.

Hannah ran her hand down the barrel of Stephen's gun, picturing him holding it by his side, raising it to his shoulder, taking it apart to clean. It was as much a part of him as his own arm, always just as near. She wondered if he had gotten off any shots before going down.

"The redskins ambushed 'em in their sleep," Purcell said, reading her thoughts. "Likely they never knew what hit 'em."

"Stephen Cole would never be taken by surprise," she stated. "He was too good for that."

Purcell bowed his head, deferring to her pride.

Hannah rose and lifted her shawl from its peg by the door. "I must go tell my sister this news, Mister Purcell. I would be pleased, though, if you would stay to dinner."

"That's mighty kind of you, ma'am, but I don't want to put you to no trouble. Not at a time like this."

"Sir, you have traveled a thousand miles on my behalf. Feeding you dinner seems the least I can do."

Picking up Stephen's gun, she closed the door behind her and trudged down the road to Phoebe's cabin. Halfway there her grief forced its way to the surface. She fell to the ground, pounding the dirt with her fists and berating God. How could He let this happen? How? Hadn't she suffered enough? Wasn't it enough to take her husband in the prime of his life? Why must He now take her son just as he was becoming a man? She huddled on the hard-packed earth, the frost seeping into her clothes, until her anger was spent. Finally, getting to her feet like a creaky old woman, she continued on.

When Phoebe opened the door, her gaze fell immediately on the rifle Hannah carried. "No!" she moaned. "No, please God, no!"

Hannah took her arm and propelled her to a chair. Turning to the fireplace, she replaced Stephen's gun on the pegs above the mantel, the only place it had ever rested besides the crook of its owner's arm. Phoebe rocked back and forth, clutching herself.

"Sister," Hannah said, wrapping an arm around her, "let me tell you what has happened."

When she was finished, Phoebe collapsed across the table, her thin body jerking with sobs that seemed too powerful for such a small woman. *Why can't I cry like that?* Hannah thought. *What sweet release it would be.* She stroked Phoebe's back, trying to lend comfort.

Suddenly Phoebe reared up, her eyes wild. "It's your fault! Your fault he's dead! You bewitched him, made him lose his senses!"

Hannah stared, not believing what her ears heard.

"He went West because of you . . . to get away from you! Now he's dead because of you!"

Drawing her hand back, Hannah slapped her sister across the face. "How dare you say that? You've lost your mind!"

Phoebe clutched her cheek, looking at Hannah with pure hatred. "He always loved you. Anyone could see it. He had to leave because he couldn't bear to be close to you when you could never be his!"

"That is a lie!"

"Is it? Do you deny that he loved you? That you loved him? Do you?"

"Yes . . . that is . . . it is not what you

think!" Hannah stepped away, but Phoebe was right behind her, squeezing her arm with surprising strength.

"Don't lie to me, Hannah. Do you think I didn't know? The way you and Stephen looked at each other, the way you always found ways to be together. He tried to be honorable, I reckon, but you led him on. Admit it!"

"No, Phoebe!" Hannah wrenched her arm away. "That is not how it was. Stephen and I were close, that is true. Perhaps closer than most in our situation. But nothing ever happened between us that would bring dishonor to either one of us, or to you and Temple. I swear that is the truth!"

"Clean hands, unclean thoughts? It's still a sin."

Oh God! Phoebe was right. What worse sin was there than to covet your sister's husband, your husband's brother? There was a time in her life when she had committed just such a sin. Somehow, even though she had always loved Temple, she had never been able to get Stephen out of her blood.

Gathering her shawl around her, Hannah stood in the doorway. "You know, I have paid a price for anything I have done wrong. I have lost a son."

Phoebe pointed at the door, her finger shaking. "Leave this house."

Hannah's Journal
November, 1825, Boonslick

My dear Dolley,

This shall be my final entry in the journal that was your wedding gift to me. It has served me well all these years, just as you predicted. I have spoken to you through its pages, and somehow felt that you heard and understood and forgave. I ask your indulgence one more time, and then I shall close the cover and lock this book away where no eyes shall e'er plumb its secrets.

You and I are in the twilight of our lives, Cousin. We are no longer at the center of the swirling storm. You and your husband have retired to your home in the country to be, once more, simple farmers. And I have moved to the country as well, with my devoted Lucy and my darling Elenor. When the town of Franklin began to sink into the river, people and businesses migrated to Boonville. Soon, my little cabin was right in the middle of town! I gave it over to my daughter and her husband and found a quiet place on my son's land some miles away. After all those years of struggle to put food on the table and clothes on our

411

backs, it is heavenly to be leading a life of comparative ease. For, in faith, it takes scant effort to keep three women fed and clothed. There are times now when we have naught to do but sit around the fire and listen to Elenor read from her book.

Ah, the good Lord knew what he was doing when he gave me my Elenor. I often think that, of all my children, she is the most like her father. Perhaps, as he lay wounded and dying, Temple's final thought was of the babe in my womb, and, not wanting her to grow up with no knowledge of her father, he willed himself into the blood flowing through my body and that of our unborn child. It sounds fanciful, I'm bound, but, if you could see Elenor, you would understand what I mean. Her laugh, her bright eyes, the way she shakes her head are all of a piece with my dear Temple. The resemblance is uncanny.

Were it not for my daughter's cheerful presence, I fear I would sink into a despair too deep to describe. When I wrote in this journal years ago of my sorrow upon the death of your baby boy, my sentiments were genuine, but naïve. Only a mother who has lost a child could truly understand the heartache oc-

casioned by such loss. And I am now one
of those mothers. Not a day, nay, not an
hour goes by that I do not feel my
Stephen's absence — feel it like a vine
wrapped around my heart squeezing the
very life from me. That he died violently
and so far from home only makes it
worse. My only comfort, such as it is, is
that he was not alone. His uncle, a man
he idolized and who, I believe, loved him
like a son, was by his side as they met
their fate.

Yes, dear Dolley, your cousin, Stephen
Cole, is dead. You once told me of your
youthful fascination with him. I cannot
blame you — he was, I reckon, the most
fascinating man I ever knew. To some he
appeared gruff and harsh, I'm bound. It
is true that he did not suffer fools gladly.
Yet, was there ever a more courageous
man, or a more determined one? Stephen Cole never answered to anyone but
himself and God. He was his own man,
and, though he would be the first to
admit he made mistakes in his life, he
never walked away from them. He was
true to his own nature to the very end.

Alas, his poor wife did not see it that
way. She believed Stephen meant to
abandon her when he chose to journey

West. Such nonsense! Stephen Cole would never have abandoned his wife, even such a wife as Phoebe, and he certainly would not have quit his beloved children. He would have come back to his family had tragedy not befallen him. This I know as well as I know the call of the mourning dove outside my window. But Phoebe lacked faith. Faith in him, faith in me, and faith in herself.

God will judge the actions of Stephen and myself, and, I pray, not find us wanting. Even more do I pray for my poor sister's soul. Oh, Cousin, this is the hardest part to tell. In the days and months following the news of Stephen's death, Phoebe turned away from life. She quit speaking, refused all but the barest sustenance, and spent hours huddled in a chair by the fire rocking back and forth, back and forth, like a person possessed. One morning, she was gone. Her children could not find her anywhere. Days later, her body turned up in the river miles downstream.

What happened? Was it an accident? Did she stumble outside in the middle of the night and in her confusion somehow make her way to the riverbank? Did she slip and fall into that mighty stream whose thick waters would have quickly soaked her skirts and pulled her weak body under? Or did she willingly go to her death? Were her heart and mind so broken that life was no longer worth living?

I shall go to my own grave with these questions unanswered. But they no longer torture me. I have made my peace with Phoebe. She lived her life the only way she knew, as have I. As did Stephen. Though our understanding of each other was insufficient here on earth, I am bound we shall reconcile in heaven.

In the meantime, there is much to do. I must weed my garden and bake my bread. I must help Lucy chop kindling. I must cut out a new dress for Elenor. I must look to the west, across my son's well-planted fields, and thank God for this blessed country.

Good bye, my dearest Dolley.
Your fond cousin,
Hannah

EPILOGUE
1843

The body lay in a room dimly lit by candle-light. Heavy curtains shut out the weak midwinter sun. The simple pine casket, supported by two trestles, occupied the center of the room. Chairs and tables were pushed back against the papered walls.

At the foot of the casket, sitting in a ladderback chair, Lucy kept vigil. She had sat there for three days, leaving only when necessary. Others came and went, paying their respects, but Lucy stayed, gazing at her hands crossed in her lap. The only time she lost her composure was when Isaac came. Her son stood behind her, his hand on her shoulder. She placed her own hand over his and felt the tears wet her wrinkled cheeks.

Miz Hannah had passed away three days ago in the upstairs bedroom of Samuel's house. Still hale and hearty at the age of seventy-three, she had caught a cold and, in typical fashion, let it go untreated. It settled in her chest, cutting off her air, and took her quite suddenly.

Lucy could not believe her mistress had succumbed to such a simple thing as a cold. Not Miz Hannah who had hardly been sick a day in her life. There was that time she went to live with the Boones, but that had been a sickness of the heart, not of the body. Looking at her in the coffin, her cheeks still firm, her face remarkably unlined, it almost seemed as though she would sit up and smile, wondering what the fuss was all about.

Lucy had been at her bedside when she died, as had Samuel and Samuel's wife Sarah. After praying over his mother, Samuel had quietly left the room. Sarah had crossed Hannah's hands over her chest and followed him out. Lucy waited for a moment, then rose and picked up one of the chilled hands. It felt like a rock dug up from the bottom of the river, heavy and smooth. She turned it over, noting its lined palm and cracked nails. It was the hand of a hard-working woman. She remembered when she was a little girl and that hand had sometimes been raised in anger against her. How she had wanted to strike back because she was angry, too. Angry that, due to an accident of birth, she was destined for a life of sorrow and servitude, while this other young woman, her mistress, was free to do as she pleased, within the bounds set by society.

But they had changed, these two women. The mistress had suffered the vagaries of life, and began to see that all was not black and white. The slave had recognized the futility of rebelliousness, and realized that her loyalty would be rewarded with kindness and even respect. The two had formed a bond, made even stronger when Master Temple had died. Suddenly Lucy was the only other adult in Miz Hannah's household. Miz Hannah came to rely on her more and more. Not just for help with the endless, back-breaking work, but for companionship as well. There were things Lucy knew about Miz Hannah that no one else in the world knew, or would ever know.

Silently Lucy laid the hand back on the still chest and turned to the bedside table. A small box made of oak with delicate inlaid wood on the lid — a gift from Hannah's son James — sat on top, next to a pair of spectacles. Lucy opened it and fingered its contents — a tiny wreath made of hair, a bit of faded cloth, a mother-of-pearl handled comb — until she found what she was looking for.

Picking up the key, she inserted it into the lock of the table's drawer. Inside, beneath several lace-trimmed handkerchiefs, lay a leather-bound book, its pages yellowed and curled — her mistress's journal. Lucy removed the book, closed the drawer, and replaced the key in the little box. She barely had time to slip the book under the bedcovers before Sarah entered the room again, carrying a basin of water.

"We must prepare the body."

For three days, Lucy kept the journal hidden. She knew what she must do with it, and she bided her time. If she moved too soon, it risked discovery. Finally, on the third day, minutes before the preacher was to arrive to conduct the burial service, Lucy found herself alone in the parlor. Removing the journal from the folds of her dress, she placed it in the coffin, secreting it beneath the quilted lining.

"Dere it is, Miz Hannah. It's done, jus' lak you tol' me. Now you kin res' easy."

The door opened and Hannah's family filed in behind the preacher. The coffin lid was nailed in place. Hannah's four surviving sons — James, Holbert, Samuel, and William Temple, Jr. — carried their mother's body to a waiting carriage that transported it down the road to Sarah's family's cemetery.

There, in the black Missouri soil, Hannah Cole was laid to rest.

AUTHOR'S NOTE

On Highway 5 in central Missouri, twelve miles south of Boonville and just north of the intersection with Road E, there is a tiny roadside cemetery. It is dominated by a large, cylindrical stone marker designating the final resting place of my great-great-great-great grandmother, Hannah Allison Cole. The marker faces east where the view is of a farmer's well-tended field. Behind it, to the west, is a thick tangle of woods. I have always thought it fitting that Hannah should be buried in this spot — between the settled, civilized East, and the wild, untamed West. Family lore has it that her slave, Lucy, is buried at her feet, although her presence there is unmarked.

In the center of Boonville, a statue of Hannah, "Breaking New Ground", was recently unveiled. The dedication ceremony was attended by over 200 of her descendants. This event celebrated several "firsts" for Missouri women; the keynote speaker was Representative Catherine Hanaway, the first female Speaker of the Missouri House, and "Breaking New Ground" is the first life-size statue of a woman in the state of Missouri. Perhaps we should not be surprised that 161 years after her death Hannah Cole is still breaking new ground.

As with any novel based upon the life of a real person, questions arise as to how much is fact and how much is fiction. This is particularly true when, as in Hannah's case, few details of the subject's life are known. For example, although her gravestone gives 1762 as her year of birth, recently discovered records indicate 1770 is a more reliable date. Similarly there is no record of the date of her marriage to William Temple Cole. But a lack of details fails to detract from the impact of her incredible story.

Historians will no doubt focus on the authenticity of two of the storylines in this book: the kinship between the Coles and Dolley Madison, and the nature of the relationship between Hannah and Stephen Cole.

With regard to the former, there is some evidence that Dolley's mother, Mary or Lucy Cole(s), was a sister to Temple's father making Dolley and Temple first cousins. For a fuller explanation of this possibility, see "Living on Hominy and Sweet Milk: The Cole, Allison and McClure Families on the Virginia and Missouri Frontiers — Part I," by William H. Lyon and Eleanor Leiter Vallieres, *Boone's Lick Heritage,* Boonslick Historical Society Quarterly, Vol. 6, No. 4, December, 1998; (Part II — Vol. 7, No. 1, March, 1999).

Concerning the relationship between Hannah and her brother-in-law, Stephen Cole, their attraction to each other as portrayed in this book is purely a figment of my imagination. My theory was that two strong-willed, action-oriented, risk-taking individuals like Hannah and Stephen would have naturally been drawn to each other, but that is only speculation.

Finally I would like to thank my uncle, Dr. William H. Lyon, for his tireless dedication to uncovering Hannah's and Stephen's story, for sharing his research with me, and for keeping after me to write this book.

ABOUT THE AUTHOR

Raised in the Midwest, **Suzanne Lyon** moved to Colorado at seventeen to attend The Colorado College. She worked as a lawyer for, among others, the National Park Service before turning her talents to writing. Lured by the landscapes and legends of the West, Lyon's interest is in Western historical fiction. She told the story of Butch Cassidy in *Bandit Invincible* (Five Star Westerns, 1999), her first novel, and *El Desconocido* (Five Star Westerns, 2002). With *Lady Buckaroo* (Five Star Westerns, 2000) she recreated the world of rodeo riders from the woman's point of view. She resides near Denver with her husband and two children.

The employees of Thorndike Press hope you have enjoyed this Large Print book. All our Thorndike, Wheeler, and Kennebec Large Print titles are designed for easy reading, and all our books are made to last. Other Thorndike Press Large Print books are available at your library, through selected bookstores, or directly from us.

For information about titles, please call:
  (800) 223-1244

or visit our Web site at:
  http://gale.cengage.com/thorndike

To share your comments, please write:
  Publisher
  Thorndike Press
  10 Water St., Suite 310
  Waterville, ME 04901